D1795514

CYBORG

CYBORG

Wolodymyr Mohuchy

Library of Congress Control Number:		2021945952
ISBN:	Hardcover	978-1-6641-9164-8
	Softcover	978-1-6641-9163-1
	eBook	978-1-6641-9162-4

Print information available on the last page.

Rev. date: 08/28/2021

To order additional copies of this book, contact:
Xlibris
844-714-8691
www.Xlibris.com
Orders@Xlibris.com
833606

Герої не вмирають!

Heroes do not die!

CONTENTS

УКРАЇНА - UKRAINE

1

Promise Kept

"Good evening. Welcome to the *Eleven Madison Park* restaurant . . . Yes, I do have your reservation, Mr. Adams—party of three . . . Your table is ready," said the head waiter as he made an entry in his ledger. "Please follow me."

He ushered them to a corner table adjacent to the enormous ceiling-high window with an unobstructed view of the entire dining area. A background of lively chatter permeated the air.

"We will start our evening with champagne," Terry said to the head waiter when they were seated.

"I will gladly relay your request to the sommelier," he replied. "Have you dined with us before?"

"Yes, I have and, if I may say so, I enjoyed the evening immensely," Terry replied.

"Excellent, welcome back! I will not bore you with describing the details of our program with which, no doubt, you are familiar. The server will be with you in a moment to guide you through this evening's fare. I will pass along your kind words to Chef Humm. He may want to thank you personally for your kind words." He nodded with aplomb, wished them *bon appétit!* and departed.

Details of our program, a curious choice of words Terry thought but not at all inaccurate. Indeed, the evening would be to some extent a combination of gastronomic entertainment and flamboyance, the only one of its kind on an island of no less than a thousand restaurants.

Declared as a seasoned patron, Terry began explaining the extraordinary aspects of the establishment. "There are no menus," he said. "Based on your preference of the main course, as the evening progresses, the server will describe the dishes, course by course, that will compliment your dinner selection. Each dish will be individually prepared and seasoned to your taste."

Both of his companions received the explanation with discrete eye contact and slight, bemused smiles on their lips as if to say, "Yes Terry, we know!" Neither one was about to interject and begin the evening on a sour note. In the *Google* age, such details were a mere click away.

Nestled comfortably beneath the soaring dome, Vika and Maya, inquisitive tourists at heart, gave way to first visit exploration. They enthusiastically appraised the massive two-story open space which had an imposing chandelier, art deco décor, terrazzo floors, strategically placed partitions, and outsized floral arrangements that diffused the enormity of the dining chamber and embellished the experience with convivial, intimate ambiance. The flower arrangements, in particular, drew their attention and praise. The towering bouquets of stemmed sunflowers evoked a cheerful mood in the diners and cast adrift their imaginations in the atmosphere of the roaring twenties. In homage to *Great Gatsby*, exotic cocktails and Long Island iced tea flowed freely from the creative purveyors of the extraordinary concoctions.

The sommelier dutifully appeared at Terry's side with a thick, leather-bound wine list in hand.

"The maître d' informed me that you wish to begin with champagne. May I assist you with your selection?"

He proffered the volume to Terry.

"Thank you, but there is no need for the wine list. I dined here recently," responded Terry. "We had the *Krug Grand Cuvee*, I believe. It was very pleasant. I think the ladies would also enjoy it,"

"Why, of course, *Grand Cuvee—Reims*," the sommelier rejoined. "It is an excellent choice. *Krug Grand Cuvee* it is, then!"

"This is an amazing place," Vika commented when the sommelier left. "They kept true to the art deco motif, down to the minutest detail. And the place is packed! Maya, how far in advance did you have to book this place?"

"I called two weeks ago. This was the earliest available opening."

The sommelier returned bearing a tray with stemware and a bottle of champagne in a polished ice bucket and placed the tray on the table. He distributed the crystal flutes and ceremoniously displayed the well-known *Krug* label, popped the cork, and filled the glasses. A server followed him with a stand which she set adjacent to the table. The sommelier deposited the ice bucket and the remaining bubbly on the stand and covered them with a linen cloth. He picked up the tray from the table and concluded his task stating deferentially, "Enjoy your dinner. Elizabeth will take your order when you are ready."

The server remained at the table with pad and pen in hand. Terry addressed her congenially, "Elizabeth, please give us a few moments."

Elizabeth said, "I will return when you are ready." She stepped away but remained within sight.

Terry turned to his companions, raised his glass, and said, "To you, ladies, in appreciation of your dedication and hard work."

"To the man of his word and to many more celebrations to come," Vika added cheerfully as they clicked their flutes.

"I appreciate your good wishes, but, I confess, I would not wish on my worst enemy any more successes like the Sobolev outcome. To quote the incomparable Yogi Berra, or whoever coined that disparaging piece of wisdom, 'The operation was a success, but the patient died.' Unfortunately, in that sense, the investigation left a foul taste in my mouth."

For weeks Sobolev's demise haunted his restless nights. The failure to save his client's life left him with a sense of guilt and made him question the entire conduct of the investigation. Was he indiscreet in protecting his client's identity? Did he inadvertently misspeak to Timur, his Chechen connection to the Brighton Beach mob? Or worse yet, did he leave a trail for Mustafa Chubarov's henchmen that compromised Sobolev in Las Vegas? The wily mob boss must have figured him out from the get-go and strung him along until he trapped his quarry. It may very well have been the Wi-Fi interloper listening in across from his office who overheard something and passed on a crucial lead. In any case, the entire affair undermined his confidence. Once again it had been a mistake to get involved with the Russian mob. Burned once—chalked up to experience. Burned twice—he would never get involved with those gangsters again!

"We all have our disappointments," the sage in Maya spoke out, "the key is not to brood about them but to put them behind you and go on with your life."

"Here, here," Vika chimed in. "I'll drink to that. Besides, look at the bright side. You solved a complicated mystery, and we all were paid handsomely to boot. And our grand excursion to Las Vegas, I will always cherish those memories . . . And besides, he got what he deserved. Justice was served if you want my opinion."

The crystals clicked and the effervescent bubbles stimulated the palate.

Elizabeth appeared out of nowhere and refilled their flutes.

"I suppose we should concentrate on dinner before we get too carried away. Elizabeth, what are this evening's offerings?"

"As always, the selections are excellent. The fish selections are fresh catch of the day is Jersey flounder and our staples are lobster, deep-sea scallops, striped Chilean bass, Atlantic halibut . . ."

Maya chose butter-poached lobster with dandelions and ginger, Vika opted for seared scallops with roasted cauliflower, and Terry, he settled for the Finger Lakes lavender duck.

With the evening's major decision out of the way, Maya's curiosity got the better of her.

"Vika, do you need to visit the powder room?"

"No, not really. You can fill me in on your return."

"Suit yourself. And please finish the champagne yourselves. I am beginning to feel a little woozy," she said as she rose from the table.

"Will do."

"Maya never fails to amaze me. Somehow she always finds a way to unravel my doldrums by her unwavering example or a timely barb like the one she just thrust in my direction," Terry spoke with admiration. "With all her ailments and challenges at home—did you know her mother lives with her and she is senile as well as bedridden—she seems unfazed and manages to be upbeat at all times. And she also maintains a wide range of interests. Besides being active in the church and Ukrainian women's organizations, one of her favorite pastimes is *The MET.* She has actually become a lifetime member. As a matter of fact, tomorrow, she and several of her friends will attend the *Masterpieces from the National Museum of Korea Exhibit*, followed by lunch in the museum's restaurant. I don't expect her to appear at the office until late afternoon, if at all." He added with a sigh, "I often marvel how she does it."

The diminutive bundle of energy, standing just under four and a half feet in her stockinged feet after the untimely death of his wife Alicia from cancer became his confidant and his tower of strength. She was an efficient, highly organized, self-motivated secretary, but most of all, she was a soul mate during his bouts of depression and self-recrimination. She was an indispensable part of his core as once was his beloved Alicia.

Elizabeth appeared at the table, poured the remainder of the champagne, and disappeared with the stand.

After a sip, Terry said, "I have not heard from you since we concluded the Sobolev fiasco."

"I was waiting for your call," said Vika with a reprimand in her voice.

"I must apologize to you. I have not been myself lately. That whole disastrous affair . . . Oh well . . . I honestly thought that the current bull marked had you on the go 24/7."

That lame excuse was the best he could muster on the spur of the moment. After the trip to Las Vegas with her, he began to see his stylish, no-nonsense companion in a different light and his attraction to her grew stronger each passing day. He did not want to spoil a possible working relationship in the future with some juvenile romantic notions or for that matter, lose a good friend in the process. But he was not yet ready for that chapter in his life even though the mourning period for his beloved Alicia should have ended a long time ago.

"It's not as hectic as you might imagine. Don't forget, I invest for a limited clientele, and I will not accept new clients unless they are financially sound and are related to those who are my customers. I also employ a highly dedicated and skilled team to handle day-to-day operations. We invest the major portion of assets in mutual funds with the best yields and in companies with high degree of growth potential. I was fortunate to have a substantial position in *Facebook* and *Tesla*. I just spent last week in the Bay Area with venture capitalists evaluating the next technological breakthrough. It could very well be as simple as safe, high capacity Lithium batteries or another promising internet startup."

"Perhaps it is time for me to join your team?"

"You know my answer to that. You suggested that before. I would not feel comfortable investing your money. I would be too guilt-ridden in a financial downturn. With your market savvy, I am sure you are not doing badly. But I am not above passing a hint or two on a new opportunity."

"You are a tough nut to crack, Victoria."

"To change the subject, I will remind you once again, Taras Grigorovich. I very much enjoyed traveling with you and will gladly be your beard on your next adventure."

"I will keep that in mind. I have a meeting with Sol tomorrow. Something may come up. I need a tough case to get me out of this rut."

"My bags are packed."

2

Back in Harness

Terry awoke groggily to the relentless pinging of his cellphone. For the first time in weeks, he slept soundly through the entire night without enduring the haunting images of Rinat Sobolev's incredulous tumble from his penthouse balcony that dominated his twilight sleep, images quite similar to those conjured by Alfred Hitchcock in his acclaimed nail-biter *Vertigo.* The antidote that mollified his subconscious this restful night was, in all likelihood, the four *Montauk* cocktails which he casually imbibed on the previous evening at the *Eleven Madison Park* restaurant. He had always been predisposed to gin, but the less potent *Pliny the Elder* cocktail, which he enjoyed on the prior visit with his good friend Jeff Bulgier, an account executive at JP Morgan-Chase, was no longer on the list. Like the ever-changing menu, the cocktail selections were revised to complement the current fare. *Montauk* was also gin based but with an added blend of sweet and dry vermouth and bitters. The cocktail originated at Waldorf-Astoria in 1931 and was revisited in keeping with the restaurant's art deco theme. His companions Maya and Vika decided to indulge in the wine pairings that were the recommended accompaniment to their twelve-course tasting dinner.

The conversation at the table became livelier and more animated with every course and wine pairing. Vika was in an unusually nostalgic, talkative mood. At some point in the conversation, she disclosed to be of Ukrainian descent. For all the years that Terry had known her, including their jaunt to Las Vegas, her ancestry had never come up. For Terry it was an unexpected and welcome revelation. He was pleased to discover that beyond the growing admiration he had for her, they also shared common roots.

Vika's parents lived in the Podil District of Kyiv in the squalid Jewish ghetto where tradesmen plied their craft and were identified by their skill rather than by their given name. Thus her father was commonly referred to as *Kozhemyak,* one who works with leather. Some were tinsmiths; some were shoemakers; some were tailors. He was a *Kozhemyak.* He hand-crafted custom ladies' handbags and purses and men's billfolds. The meager household income was not sufficient for them to escape from the deprivation of the slums. Her mother was highly accomplished in the preparation of traditional foods. She augmented the household money by selling *perizhky* in area street markets frequently referred to as potato knishes.

In the heat of World War II when Kyiv was being pulverized by both Nazi bombardment and Soviet scorched earth, her parents, like thousands of other Jews, heeded the Soviet propaganda and slipped out into the countryside with nothing but the clothes they wore and a handful of precious memories. They found refuge with a farmer who hid them in his cellar until the country was liberated. When they returned to Kyiv, Podil, like the rest of the city, was in rubble. Not a timber of their hovel remained upright. They struggled for years until America offered them sanctuary. They settled in Brooklyn among other Soviet refugees. Both her parents were now deceased, and after a brief, tumultuous marriage, details of which she did not volunteer to share, she remained unattached.

Terry proceeded to the kitchen and poured himself a cup of coffee which he set up before retiring and swilled it black to moisten the dryness in his mouth. He shaved, washed, and slipped into his sweats. He stuffed a pair of shoes and a fresh shirt into his gym bag and left. He would dress formally in his uptown office where he maintained several suits and ties in his closet before embarking on the day's business.

He attacked the two flights of stairs, not quite in the manner of James Cagney, nevertheless in a spirited, jubilant descent. On exiting through the front doors, he saw that the steel shutter over the front entrance to his office was down and padlocked. He recalled that Maya was spending the day at the museum. He continued down the half-dozen steps unto Second Avenue.

It was a spectacular spring morning: mild temperature, no humidity, no eye-tearing, noxious exhaust fumes in the air. He was tempted to quick walk the fifty-odd blocks to the gym and follow up with steam and shower. He was not in a hurry since Sol did not specify an exact time that would imply a formal meeting. And he did not want to arrive too early and appear overanxious even though he was eager for another challenging assignment.

Still undecided whether to walk the distance, he proceeded along Ninth Street past the Cooper Union to Astor Place and from the force of habit, turned into the subway station that was still referred to by the locals as the Lexington Avenue line but now carried the 4, 5 and 6 trains. He would get off at fifty-first and walk the rest of the way.

Smartly dressed, he even tucked a matching handkerchief into his breast pocket. He greeted Camille, the *Wilson, Stern & Abrams* receptionist, with a hearty good morning, how have you been, long time no see.

"Is Sol very busy?" He quickly got down to business.

"He is expecting you. Go right in."

Solomon, the Abrams of *Wilson, Stern & Abrams*, was his bosom buddy since the days they were rookies on the city police force. Sitting behind his desk with folders stacked in piles, he projected an image of a mature researcher racing headlong to an imminently critical discovery. Unlike Terry, the younger of the two revealed an abundance of gray along the temples and hints of a receding hairline. His vigorous face showed traces of the good life but not disfigured by crow's feet around alert hazel eyes. His *Brooks Brothers* suit jacket was visibly snug about the chest and shoulders.

He rose, removed his eyeglasses and came around the desk, and heartily embraced Terry.

"Ahh, Taras . . . good to see you . . . where have you been hiding?"

"Just biding my time, getting ready for the next challenge."

"Why don't you take a seat? We have several opportunities for you in the works. The most imminent is one that I'm sure you will appreciate. It's right up your alley. It has to do with one of those newly minted, international businessmen. It seems the gent wants to upgrade to a newer trophy. The wronged maiden was offered a paltry sum for an uncontested divorce. She feels that there are hidden millions to which she is entitled. The last thing her erstwhile spouse needs is to appear in court and divulge the offshore sums and attract your friendly tax collector and the boys from the Justice Department. All she wants is her fair share—no courts. We need to determine what that fair share is. We should have the preliminaries settled in a couple of weeks before you can start. Meanwhile I have a family matter that I urgently need your help on."

Oh no! Signals of doom exploded in Terry's head.

"Family matter? Not Rachel!" he burst out.

"No, no—nothing that insane. Don't you even think it! It happens to be Rachel's twice-removed cousin. In a nutshell, this cousin's husband is a recent immigrant. He works in the jewelry trade. His and his family's life has been threatened unless he cooperates with parties unknown in some outlandish break-in scheme where he is employed. Needless to say, he is frightened and does not know where to turn . . . You know how clannish our families are. Well, here I am, an ex-policeman and a high-priced lawyer. The entire extended family is looking to me for a solution, and they are driving me out of my wits. And worse yet, even Rachel is nagging me to do something. She just won't let up.

"I keep telling them to contact the police. To these people contacting the police—you might as well tell them to put a gun to their heads. Besides, they are hounding him at night with telephone calls with blocked caller IDs and heavy breathing—can you believe it, heavy breathing? And in the daytime, he is being brazenly watched by shadowy figures.

"I am at a loss. I don't know what I can do in this situation. I am a divorce lawyer for Christ's sake. I would not know where to even start . . . That's the reason I called you."

"Hmm. There is no question that I will help. What kind of friend would I be if I didn't?"

"Thanks, Taras. I know I could count on you!"

"I suppose we have to start at square one. I will need to interview this mysterious distant relative of yours. Does he at least have a name?"

"His name is Asher, Asher Feldman," said Sol, then added a throwaway line, "And when you get to know him, you will be pleasantly surprised and be glad to help him."

"You are not trying to snooker me, old chum? I said I will do it. Now how do I get in touch with him?"

"I thought of that. I knew you would not disappoint me, so I invited the entire cabal to my house for a barbecue on Sunday afternoon. You should be aware that most of them, including Asher, are devout Orthodox Jews, so Sunday is the earliest we could get together. Your meeting will be entirely incidental and above suspicion. You can start from there. I hope it does not interfere with your plans. I just can't take this harangue anymore."

"I'll change my plans. Rest assured that I won't let you down, Sol. I'll be there on Sunday afternoon.

"Good. That's settled." He glanced at his *Swiss Army* desk clock as he spoke. "It's that time. How about I buy you lunch, and I can fill you in on our prosperous businessman."

"Had I not exercised this morning, I would drag you down to the gym. You are getting too soft, my friend. It's a small Greek salad and a glass of white wine all around."

Terry returned home not as chipper as he had left. In fact, he was downright depressed. As much as he had foresworn not to get involved with the Russian mob, he had no recourse but be drawn into the quagmire once again. How could he refuse to help his best friend in a family crisis! Asher Feldman, recent immigrant, life threats, jeweler—what else could it be but the mob? In the least, he would listen and minimize the stress on Sol and Rachel.

He was less concerned with the "international businessman". That would be duck soup. For some reason, those thugs were drawn to Cyprus and the Greek banks. Depending on their standing with the Kremlin, which could change at the drop of the hat, they would stay clear of havens such as Kyrgyzstan where the financial institutions were, de facto, in the hands of the FSB and the funds could be frozen or entirely confiscated without warning. And for all he knew, the banking details of his potential target may already be on the flash drive in his safe which he brought back from Nicosia.

As he crossed Second Avenue, he noticed a bent shape sitting on the bottom step of his building. For years the exterior staircase served as the hangout for an array of questionable characters, both in daylight and on warm nights. You literally had to request in a friendly manner to gain passage. God forbid you should be impolite or show contempt. An abusive argument was sure to follow. Finally the landlord relented and installed a wrought iron barrier above the first step. The move eliminated the social gatherings and relegated the first step to solitary, out-of-luck lost souls.

"Zachar . . . Greetings! I haven't seen you in ages. Where did you disappear to? Have you been ill?" Terry exclaimed in a friendly tone. "What you up to these days?"

"I've been away," said the young man with glazed eyes, who looked twice his age, his hair overgrown and flaring out in clumps every which way, his face not overly clean and covered with scruffy facial growth, and his clothes soiled and slept in.

"Where did you go?

"I lived upstate with my mother ever since those greedy idiots blew up the place and killed several people," he said acrimoniously while pointing with his index finger down the avenue to the fenced-in space on the corner of Seventh Street. "And for what? For a few pennies of stolen gas! I hope they put them away for life for the misery they caused. Mother and I lived in the big corner building which the city declared unsafe and demolished it. We had to move. So we went to live in her cottage upstate. She died a couple of months ago."

"I am sorry to hear that. May she rest in peace . . . What are you doing in the city?"

"Oh, I'm just getting by."

"Well, if there's any way I can help, just let me know."

Zachar said without hesitation or embarrassment, "I would appreciate it if you could lend me five dollars. I haven't eaten in a while."

"You know I can't give you the fiver, but I will gladly buy you a decent meal. Come along with me."

Zachar followed him listlessly to the corner of Ninth Street, disappointment obvious on his face. Terry sat him at the outermost outdoor table of Veselka restaurant. He motioned to the waiter.

"Please give my friend a full lunch of his choice and add a twenty percent tip for yourself. Give the bill to Jason and tell him I will stop by later and pay it. Thanks."

The waiter nodded and said, "Okay."

He went back, opened the gate, and ascended the staircase to the office. The door shutter was up. Maya was at her desk.

"How was the exhibit?" Terry greeted her with a smile.

"It was terrific. You should have been with us. You would have enjoyed it. The Koreans have a culture they should be very proud of."

"I definitely want to hear the details and examine the brochure, but I need you to do something for me right away. I have to go to Sol's house on Sunday, and I need to bring something for the kids. I don't dare go empty-handed. The twins are now in middle school, so toys and video games are out. I thought you should go to *Barns and Noble* and get an age-appropriate book for Megan and perhaps, a kit on magic tricks for Sol junior. But use your judgment and don't forget to get a gift receipt, just in case."

3

Barbecue

Up the FDR Drive, the New York State Thruway, and eventually Route 9, Peter, the unflappable *Uber* driver, negotiated the light Sunday afternoon traffic with gusto on his way to Tarrytown. *This is what an enjoyable Sunday outing was meant to be*, Terry thought, securely fastened in the shotgun seat, filtered from the relentless morning glare with his favorite wraparound *Wiley-X* sunglasses.

It was indeed a perfect day for an outing. The sun glittered in bursts of silver and platinum along the hood of the vehicle in between cotton puffs floating languidly against the azure canopy. The early May breeze raced refreshingly through the open windows. And the intimidating sentinels, the guardians of road decorum, remained out of sight perhaps in deference to the Lord's Day. Ten miles above the speed limit and minimal stoppage at red lights on Route 9 brought them comfortably to the Abrams' front gate in no time at all.

Sol's domain was a sprawling four-acre compound populated with evergreens, red-leafed maples, and leafy tall oaks. Manicured lawns were extended to the perimeter on both sides of the cobblestone driveway with carved out plantings of spring flowers and golden yellow forsythias scattered symmetrically about the grounds. The fruit trees were at the peak of bloom, dazzling the eyes with pinks and reds and whites.

The house was a spacious modern structure blended into the rustic surroundings. It was positioned on a rise to allow a view across the mighty Hudson from the upper-level bedroom balconies.

Terry exited the car and told Peter to return home. He was not sure when he would be leaving. But no matter the time, the evening drive home on such a glorious day would be packed bumper to bumper with weekenders. Peter's objections to the contrary, it made more sense for Terry to return home by train in the evening. Sol would drop him off at the station.

Before he could comb his windblown hair into place, two eager Great Danes were at his side snuggling for attention. The man-sized canines, their glossy black coats glistening in the afternoon sun, their ears drooping and their stubby tails uncontrollably gyrating, rubbed their muzzles on Terry's hips and murmured sounds of recognition and contentment. Terry reciprocated in the outpouring of affection. He stroked them in turns below their chins, bent down and rubbed his nose along their snouts and repeated, "Yes . . . yes . . . I love you too."

The waist-high mastiffs were in top form. Their muscular bodies were lean and well-exercised as they had free rein of the property. Each wore an electronic collar that confined their movements within the perimeter. They barked fiercely at unwelcome strangers. But with those who were familiar, they were merely overgrown domestic puppies eager to nuzzle and play.

Terry heard music from the backyard and proceeded around the house armed with two *B&N* tote bags in his right hand and flanked by the two enthusiastic bodyguards at his side.

"Uncle Terry . . . Uncle Terry!" Hugs were given around his waist.

"Now let's see. What do we have here?" The favorite uncle put forward the *B&N* totes. "I suppose the pink one is for you, Megan. Then this one must be for you, Sol," he proclaimed good-humoredly.

There were enthusiastic thank-yous and frantic unwrapping of packages, no disappointments on their faces. The gifts hit the mark. The recipients took flight.

The proprietor was immediately at his side as well as the hostess, hugs and cheek-to-cheek air kisses.

"Glad you made it."

"You didn't think I would?" He looked about and said, "This is quite a gathering. Did you bring them here by the busload?"

Sol burst out laughing.

"As a matter of fact, I did. I chartered a bus. It's parked behind the garage. I told you it's the extended family, the entire extended family," Saul said with exaggeration. "When you live in Brooklyn, you don't necessarily own a car . . . Come I'll introduce you. But don't make a fuss when I present you to Asher. He insisted on minimum interaction. He feels this is not the time nor the place—just an incidental get acquainted."

"Sol, is he paranoid? Is he suspecting someone in his circle?"

"I don't know what he thinks or suspects. But he seems overly cautious. So act with detachment . . . Now, for starters, can I at least get you a beer? I have your favorite Brooklyn ale on ice."

"Give me just a minute to get my bearings. Which one is he?"

"He's in that group of men standing with his back toward us."

Terry was not surprised that the men socialized in a separate clutch from the women. He was no stranger to the customs of the ultraorthodox.

"Oh well . . . might as well bring me a cold one. I'll stay put and concentrate on my bosom buddies in the meantime."

He squatted in between his guardians, who were spread eagle at his feet with their chins planted on the grass between their paws and fondly patted them. He keenly scrutinized the gathering from his vantage point and marveled at the cultural diversity he was witnessing within the Adams clan.

Sol wore a colorful Hawaiian shirt, navy-blue Bermuda shorts, and matching deck shoes without socks. Rachel complemented her husband's picnic attire in a bright-yellow blouse, white shorts, and white *Sketchers*. The men were all dressed in white shirts, black trousers, and black shoes, and of course, black yarmulkes. Several had tzitzit overhanging their belts. The ladies, with one exception, were head to toe in traditional gray and black, wigs included. The one exception was a statuesque, attractive woman wearing a flowery knee-high dress, matching cutoff socks, and sandals. Her auburn hair was pulled back into a loose bun. Unlike the men, the women were dispersed on canvas recliner chairs and wicker lounges randomly scattered across the divide. Some were in pairs. Some were in clusters. Others roamed with chilled fruit drinks in their hands and partaking kosher hors d'oeuvres that continuously flowed from the gourmet kitchen. All were conversing and giggling and keeping a close eye on their brood.

The children, outnumbering the parents by at least a factor of three, reflected the dress code of the parents. The Adams twins favored *Under Armour* tees, shorts, and sneakers. Two boys, identical twins in appearance, were Sol junior's age. They wore current-style sportswear and no yarmulkes. The twins and Junior were playing catch with lacrosse sticks. The other children, dressed in grays and black and sandals, were kicking soccer balls and improvising games around the outdoor swing set. All the boys wore yarmulkes. The only disappointment of the day was the unavailability of the pool. It was still covered with a tarp.

"Okay, master of the hounds, here's your ice-cold brew—just the way you like it. How about a bite to eat? We are all way past the first round, so you need to catch up."

Terry stood up, gulped a swallow, and said, "We better do the introductions. I sensed some uneasy peeks in my direction from both sides of the gathering . . . By the way, who is that striking woman in the colorful dress?"

"That happens to be Asher's wife Zina."

"I kind of thought so. She seems to be quite a social butterfly, going from flower to flower, and spreading good cheer."

"Your insightful metaphor is on the mark. She is very sociable and popular among her kin. Even though she happens to be a highly accomplished physician, she is not aloof or pretentious. On the contrary, she is rather solicitous, and her keen sense of humor bodes her very well as you can see for yourself. You notice her boys, those two that are tossing the ball with Junior, they also differ in their upbringing and worldly outlook even at their tender age. But they are kin. They stick together with their distant cousins. and they all get along famously."

"All right. Let's go on and get the ball rolling."

"Don't forget, just a casual handshake. Let him make the first move," said Sol as they approached the men.

"Gentlemen," said the host, "let me introduce you to my dear friend Terry. Terry this is Chaim . . . Joshua . . . Ben . . . Asher . . . Gabe . . ."

Handshakes, smiles, nice to meet you, how are you doing—not the Brooklyn *hayadoin'*— and a bit of small talk were exchanged.

Terry casually sized up his quarry, above-average height, broad, muscular shoulders, trim at the waist, pleasant, round-faced, had a neatly trimmed beard, mustache, and sideburns, full black head of hair partially covered with a yarmulke, and clothes smartly pressed with sharply creased trousers.

In a short while, Terry lifted up his head and sniffed the air with exaggeration. "Sol, perchance, are those *Nathan's* finest I smell in the air?"

"Your favorite. I had Yolanda throw a half dozen on the grill. Is anyone else game for some before we treat the kids to another round? Come along, Terry. I'll introduce you to the ladies after you have a bite."

"I can't resist. Would anyone care to join me?"

The men looked at each other with confusion and politely declined. Asher volunteered, "I can use a bite if you don't mind me joining you."

"I would love your company."

Sol moved quickly to the grill. Terry and Asher followed casually.

"Taras Grigorovich," Asher said softly in Ukrainian to Terry's amazement. "I want to thank you sincerely from the bottom of my heart for coming and hopefully helping me with my troubles. I am still a stranger in this country, and I have no one to turn to."

"I'll be more than happy to do what I can. I am impressed with your flawless Ukrainian. Where exactly do you hail from?"

"I was born in Mariupol, but for most of my adult life, I lived in Kyiv. We use the mother tongue interchangeably even though Russian predominates."

"Surprise, surprise . . . Then I am doubly pleased to help you. How is your English?"

"I am still learning. I can make myself understood. But in my community and at work it's mostly Russian. Languages come easily to me. In time I will be proficient. Why do you ask?"

"I regret to say it, my everyday language is English. I do speak Ukrainian, but I lack more sophisticated vocabulary. I do understand Russian to some degree when it is spoken slowly. Let's stick to English and if you have difficulty expressing yourself accurately, you can fall back to whatever you are comfortable with."

As they approached Sol, he was finished warming the buns and stuffing them with grilled-to-perfection Coney Island treats and placing them on plates next to the grill.

"Help yourselves. There's sauerkraut and whole-grain Dijon mustard and half-sour pickles to your liking. You can sit at that table. I'll bring beer for both of you."

"Let's get started," Terry said after several bites and a mouthful of ale.

"I don't really know where to start," Asher said nervously.

"First of all, relax," Terry spoke calmly. "You are among friends. Solomon told me that you and your family have been threatened. Just tell me briefly why and what are the demands. We will need to meet later, get to know each other better, and have a serious discussion. I worked out a plan for our next meeting that will not compromise you in the least. Now, what is this all about?"

"I am a diamond cutter by trade and work for a jeweler in the diamond district on Forty-seventh Street. Three weeks ago a man approached me on my way home from the subway and told me to get familiar with the details of the building, the alarm systems, and exits. I would receive further instructions in due time. I was to keep it to myself and God forbid, go to the authorities. Then he threatened my boys and my wife by name.

"I have been at the doorstep of death several times in my life and have no fear of dying. But my wife and my children—I panicked. I am a stranger in this wonderful country. I don't have close ties to anyone who could help."

"Did he speak to you in English or in Russian?"

"He spoke in Russian, street Russian—obscene vulgarities every few words just to underline his point and muttering strings of blasphemy every now and then. He knew my family details here and back home. Later they used scare tactics on the telephone to unnerve me and soften me up. I am constantly being followed by different individuals in full view, which is driving me up the wall. Last Thursday the same man accosted me again and handed me a cell phone and a set of diagrams of the building. He gave me a month to mark up the plans and photograph the alarm panels and camera locations."

"That does not give us much time, but we'll put it to good use. Under the circumstances, it would not be wise to meet after work since you are being watched. Obviously Saturday is out. That leaves Sunday. I will use the week to try and find out from my contacts what is going on. You and I will meet on Sunday. Next week is the annual Ukrainian festival on Seventh Street. It will run for three days with crowds from the entire metropolitan area. We will use that as our cover. Are you familiar with the National Home?"

"Yes, of course."

"Good. I live next door. Here is what we will do. Exactly at noon, I will be in front of *McSorleys*. Do not acknowledge me. As soon as we make eye contact, I will make my way down the street to Second Avenue. Follow me at a safe distance to my apartment. It's between Eighth and Ninth. Go up the brown steps—they are the only steps on the block—and enter the double doors. The doors will be open and I will be waiting for you in the hallway. Do you follow me so far?" Terry said with confidence in a reassuring, can-do tone.

There was an affirmative.

"By the way, do you have an embroidered shirt?"

There was another yes.

"At some point along the way change into it, but don't leave in it from the house. You will blend in better with the crowd. I really don't think anyone will be following you on a Sunday . . . Now, Asher, that's settled. Do you have room for another dog?"

4

Street Fair

Saint George's Festival had evolved into an annual, not-to-be-missed celebration of Ukrainian tradition, culture, arts, crafts, and mouth-watering cuisine, highlighted by *varenyky*, the renowned potato and cheese dumplings drenched either in caramelized onions. dollops of sour cream, or sizzling butter.

For three days in mid-May, Seventh Street in the East Village was blocked from traffic between Second and Third Avenues. An elevated stage was erected across the street adjacent to the church on which were continuous performances of professional and amateur dancers, decorated singers, and artists from the mother country, and local political well-wishers. The entire street was draped in blue and yellow flags, streaming from the tenement windows and lamp posts and framing door entrances. Both sides of the street were lined with kiosks offering homemade foods, ceramics, wood carvings, embroidery, and ethnic jewelry. The entire space was occupied shoulder to shoulder with revelers from as far away as Maryland.

Terry was on post near *McSorleys* since the day's opening ceremony, soaking in the atmosphere and emptying a steaming container of *varenyky* smothered in his favorite caramelized onions. At the moment the master of ceremonies was introducing the *Iskra* dance ensemble to entertain with the classic *hopak*. Music erupted to the high heavens with an ear-piercing medley that surely would even rouse Grant in his tomb. The young men and women, resplendent in their embroidered finery, danced with abandon, twirling and leaping effortlessly in the air.

Terry was mesmerized with the performance and enthusiastically clapped in cadence with the music, feeling his muscles pulsate to the rhythm of the drumbeat. He noticed Asher punctually turning the corner from Third Avenue. On eye contact, he turned about and proceeded down the street.

The day could not have been any more ideal for an open-air event. An unblemished cobalt sky combined with a gentle breeze flowing through the cavern from the East River—a made-to-order inducement to enjoy the outdoors, and it seemed that every path led to Seventh Street.

Terry waded exasperatingly slowly through the crowd. He shuffled along sideways and excused himself at every step until he finally broke out from the pack. He made his way up the Second Avenue without looking back, up the stairs, and entered the building leaving the front doors unlocked.

Asher was not far behind. He ascended the stairs and walked through the double doors.

"Good day, Asher. You are safe and sound. I did not notice any tails," Terry said.

"Good day to you too, Taras," said Asher calmly. "You were right about the watchers." He added with a slight grin on his face. "Sunday must be their day of rest—perhaps they went to church. What do you think? I did not spot any of them since I left my house."

Asher reached into his bag, took out his yarmulke, and covered his head. He was dressed in an intricately embroidered shirt, hand-stitched in blue and yellow thread.

"That's good to hear. My apartment is two flights up," said Terry as he locked the front doors and began to scale the stairs. He noticed that Asher negotiated the stairs laboriously with the aid of the banister and was favoring his left leg. However, he seemed to be in good physical shape. He moved vigorously and did not appear winded from the effort.

He unlocked first the upper deadbolt, then the door brace, and then the door latch dating back to the nineteenth century—finally opening the metal-clad door into the apartment.

"Welcome to my humble abode. Make yourself comfortable in the living room while I get some refreshments. What would you like to drink?"

"I'm fine, thanks."

"Now, Asher, you are a guest in my home. Don't feel that you are imposing. Personally, I am parched and need something wet and cold. I have Brooklyn ale in the fridge. How about seltzer or a mixed drink?"

"I'm not much of a drinker anymore. But if you insist, I will join you in a glass of ale."

"Would you prefer a glass or would you rather drink from the bottle? I also keep a set of glasses in the fridge. If you want yours on the warm side, I can do that."

"I am getting used to the American ways. I'll have it cold but not too cold."

"Okay."

Terry brought out a tray of food which he bought earlier at the fair and a bowl of crinkled potato chips. One of the beer glasses was covered with frost, the other exposed the unmistakable brewer's green logo.

"Na zdorovya [to your health]," Terry said as he lifted his glass.

"Slava Ukraini [Glory to Ukraine]," replied Asher.

"Heroyam Slava [to the heroes glory]," replied Terry and knew exactly where his guest stood. "I am hoping to spend the rest of the day with you if you don't mind, to get to know all there is to know. There may be a clue somewhere in your past. I'll throw some steaks on the grill later on . . . By the way, I can't help admiring your wyshywanka, such rich detail, and such patriotic colors."

"That is who I am," was Asher's unequivocal response.

5

Asher

I was born in Mariupol to a working-class family. My father was a proletarian to the core. He was a card-carrying member, working since his teens at the *Ilyich Steel & Iron Works*. He wholeheartedly embraced the *Stakhanov* myth by exceeding the norms of his assignments even though after Stalin's death, the ploy to increase productivity during the First Five-Year Plan was discredited and proven to be merely a staged propaganda maneuver. Nevertheless, through his zeal, he rose rapidly in the ranks from a gofer to a position in the worker's union. Life was comfortable by the day's standards.

I did not see much of my father in those early years. He left to the plant before sunrise, then remained at one meeting or another after work. On his days off he slept into the afternoon and then, after a hearty meal, he disappeared for the rest of the day and returned at night in a drunken state and plopped down on the bed. I learned early on that silence was golden when he was in the house. God forbid that I should interrupt my father's slumber. I dread to think of it even now. And if Mother interceded, then both of us would feel his heavy hand.

As difficult as my upbringing may have been, nothing compared to what followed after December 25, 1991, when Gorbachev literally pulled the rug from under my father. I was only six years old at the time, but I remember it as if it was only yesterday. Privatization took away all his privileges, stripped him of his manhood, and stranded him in the labor force. As irritable and thin-skinned as he used to be, he became morose and downright mean. He could be provoked into a rage with a disrespectful glance or a reply not to his liking.

His clothes, his hat, his shoes were always in soot. He lost weight and his face thinned out and attained a cruel look with deep furrows across his brow and sunken cheeks and crow's feet narrowed his eyes into a permanent, sinister squint. His hands and face were blackened to the extent that soap could not entirely scrub out the grime. At times he coughed uncontrollably and expectorated black mucus.

He was having difficulty accepting the collapse of the Soviet Empire and cursed Gorbachev at every opportunity. But worst of all, he buried his discontent in the bottle—the panacea of his fellow countrymen. He came home drunk; he went to bed drunk and he returned to work drunk on the following day.

Mother bore the burden of maintaining body and soul together. The household finances were in shambles. She used the patch of land behind the house to the maximum extent—planting, harvesting, and preserving for the winter months. She even had a neighbor rig a small fenced-in chicken coop at the back of the property for a daily supply of eggs. She was an accomplished seamstress, a trade she learned working for a dressmaker after she wed. She acquired her own rickety Singer sewing machine, and she put it to good use. Word spread in the neighborhood and filled her day into the night. She let it be known that she preferred not to be paid in coins because Father had a knack for sniffing out every kopek and immediately depositing it in a gin mill. Barter put bread and occasional meat on the table.

Eventually father's health took a downward spiral. He refused to see doctors even when he began spitting up blood. When the chest and belly pain became excruciating, he was taken to the hospital by ambulance. On examination, the doctors concluded he was damaged beyond repair. He did not return home and died several days later. As he was a lifelong professed atheist, Mother had his remains cremated.

His death put an end to the worst four years of my life.

Tranquility returned to our house. But it did not last. Mother had a delicate constitution to start out with. She was orphaned at an early age and was taken in by some distant relatives. They treated her more like a servant than a daughter. When she became of age, they saddled her with my father, sight unseen, through an arranged marriage. In effect she led a life of servitude since childhood.

In retrospect I was the only bright spot in her life. I realized this and made every effort to make her proud. I attended school regularly and stayed away from trouble. My grades were very good. The report card always put a smile on her face, and she rewarded me with a warm caress. I tended the garden after school and fed the chickens. I never refused any task that she would ask of me.

The unthinkable happened. Usually Mother would rise early, collect fresh eggs, and start breakfast before waking me. But when I woke, the bedroom was flooded with the morning sunlight; there was no activity in the house. I peeked into her bedroom. She was peacefully asleep. I washed, dressed, and went to collect eggs and feed the chickens.

I hated to wake her. She looked so comfortable. I gently shook her arm and said, "Mother, wake up. It's getting late." Her arm was cold. I touched her forehead. It was ice-cold. Her face was drawn and ghost-like.

I knelt beside the bed in tears and kissed her cheek. I was at a loss for a prayer. I knew none. I merely cried out, "Oh god! Oh god!"

I ran to my next-door neighbor Avraam. He tried to console me with words I did not hear. When I was a bit calmer, he said, "She was a good woman. She deserves to be properly laid to rest. Don't worry, I will take care of everything."

He was a religious man, dressed in a traditional white shirt with the knotted tassels from his undergarment spilling over black trousers. I never saw him with his head uncovered.

"Masha," he called out. "please come here."

Masha came in from the kitchen, wiping her hands on her apron. "What is it? What's wrong, Asher? Why are you crying?"

"Zoya died in the night," said Avraam. "Masha, let Asher stay here with you. Give him something to eat. I will make all the necessary arrangements with the *Chevra Kadisha*—the burial society. Don't let the boy go back to the house. I'll be back as soon as I can."

I remained in the house next door while Mother was being prepared for her funeral. I was in a complete daze. I remember only bits of what happened. A plain pine coffin was suspended over an open pit surrounded by mourners, men and women dressed in shades of black. I was also in black and wearing a yarmulke for the first time in my life. A man was reading Hebrew at the foot of the grave, and then he spoke about my mother in Russian, our everyday language. When the coffin was lowered, the men, including myself, shoveled the grave with soil. The rabbi began the *Kaddish* prayer ritual, and I joined the mourners in affirming the scripture by testifying, "Amen."

We returned to our house from the Jewish cemetery to honor my mother's passing in the traditional *Shiva*—the mourning ritual. A small crowd greeted us at the door and expressed their condolences. I was overwhelmed that the house was prepared in my absence in solemnity, black ribbons around the walls, and trays of food on the parlor table. Neighbors came in for a brief remembrance. Despite my state of confusion, I was deeply moved that my mother was so well respected and would not be soon forgotten.

6

Ruslan

My mother's untimely death, despite all the well-wishers, left me alone to fend for myself at the ripe age of fourteen. Lacking any direction, I completed the school year and took to the street for subsistence. I had grown to a manly stature and thanks to my mother, had sufficient meat and muscle on my bones to take on a variety of physically demanding jobs.

My favorite daily routine centered at the Azov Seaside. At sunrise I tended to the chickens, ate fried eggs with bread and whatever else was on hand, took my rolled beach mat underarm, and headed for the seashore on foot. I would not waste the few dearly earned kopeks on carfare.

Hotels like the *Poseidon*, *Grand Hotel,* and *Spartak* were booked solid from May through September where menial kitchen work was always available. Lunch and dinner preparations needed peeled potatoes and vegetables. And there were always greasy pots and pans and at times, substituting for the less than reliable dishwashers. My reward was a bellyful of leftover food at the end of the session and a portion or two to take home. Several times a week the kitchen floors needed scrubbing after hours. The payment was in the coin of the realm. I actually saved enough for a rickety motorcycle that made my life much easier.

In the afternoons I headed across the Primorsky Boulevard with my beach mat and roasted to my heart's content. I became a familiar face with the kitchen personnel of several hotels as a reliable, trustworthy individual. On the beach, I saw an opportunity to augment my earnings.

Forgive me for being somewhat immodest, but I must admit that nature was very kind to me. I had a spurt in growth to what you would consider about six feet. I was also fortunate to have my mother's genes surging through my veins that molded my character and sculpted my face with good looks and capped it with a shock of curly reddish hair. A mirror would not distinguish me from one of the *Corsican Brothers*, bursting with the passion and flair of a swarthy gypsy. My body was muscular and erect. Eventually, I put it all to good use.

Every concierge along the shore had me on top of his list as a tourist guide or an escort with the expectation of a healthy kickback. On the beach, I was ready with a lounge or an umbrella or a mat or an intriguing drink. I was, as you Americans would say, Johnny-on-the-spot, dressed in a bright-yellow open-collared shirt and white shorts.

My moniker became Ruslan. That name was as romantic as *Alexander Pushkin's* vivid imagination could conjure. The women loved it. But I did not think I was yet ready for my *Ludmila*.

In high season, I was at the peak of my earning powers. After breakfast, I canvassed the beach and collected a modest number of tips. By noontime the rest of the day was booked solid, tour after lunch, nightclub into the wee hours after dinner. The fees and tips stacked up to the point that I decided to treat myself to a new motorcycle—well not exactly a brand new one, but a slightly used one. One of the bartenders, a tough tattooed biker who used to slip me a free drink once in a while, steered me to a Harley—a Harley nonetheless. His friend died recently from a liver condition, and the wife was strapped for cash. I just had enough to meet her demands. I even threw in my old bike, which I babied into good shape so that she would not be left without transport. She was so pleased that she included her husband's helmet with the deal. From then on, I had respect on the road not only from passenger vehicles but also from the police who gave me quizzical looks but did not have the nerve to stop me for a shakedown. The boys with skulls and swastikas on their helmets never failed to tip a salute even though I scraped off that hideous insignia from my helmet and replaced them on the sides with blue and yellow patches overlaid with the national trident at the center. I left the skulls on the front and back of the helmet just for the fun of it.

One spectacular summer morning fate entirely changed the course of my future. The change was by no means something dramatic like a spark from a bolt of lightning or a divine revelation. It was more of a protracted emotional longing that drew me to the inevitable.

I noticed three young ladies crossing the boulevard from the *Poseidon* dressed in beachwear and carrying stuffed beach bags. It was rather early. Breakfast at the hotel was still in session. The beach was empty. I did not want to appear too anxious, so I remained by the kiosk exchanging few pleasantries with the proprietor.

It was obvious that they were new arrivals, and this was their first outing. They went straight to the water and waded in. Satisfied, they chose a nearby spot and set down their bags on the fine-pebbled sand.

I hastened to them.

"Welcome to our beach. Would you young ladies like lounges? The lounges would be compliments of the hotel." I said pleasantly. They looked awfully young, at least to a seasoned hand like me at the ripe age of eighteen. I knew they would respond favorably to being called ladies.

"No, thank you," they seemed to say in unison. "We prefer laying on the sand."

"Then let me get you some mats and later when the sun is more intense, I will bring you umbrellas."

The threesome vigorously applied sun protection while I casually tried to make idle conversation since my regular sun worshipers were yet to make their appearance.

On closer look, my first impression was somewhat off the mark. They were older than I first thought. They were likely in their late teens, perhaps even my age. They were trim and sported stylish hairdos. Their bathing suits were modest, not vulgar as some girls had a tendency to wear. And they were lookers, each in her own right. They hailed from

Kyiv. The two natural blondes were Lena and Olia. The brunette was Zina. I, of course, for all practical purposes was Ruslan.

They were not the giggly types. Neither were they trying to impress me with some silly comments to elicit a reaction. They were obviously well-bred both in their demeanor and language. They were best of friends on their first outing without chaperones.

Predictably the subject revolved around the attractions in Mariupol and more specifically on the nightlife. I obliged in fine form.

People began to drift in. Before leaving the girls and attending to my customers, I suggested that they speak to the concierge and get a reliable guide, not only for their own safety but also to gain access to the more popular clubs which required advance reservations even on weeknights and most likely would not be let in without an escort because of their age.

That afternoon I had a lengthy tour with a middle-aged couple from Kharkiv. The well-heeled couple was pleased enough to give me a generous tip. They paid the cost of the tour to the concierge which we split as usual and included a share for the driver.

The concierge informed me that there was a change in the plan for the evening. Three cuties requested me by name and would not take no for an answer. They happened to be staying in one of the top-floor suites. How could I refuse such refined beauties?

I met the threesome in the lobby toward sundown. I wore my eat-your-heart-out Travolta whites but without the bell-bottoms, a yellow open-collar silk shirt, and white Italian shoes—dressed to kill and be noticed.

The young women, elegantly dressed, stepped out from the elevator and captivated every eye and every fertile imagination in the lobby. They wore summer blouses and skirts of modest length and strutted with a flourish on fashionable high heels. There was little evidence of makeup or lip rouge on their mildly tanned faces. Their hairdos were stylish. They were merely fluffed by a hairdryer—a vision of radiant natural beauty in triplicate.

Olia, the more outspoken of the three, said enthusiastically when she saw me approach, "Ruslan, I hope you will be our escort this evening, are you?"

"Indeed I am."

I told Yuri, the driver, to head for the *Coral Casino* compound. Our first stop would be the *Coral Travel Club*. I had no reservations, neither did I think I need one.

The doorman said, "Ruslan, we did not expect you. Why didn't you call ahead? The place is packed."

"Forgive me, Sasha. This was last minute."

"Come along. I'll see where I can squeeze you in."

The *Coral Club* was a pop and R and B establishment. The place was jumping. We wound up parked at the bar. I brought along our driver to help entertain the ladies on the dance floor. He was more than happy to oblige. Drinks all around.

The girls were enraptured with the place. I engaged another volunteer to assist with the dancing. I remained at the bar for a while chatting with Zina before joining the mayhem. There was something about her that attracted me in an unusual way. I have been with many girls who may have been more alluring. But this feeling was new, confusing, and at the same time refreshing.

We winded through the week in a blink of an eye. We hit the *Armadillo* with its reggae music, clubs *Zebra* and *Barbaris* and *Ron Cubano* and *the Imperial* to exhaustion. We spent a few hours in the *Coral Casino*, but the girls were not too keen on gambling. Somehow we ran out of time to visit any other must-see city attractions.

Yuri and I eventually escorted the girls to the airport. It was time to get some sleep and rejuvenate myself for the next crop of eager beauties. Yet Zina's image kept dominating my twilight dreams. "Out of sight—out of mind" did not seem to have much of an effect. I kept reprimanding myself for not asking for her address or at least for her wireless.

Three weeks went by when the front desk attendant of the *Poseidon* excitedly waved a letter in my direction.

"Ruslan, it's for you," he said as he exaggeratedly sniffed the letter and rolled his eyes. "From Kyiv, nonetheless."

The fragrance was pleasant indeed, but the return address on the envelope was even more so. My heart skipped a beat—Zinaida, Kyiv, Mezhyhirska Street 47, Podil District. The letter was innocuous, recounting the memorable experiences—a heartfelt thank-you from all three for a wonderful time. They were planning for a return visit next year, sometime in late June. She ended with listing her cell phone number if ever I was in Kyiv. But the biggest surprise was a photo of herself. That sealed the deal, at least in my mind. My heart skipped a beat. My *Ruslan* may have found his *Ludmila*.

7

Podil

The following summer could not come soon enough. Surprisingly this time Zina came alone. I was glad—I would have her to myself. I vowed to be on my best behavior.

She was more attractive than ever. Signs of maturity were evolving on her face as baby fat was diminishing. She seemed a bit more reserved without her girlfriends, but still she was friendly, cheerful, and more outgoing. Yet something was obviously on her mind.

We spent most of the days at the beach until late in the afternoon. She had the *Poseidon* prepare food baskets for us, and I bought refreshments from the vendors at the seaside. We talked, we frolicked in the sea, we talked some more about our visions of the future, and we daydreamed in the shade of a beach umbrella. She informed me with pride that she was accepted to the *National Medical University* in Kyiv and would begin her studies in the fall semester. She was somewhat apprehensive about the new challenge. Perhaps that explained her uneasiness.

Unlike the evenings of the previous visit, this time they were not as hectic. We did the nightclub routine, but the revelry ended well before the usual closing time. We actually skipped two nights just lingering over late dinner and then ending the evening on the hotel verandah watching the silvery crescent sail over the sea.

I was in a melancholy mood on the final day of her visit. I sensed Zina was feeling the same. We did not say much, just daydreamed at the seaside and soaked in the sun. In the evening we had dinner at the hotel in a quiet corner of the dining room. Neither one of us wanted to go anywhere. The waiter did not rush us. We did not speak much between imbibing sips of Crimean pinot grigio from the *Massandra* vineyard.

While I was happy for her acceptance to medical school, the newscast had a dark shadow on any future that I naively envisioned with her. What future, what happiness could there be for a school dropout and a sophisticated doctor of medicine? As it were, my current prospects were nil. She may have come to deliver the bad news in person. If that was the case, I gave her a lot of credit and admired her for it.

There was no sense in sitting and moping. So be it if that was the way it was. She would have her last fling. I owed her that much. I would see to that. First, I needed to become who I was, not some imaginary curly-haired gigolo named Ruslan.

"Zinochka dear," I said, putting on a cheerful face, "let's end our last evening together with a bang. Let's finish the wine and head to the *Coral Club* and dance until they throw us out and then greet the sunrise on the beach. But first I must confess to you who and what I really am. My real name is Asher Feldman. I am a Jew."

Her hazel eyes nearly popped the sockets. She burst out, "That is wonderful! I love that name—Asher . . . Asher Feldman. What a wonderful ending to a bad dream. This makes everything magical. I honestly thought you were a gypsy."

I was stunned. I did not know what to make of it or what to say.

"You have taken a heavy burden off my shoulders, darling Asher. I also must clarify something. Did you notice in my letters that I never used my family name? It is Stein. I was afraid you would assume that I was Jewish and your attitude toward me would change and I would lose you."

A million implications raced through my head. Mixed marriages were nothing unusual in our society. I had a number of friends who did just that. There had to be something more to it. I would not interrupt her. I reached across the table and held her hand.

"My father is a religious man. He would not have his only child wed outside his faith. I had the worst emotionally stressful year of my life. I finally got his consent but only if you would convert to Judaism. This is why I came here to plead for your conversion. You cannot imagine how relieved I am. I should not admit this, but I fell in love with you from the first moment I saw you."

"My precious Zinochka, you were always in my thoughts. I was so thrilled when I got your first letter. For some reason, I dared not call. Your letters kept my hopes alive. It has been a long year for me also. Now I am at a loss. I dropped out of school when my mother died and lived by my wits. I am afraid it would not work for us."

"Don't be so negative. My father owns an established jewelry business. He also started with nothing. Now he is probably the most sought-after jeweler in Kyiv. He will teach you the trade. Come to Kyiv. Meet my father and see what you think. We own the apartment building where we live. You can have your own place. And if you are not satisfied, you can always return."

I waited for the tourist season to end before embarking on the journey. In the interim I converted every hryvnia that I had to dollars and euros and sold the house, furnishings, and the chickens. Whatever was left I gave to my neighbor Avraam.

My tattooed friends, with whom I occasionally rumbled on outings on the Harley, were most solicitous about my trip. They outlined the safest route for me on a map and identified reliable places along the way where I could stay without fear of being robbed. They also gave me a list of cell phone numbers in case I needed help.

One of the burly toughs came up to me and said on the QT, "Asher—I was Asher in the group—come here. I want to show you something I suspect you didn't know."

He led me to the rear left of the bike and stopped at the hard saddlebag. "Look here," he said as he squatted and reached underneath. He twisted a knob and a flap opened. On it was a pistol and a spare clip. He tapped his nose and said with a devilish smile, "Just in case, keep it under your pillow at night. You never know."

As daylight got shorter and the Azov seawater temperature could not sufficiently recover from the night chill, I strapped all my worldly possessions on the bike, donned my patriotic helmet and goggles, slipped into my new biker leather jacket and gloves, and set out on the five-hundred-mile trip. I headed north to Donetsk on a potholed secondary road and further to Artemivsk. That connected me to a well-maintained national highway leading to Kyiv through Kharkiv. The Harley roared like an enraged beast charging through the tundra at attack speed.

At that pace, I could have managed the distance in one long stretch, but arriving late in the evening on the first get-acquainted visit made for a bad impression. So I stayed at an inn sixty miles from the city that was on my list. To my surprise, the receptionist was expecting me. He received a telephone call from a friend. He even told me to put the bike in the shed and handed me a padlock. The boys took care of me, and I owed them.

I arrived in the Podil District the next morning after the rush hour. Zina agreed to meet me in front of their building after her morning classes, and she would introduce me to her parents over lunch. She would be waiting for me at noontime.

With several hours to kill, I decided to familiarize myself with the lay of the land. But first I took off my biker jacket and wrapped it inside out around the bundle on the back seat. I covered my helmet with a camouflage cloth to avoid unnecessary attention.

I crossed the Metro Bridge into the old city and followed the Dnipro shore road until I exited at the main thoroughfare of the district. Podil was a densely packed neighborhood where expansion had nowhere to go but skyward. Construction cranes despoiled the horizon in every direction. I meandered around until I came across Mezhyhirska Street which I slowly traversed until I passed Zina's address. It was an imposing multistoried apartment building with two burly uniformed doormen at the entrance, obviously posted there not merely to greet visitors and open doors. Further up the street, a mere stone's throw from her residence was the magnificent, jaw-dropping façade executed in a Neo-Moorish architectural style. This was the entrance to the *Great Choral Synagogue of Kyiv*. The sprawling complex on Schekovytska

Street survived its share of woes during Stalin's repression and later was subjected to the ultimate desecration by the Nazis as a horse stable. This was the very same humiliating tactic applied to independent Ukrainian Orthodox Churches by the Soviets in the nineteen thirties.

Whether I was feeling the fatigue from the previous day's journey or the anxiety of facing the inquisition in less than an hour, I needed to get off the bike and regroup. I remembered passing a large plaza on my way into the district. I doubled back to the shore road and looked for a place to park. I saw a row of motorcycles along a railing overlooking the river adjacent to the river terminal. I pulled over, parked, and took in the view of the tourist boats anchored at the port and the entire square across the highway. This appeared to be a magnet for tourists judging by the wall-to-wall wandering crowds. Zina and I would join the crowd on more than one lazy afternoon once I settled in.

The plaza was named Postal Square in recognition of the century-old district post office located at its center, which, in the present day, functions as a compact art gallery. Adjacent to the stucco building was the bright-yellow domed *Rizdvo* (Christmas) *Church* and its equally distinct bell tower. The five-star Fairmont Grand Hotel anchored the open space. Red-tented food and souvenir kiosks were scattered throughout with the newest McDonalds eatery at front and center. On the southern perimeter of the expanse, adjacent to the Riviera Hotel, was the main tourist attraction. It was the renowned *Kyiv Funicular*. The word Podil literally translates to below. The district is below or at the bottom of a steep incline from the old city. In the past the funicular was the central pedestrian connection between the two parts of the capital. The opening of the metro station at the square relegated the funicular to the tourists. A long line of sightseers could be seen patiently shuffling along the stepped walkway to the entrance, awaiting to experience the curious ascent.

Instead of clearing my mind and regaining my self-confidence, I felt a tightening in my chest as I looked nervously at my wristwatch for the tenth time in the last five minutes. My imagination was racing through a murky forest of self-doubt and the folly of my naiveté after gaping at the citadel Zina flippantly called home. It would be laughable that I had the gall to aspire so far out of my reach if it was not so painful. Yet I made the move and now it was time to face even worse disappointment.

I circled around the square and headed westward on side streets until I flowed into Mezhyhirska. I checked my watch and saw that I was on time. I pulled up in front of the building, killed the engine, took off the helmet and cutoff leather gloves, and began to disembark. The two centurions began walking slowly in my direction. That was all I needed was to start a ruckus. I set the bike on the kickstand without giving them notice.

Fortunately I heard Zina's voice as the front door opened, "Asher darling, I did not expect you to be so punctual!"

She ran up to me and we kissed.

The guardsmen stood still looking at each other in confusion. They reminded me of my biker friends in Mariupol—solid blocks of granite from head to toe, full no-nonsense faces. The only difference was that they had no visible tattoos, good people to know for future reference.

"I am so happy you are here. I just this minute walked through the door. I did not even have a chance to make myself presentable."

"You look ravishing!"

"I do believe you missed me." She giggled. "Let's go in. We'll have the rest of the day to ourselves. I will hold you personally responsible for missing my afternoon classes."

"I just can't leave my cycle and valuables out on the street."

"Not to worry. Boris will find a place for the motorcycle. And he will bring your belongings to your apartment. You are in safe hands."

She went over and spoke to one of the strongmen. He nodded and tipped his hat.

"It's all settled!" she assured me.

"Thanks . . . Did you mention something about an apartment?"

"Yes, Father keeps a furnished apartment for out-of-town visitors. He does business worldwide. It's a matter of convenience and safety for them to stay here. The apartment is yours for the duration . . . We had better go in. I am sure my parents are anxious to get acquainted."

The bulky double door outfitted with polished brass hardware opened into an entrance hall brightly illuminated with a central candelabra and crystal wall sconces. A round table was planted below the candelabra with a large bouquet of freshly cut flowers. Settees, upholstered in broad, patterned blue-and-gold brocaded stripes, bordered the walls. The floor was black and white marble displayed in a diamond pattern and enclosed at the perimeter in black. The walls were olive-brown marble intricately veined in ferrous pigments. The space had the feel of an upscale hotel lobby.

Along the right wall was a showroom behind outsized windows at either side of glass doors. Rows of display cases populated the interior as well as mirrored walls and tufted red velvet chairs and side tables.

I was closely following Zina, mesmerized by the brilliant sparklers radiating through the windows.

"Come along, darling," she said while pressing the elevator button at the end of the hall and cradling her school books. "You will have a grand tour after lunch."

I would be lying if I claimed positive thoughts on my way up in the elevator. I miscalculated—miscalculated badly. What in heaven's name was I thinking? I might as well make the best of it and enjoy the adventure. There was always Mariupol to fall back on.

I paid no attention to our ascent until the elevator chimed. It took an eternity to get there. I took a deep breath. Come what may—I deemed not to make a fool of myself.

A formally dressed youngish man of average height and wiry frame stood in the hallway as the elevator door opened. He wore the traditional garb of a practicing Orthodox Jew—black suit, white shirt, black necktie, and yarmulke. He had well-groomed facial growth without any traces of gray. He had a handsome face and a welcoming smile.

"Ahh . . . Zinochka, I thought it might be you. And this, I presume, is the young man you have been telling us about?"

"Yes, Papa. This is Asher, Asher Feldman," she said with a noticeable excitement in her voice.

"I am pleased to meet you at last," he said and extended his hand. "I am Isaac, Zina's father. I've heard so much about you. Welcome to our home."

It was a solid handshake. I reciprocated the greeting. First-name basis—we were beyond formal patronyms.

I noticed an electronic eye in the ceiling at the end of the corridor in full view, similar in appearance that I saw in the elevator. There was no attempt to conceal either.

"We should continue our discussion inside. I am sure mama is anxious to greet you and get to know you. I believe she is setting the table."

First impressions carry the day flashed through my thick skull. I turned to Zina and took her books. I should have done that downstairs or at least in the elevator. It was an opportunity missed.

Zina smiled.

The apartment was spacious by any standard, decorated tastefully with quality furnishings and art. It was an open layout overlooking the river to the northeast in the direction of Fisherman's Island.

"Mama, this is Asher," said Zina. "Asher, this is my mother Rifka."

"I am pleased to meet you," said I.

"I welcome you to our home. I feel I have known you for quite some time," she replied with a curious smile. "I hope you are famished. The food is on the table. We can get better acquainted while we eat."

If I wasn't told differently, I would have mistaken Zina's mother for an older sister. Their striking features, their complexions, their trim figures, their mannerisms, their taste in colorful clothes, even their eyes and hairdos were similar.

8

Ludmila

The lunch was more of an intimate family celebration than just a simple midday meal. The Steins spared no expense. In adherence to Ukrainian custom, the table literally bowed from the abundance of prepared food: meats, smoked sturgeon, salads, pickled cucumbers and tomatoes, condiments, and a bottle of Balaclava Sauvignon. All aspects of the repast were in accordance with dietary orthodox laws without exception. Notably absent was hard liquor, for which I had no particular craving. But I was asked and I dutifully declined.

My fears of intense grilling proved unfounded. The mood at the table was convivial. There were no probing questions or furtive disapproving quizzical glances between the parents. On the contrary, the parents seemed to know more about me than I cared to admit and did not cause me to be defensive or embarrassed. I suspected Zina conditioned them relentlessly since our time together on her prior year's visit to Mariupol. She had made up her mind there and then, and all their entreaties and objections faded away once they found out that I was Jewish.

The conversation mostly flowed in my direction. It turned out that Isaac's formidable years bore similarity to mine. By the time he was eleven years old, his mother died, and then several months later his father also passed on. There were no close relatives to take him in, and he was destined to spend his youth in an orphanage. An elderly childless couple stepped forward and took him in within days of his father's demise. They brought him up as their own and registered him as their son, bestowing on him their family name Stein. They did retain his father's name Leiba on the documents as his patronym. Thus Isaac Leibovich Stein was legally born again in the eyes of the law.

Those memories overwhelmed Isaac and glazed his eyes. He paused for a sip of wine, cleared his throat, took a deep breath, and fondly resumed his tale.

His foster father had a small jewelry business with a reputation for fashioning unique made-to-order costume jewelry. He was a craftsman from the old school and lovingly taught Isaac the rudiments of the trade. Isaac's interest in secondary school rapidly fell by the wayside and was supplanted by the fascination with precious gems.

The dissolution of the Soviet Empire and the declaration of Ukrainian independence flooded the marketplace with new money. With the uncertainties in the economy, the newly minted democrats had yet to discover offshore havens and sought shelter closer to home in hard currency and gems. It was not in the stones set in intricate jewelry to impress the less fortunate but in multi-carat diamonds, emeralds, rubies, and such that they could squirrel under the mattress for a rainy day and out of sight from the curious.

Supply and demand forced his foster father to rethink his approach to doing business. He felt that middlemen took the lion's share of the profits and left him pittance and without leverage to bargain for a more lucrative deal. He decided to go directly to the wholesalers. He, together with his adopted teenage son Isaac, headed first to Amsterdam and then to Antwerp to test the waters. The promise of volume purchases of high-quality diamonds opened doors and established valuable contacts for the future. Eventually they traveled to Rotterdam, Europe's largest commercial port, where emeralds, rubies, and other precious gems flowed from all the corners of the world. Platinum and gold were also available at competitive prices.

By the end of the century, business was brisk and capital reserves were substantial enough to warrant significant expansion. At that time his foster father was well beyond retirement age and in poor health. He handed over the reins to his adopted son, twenty-one-year-old Isaac. He saw no point in abandoning Podil and moving uphill to the city center. This was his comfort zone. He did not have to chase the trade; the trade came to him through word of mouth. And the most important for him, he was within walking distance to the synagogue where he could practice his faith.

A dilapidated wood-framed house became available on Mezhyhirska Street. He negotiated the purchase at a give-away price and immediately razed the property to the ground. An architect designed a veritable fortress for the burgeoning enterprise with spacious living quarters and manufacturing space.

As much as I enjoyed hearing the family history, the message was not lost on me. From time to time I glanced at Zina. Her loving eyes bathed me with enthusiasm. She seemed ready to jump out of her seat and declare victory. I felt I found my home. Indeed *Ruslan* found his *Ludmila*.

9

One of Us

I woke up early the next morning in the comfort of the spacious apartment. Once Zina settled me in, we kissed and called it an early night. She needed to prepare for a morning examination, and I was barely keeping my eyes open from the exertion of the previous day's jet-propelled ride. I shed my clothes in a pile, washed and went straight to bed. As soon as my head touched the feather pillow I was sound asleep.

Zina was in an upbeat mood, buoyed by the positive reaction from her parents, particularly by her father's emotional reminiscences of his own trying journey—reminiscences she did not anticipate to hear.

At our parting, she quipped, "Well, what do you think?"

"What do I think? I think this place is a palace!"

"No, silly." She laughed. "What do you think about what Father said? He has never delved into his past in such heartrending detail. There is no doubt about it. He and Mother have taken you to their hearts . . . I meant, what do you think of his offer to teach you the rudiments of his trade?"

"Do I have a choice?" I teased her mockingly. Then on a more serious note, I said, "This is all your doing and I love you for it, my dearest Zinochka. Don't think that I am not aware of your hard work. I assure you I will give it my best effort."

The apartment was equipped with all the amenities that a visiting traveler would appreciate, executed in the spirit of a home-away-from-home environment. The rooms were spacious and decorated in bright colors of the rainbow and enlivened with lots of daylight through the windows. The view from the sitting room was expansive, overlooking the northern half of Podil and far out beyond the dogleg in the Dnipro, much like the view from the owner's apartment. The full-functioning kitchen was outfitted with modern appliances. There was a small side table and two chairs along the wall convenient for a quick bite to eat. A bowl was on the table displaying difficult to get imported fruit: a pineapple at the center surrounded with bananas, oranges, and local seasonal fruit. The refrigerator was generously stocked with a variety of products and bottles of *Obolon* beer. The cabinets were likewise filled with dry and canned goods.

For starters I decided to scrub off the grime from the previous two days and step forward into the future cleansed from the remnants of the past. The bath was a floor-to-ceiling marbled chamber. On one side was a raised whirlpool and on the other a shower with modern fixtures including a central rain shower head protruding from the ceiling. That rain shower was my first taste of what it meant to be filthy rich. I just stood under the endless stream as if in a trance expecting the water to abruptly turn ice-cold as was the norm for the ordinary citizen. But the hot water just kept coming. It boggled my imagination—the hot water just refused to run out.

I dressed quickly in slacks and an open-collar shirt. I fried myself two eggs and simulated bacon strips. I assumed they had to be simulated—most likely they were beef strips—no pork in this household. Anyway, they tasted like real bacon. A cup of hot tea and a slice of black bread were more than enough after the previous day's eating fest.

With all the opulence about me, I would have been surprised if there was no maid service. Nevertheless, still mindful of first impressions, I proceeded to tidy up. I rinsed the dishes and the frying pan and stacked them in the dishwasher. Next I went to the bedroom. My clothes were neatly put away in the chest of drawers and my shoes were paired at the bottom of the clothes closet. My only two suits, my only formal wardrobe, the Travolta white and a dark-brown suit I wore to my mother's funeral, were hanging in the closet along with several pairs of slacks. The only possessions that were missing were my leather biker jacket, boots, and the patriotic helmet. I thought it strange. I would not make it an issue but would inquire at the appropriate time. I assumed that my toiletries, such that they were, were in the bathroom.

I made the bed and went downstairs to see what was what. By then Zina was off to school, and I was ready to take the first step into my future.

It was still early, too early for any activity in the jewelry store, even though the brilliant lighting was in full force. I went out the front door. The two centurions were already at their post. I approached the one Zina addressed as Boris.

"Good morning, gentlemen," I said loud enough for both guardians to hear.

"Good morning to you" was the friendly reply.

"Boris, I was wondering what happened to my bike."

"Not to worry, Mr. Feldman. Your Harley is safe in the garage. I can take you there right now if you wish."

"I would appreciate that. But in the future please don't call me Mr. Feldman. I was never a mister Feldman. I am Asher . . . not Asher Yehudovich . . . just plain Asher."

"Very well, sir. Asher it will be from now on. If you would follow me, I will take you to the garage so you can familiarize yourself with our security procedures at the same time."

We proceeded to the side of the building. As we approached the formidable solid door facing the street, Boris waved his hand at an overhead camera and the door began to rise.

"Normally you should use the elevator to the basement level. There is also a camera in the elevator. When you press the basement button, whoever is on watch at the time will activate the control. When you want to return to the garage from the street, stop before the door, look up if you are on the Harley. There is a speaker right there. You will be asked to identify yourself until the guards get to know you. Security is active day and night."

We descended into the concrete tunnel and passed through yet another electronically controlled checkpoint. Surprisingly the garage seemed not as large as I would have imagined in comparison to the size of the building. We headed toward several sedans parked near the back wall. The elevator enclosure stuck out in the corner on the right with the door opening to the side.

"This space seems rather small," I commented.

"Yes, it is. There is a good reason. Almost half the footprint of the building is dedicated to the jewelry business. The walls surrounding that portion of the basement are doubly reinforced with steel bars and are more than twice as thick as normal. It is accessible only by a separate elevator at the back of the showroom. A tank could not penetrate through those walls. Isaac Leibovich built this place like a fortress. It would take a small army to overwhelm this place."

"Rather a calculating individual is Isaac Leibovich?"

"In more ways than you could imagine."

We passed a black Mercedes sedan, a tan Range Rover, an empty space, and an outlived Lada coupe. Behind the automobiles stood two motorcycles. My jaw dropped at the sight. Standing next to my puny bike was a silver/black Electra Glide Ultra Classic, spit-polished as if it was on display in a showroom. I approached the machine with reverence brushing my hand caressingly along the leather-bound saddle and equally ergonomic elevated passenger seat. The control panel instrumentation was eye captivating beyond belief with the outsized touchscreen GPS display and audio system. The power plant and the chrome exhaust system sparkled brilliantly. There was not a speck of dirt to be seen, not even on the wheels or tires.

Boris stood there with a proud smile on his face appreciating the loving attention bestowed on the machine.

"My, oh my . . . This is a work of art. Is it possibly yours?"

I could sense that those words were welcomed like honey pouring over his heart.

He responded in kind. "Yes, it is. I bought the bike several months ago. It rides like a magic carpet. There's nothing like it."

"I am somewhat embarrassed to have my beat-up relic next to this beauty. The least I can do is make it presentable."

"I can help you with that if you wish. I have all the necessary preparations in my locker. By the way, your equipment is in the locker next to mine. The locker is not padlocked. There is no need for locks down here. You can leave your key on the bike without concern. Also, I did not remove your weapon from the saddlebag. It is safe where it is."

"Thank you. I'll keep that in mind. I would like to accompany you sometime when you ride out to the countryside."

"You are welcome to hit the road with us. We have a group of enthusiasts who go on excursions quite frequently. It makes for a very pleasant day. I will let you know when we will be going."

"I will look forward to it."

"Let's take the elevator up to the lobby."

10

Apprentice

As Boris and I exited the elevator I noticed activity in the showroom. I thanked him for the tour and headed straight for the double glass doors. The doors were locked. A woman was fussing with a display cabinet inside with her back turned to the entrance. I knocked. She turned and with a smile on her face came forward and let me in.

"Yes, can I help you?" said the perky young woman.

She was above average in height, slender, and well-proportioned. She was elegant from head to toe—attractive enough to be a model. Her hair was silky blond with a wave in the front and loosely flowing toward the nape of her neck and tied in a simple bow with a black ribbon. Her smile was genuine, and her blue eyes were friendly and inviting. The makeup was subtle and did not detract from her natural beauty. She wore a white silk blouse, a black skirt, and high-heeled dress shoes. But her jewelry was out of character in the extreme to put it mildly.

"I am here to see Mr. Stein. He is expecting me."

"Isaac Leibovich should be here shortly. We are expecting a special client within the hour, so he should be on his way as we speak. Is there anything I can help you with while you are waiting? Would you like a cup of freshly brewed coffee or a glass of tea?"

"I am fine, thank you. May I introduce myself? My name is Asher. I suspect we will be seeing each other quite often."

I extended my hand and she responded.

"I am very glad to meet you, Asher. Welcome to our little tight-knit family. I am Nina. I staff the showroom . . . So you are the fiancé that we all have been hearing so much about. That Zina sure has a keen eye."

"I could not possibly disagree with your astute observation."

We both chuckled.

"Forgive my impertinence, Nina," I said. "But do you normally wear that much jewelry? It seems a bit much."

"What would you say if I told you yes?" She laughed and stroked the necklace fondly with her right hand.

The necklace was a king's ransom floating on a cascade of intricate, hand-crafted white gold. Four matching sets of rectangular-cut emeralds descended from the neckline, each set progressively longer and clustered with diamonds. The two strands merged into a pendant displaying the most magnificent emerald one dared imagine and were also surrounded with diamonds to draw attention and dazzle the eye with brilliant verdant green.

Matching pear-shaped emerald earrings, bracelets on each hand of different sizes, and rings on the fingers, one oval in shape and the other marquise, encrusted with diamond baguettes rounded out the display on the walking, talking manikin.

"It does look absurd, doesn't it?" Nina said. "This is not the usual way we do business. We have this special client from Lviv who has been buying loose quality gems from us for a number of years. Well, this oligarch, as we call the newly anointed elite, recently upgraded his marital status, to put it politely. He wanted to make a statement to his new bride of his eternal love and devotion. He commissioned Isaac Leibovich months ago to create an ensemble of emerald jewelry that would attest to his generosity and self-importance. Isaac Leibovich went back and forth with him over the internet with proposed designs until they settled on what you are seeing. These stones are flawless, investment-grade gems that also took some effort to acquire, especially this transparent thirty-two-carat piece.

"As far as why I am so ridiculously decorated, our buyer is passing through Kyiv from vacation in the Greek isles and wants to see the collection in person before accepting it. He specifically asked that I wear the jewels so he could see how it would look on his bride before he would accept delivery. So here I am as you can see."

"Good morning, Nina," said my future father-in-law as he briskly entered the showroom.

"Good morning, Isaac Leibovich."

"Good morning to you, Asher. You are up and about quite early."

"Good morning to you, sir. I am an early riser."

"I see you have gotten acquainted with my niece. That is good. She knows our operation as well as I do. So you can learn quite a bit from her. Our only other associate, Misha, is not due in until later in the day. He and I cut the gems and hand-craft the jewelry . . . I had a call from Boris. He picked up Moroz at Borispol and they are well on the way. They should be here momentarily. After he leaves, I will show you around and we can talk."

In a matter of minutes, Boris entered the showroom escorting two men. One was tall, solidly built and dressed in a suit and an open-collared shirt. The other was a balding, average-looking individual, wearing a jogging suit and track shoes.

"Ahh, Fedir Petrovich," exclaimed the proprietor gregariously, proffering his hand to the balding visitor. "Welcome to our shop. It's a pleasure to finally meet you in person. I hope your vacation in the Greek islands was pleasant. We are all disappointed that Ksenia Ivanivna was feeling under the weather and could not stop by."

As the formalities continued, Boris left his post, and the tall gent, unmistakably the bodyguard, drifted over to the display case of watches at the far end of the showroom.

"She had too much sun and decided to fly home directly. That's the reason I asked for the jewelry to be worn by someone else."

"I would like you to meet my niece, Nina. She volunteered to wear the ensemble and the additional pieces we prepared for you. And this is my new associate, Asher."

Handshake with Asher and a two-handed one and a smile with Nina.

"It is a pleasure to meet you both. Nina, thank you for volunteering. Seeing the jewelry on a computer screen limits the visual impact."

He stepped closer to admire the necklace.

"Isaac Leibovich you have outdone yourself. Every piece is magnificent. I bow to your creativity. That necklace, that emerald . . ."

"That emerald is twenty-two carats, flawless and transparent. It is a rarity and an excellent investment. Nina, please take off the necklace and put it on a display tray."

She removed the necklace and placed it on the tray covered with a black felt cloth which she prepared in advance.

Isaac turned over the necklace and handed a loop to Moroz. He pointed to a spot on the pendant.

"Each piece has my initials and a unique serial number. We keep a ledger if the need ever arises for identification or the purchase price needs to be confirmed."

"I see it. Excellent. I am taking the entire grouping."

"Good. We will pack and store the jewels in our vault until all the payments are reconciled. Boris and Asher will hand-deliver them to you in Lviv."

The enthusiasm on Moroz's face vanished. He obviously intended to take the jewels with him. That was the reason he made the detour.

"As soon as I get back, I will transfer the funds to your account," he said with confidence in an attempt to mask his disappointment. "Is it the same account I used previously?"

"Yes, the bank in Rotterdam. Nina can give you the details."

"There is no need. I have it. I assume there is no change in the price?"

"As far as the price is concerned, it is what we agreed to. As soon as the transfer's clear, we will deliver on the very same day . . . Can I interest you in a bite to eat?"

Moroz looked at his watch and said, "I would have liked to very much, but there is still time to catch the next flight to Lviv if I leave now. I am sure there will be opportunities in the future. I am thinking of running for the *Verchowna Rada* (Parliament), so you may tire of seeing me too frequently."

You sly fox, I thought, *you must be one step ahead of the law and you want to buy immunity from prosecution as a member of that august body.*

"I look forward to that. I wish you success. I'll be more than happy to take you under my wing and help you get settled."

"I appreciate that very much. Now, I must leave you, good people."

"I will walk with you to the limousine," said Isaac. "Asher please help Nina pack the jewelry, and I'll put it in the vault when I return."

"Well, that's that," said Isaac on his return. "The charade is over."

He walked over to the stack of decorative boxes on the display case. He nodded with satisfaction and patted the stack.

"Thank you, Ninochka. Well done. We'll put these away in a few minutes. We won't pack them until the payment is made. But first, Asher, tell me what valuable lesson have you learned from this episode?"

I did not want to appear foolish, especially when Isaac called the multimillion transaction a charade. I replied lamely, "I am not quite sure, Isaac Leibovich. I did notice that his enthusiasm changed when you told him that the jewels would not be delivered until the payment was received."

"You are right of course. Let me ask you this. If he left with the jewelry, what would be my chances of collecting a single kopek from a man of his notorious reputation? None whatsoever, I can assure you. You always have to know with whom you are dealing. Now, take our citizen Fedir Moroz as an example. I sold him millions of dollars' worth of gems over the years. He paid, the transfers cleared, and the merchandise was hand-delivered to him. No problems. No issues. No complaints. Why then, all of a sudden, he needed to divert from his vacation trip to personally pick up the jewels? I worked with him on the details for months. He knew exactly what he was getting. Did he need to stop in? I am willing to bet that he was already booked on the connecting flight and that his trophy wife is waiting for him in a lounge at Borispol sipping a cocktail and dreaming of all that glitter.

"Several other details come to mind that you should be aware of at the outset. All those emeralds, including the thirty-two-carat gem, were given to me on consignment strictly based on my reputation, which took years to establish. This business is built on trust. Once that trust is violated, you might as well start selling costume jewelry and souvenirs to tourists because you will be dealing strictly in cash, and the quality merchandise will only be available at a high premium. I could not tie up such an enormous amount of my own money and chance that Moroz would change his mind at the last minute and not take delivery. If that were the case, I would return the gems, and I would be merely charged a token surcharge.

"With respect to the payments, transactions of this magnitude must never be done in cash for many reasons besides safety. In yesteryear Mayer Rothschild and his five sons set the precedent using carrier pigeons and journal credits to crisscross European borders unmolested. Today wire transfers serve that purpose."

"One last observation, I told Moroz that you and Boris would hand-deliver his purchase. This is true. I would like you to get your feet wet traveling, eventually throughout Europe—at times with me, at times with Boris, and once you learn the diamond business, you may travel alone. By the way, we always travel in comfort in first class. If Moroz goes through with the payment, he will in effect own the jewels. We will keep our end of the bargain. No doubt he will have his men follow you every step of the way until he takes possession at the Lviv airport. Here in Kyiv no one would dare accost you. So your safety is guaranteed."

"No one dare accost you in Kyiv" brought to mind protection beyond Boris's capabilities and at what cost. I bit my tongue.

"Now let's take these boxes down to the vault," Isaac said.

Nina picked up the boxes and they proceeded around the partition at the back of the showroom to the elevator. As they entered and the button was depressed, a voice came on, "Good day, Isaac Leibovich. Are you on the way down?"

"Good day to you, Sasha. Yes, I am . . . Meet our new associate, Asher. Asher, please look up to the camera."

"Thank you," said Sasha. "I made a photo, which I will post to inform the others. Welcome aboard Asher."

The elevator descended slowly.

The vault was indeed a formidable fortress in every sense of the word. The massive steel floor-to-ceiling structure, as wide as it was tall, could have satisfied the needs of the National Bank of Ukraine. Isaac placed his right hand on a scanner. The electronic lock clicked. He then dialed in the combination and opened the door by turning the centrally located wheel which retracted the interlocks through a set of intermeshed gears. Shelves lined the interior with trays and velvet-covered panels of what I presumed to be jewelry and cut gems. There were cartons on the lower shelves labeled with names. There were stacks of gold and silver bars and toward the rear were several stacks of bundled currency. The wealth was mind-boggling. It could very well have contained the assets of the National Bank of a small nation.

"Don't be overly impressed, Asher," said Isaac, noticing my eyes about to burst the sockets. "Much of what you are seeing is in storage for clients, including some competitors in the old city who lack safe facilities for their seasonal stock, or work in various stages of completion. Come, let me show you the rest of the basement."

As Isaac was closing the vault and arming the electronic alarm, I said, "How did you ever get that safe in here? Was it assembled in place?"

"It came as a complete unit from the factory. Now, you tell me how it could possibly wind up in here?"

It was a bad move on my part. I hated to fail my first test even though it was delivered innocently with a smile on his face. The one possibility was that the safe was brought in through the garage and set before the interior wall was erected. But it looked like it would exceed the ceiling height since the bottom and the top were poking through the cement. The vault was too tall for such a likelihood.

Convinced that Isaac tended to plan every detail of his personal and business affairs in advance and that he may have tested me with a trick question, I took a chance and replied emphatically, "The safe was set in place and the building was constructed around it."

"Asher, you have a head on your shoulders," he reacted with amazement. "Yes, you are absolutely correct."

A slight nod and approval also alighted Nina's face.

Isaac pointed at the vertical ladder attached to the side of the safe leading to a steel trap door bolted from within.

"This is an emergency escape in case of power failure and the elevator ceases to function. We have a power generator that supplies our electricity automatically, but you never know. The ladder gives you peace of mind if nothing else. We have yet to use it . . . The rest of the basement as you can see is used for the coarse molding and shaping the precious metals. The final product is completed upstairs."

The working area was well-lighted and painted in eye-soothing pastel color. Several framed collages of what I assumed to be their best designs decorated the walls. The environment did not at all feel like some medieval dungeon for concocting clandestine alchemy. Several speakers were on the walls wired to a receiver. There were a number of work tables, each with two adjustable, lighted magnifiers craning over the work space. Series of graduated eye loops and working tools were neatly arranged at each station. A rack of various molds and insulated gloves lined the wall. At the back of the space stood half-dozen electrical crucibles and hardware to manipulate them. Smaller melting vessels and soldering irons were also at each station.

Isaac looked at his watch and said, "I am afraid we must conclude this brief tour. Unfortunately, I have an appointment in the old city that I cannot break. We will just have enough time for a bite to eat before I must depart. I invite both of you to join me. Misha should be along by the time we finish. He will show you the rest. Nina, please introduce Asher to him. He is expected."

11

The Shop

Misha was an elderly man built close to the ground with a disarming smile nestled in thinning gray facial growth. Clad in traditional Hasidic garb and a black wide-rimmed fedora, he was as round as he was tall—a jolly rosy-cheeked munchkin if there ever was one.

"Asher, it has a pleasant ring to it . . . Asher," he said in a sing-song manner. "I am happy to meet you, Asher. Isaac tells me you wish to learn the diamond trade. I will do my best to make a craftsman out of you if you are serious about it. The business aspects, which are no less important in today's highly competitive world, will be Isaac's end of your apprenticeship. Have you any familiarity with gemology other than admiring gems in a jeweler's display window?"

"No, none whatsoever. To tell the truth, I was not in a position to be interested in jewelry, not even when walking past the hotel displays where I was working. But I am eager to learn the trade."

"I promise to teach you all I know. It's a skill you don't learn overnight. It requires perseverance and lots of practice and patience . . . Why don't we go into the work area and start with the basics."

We walked to the rear of the showroom, stepped behind the partition where the elevator to the basement was located. Opposite the elevator was a heavy curtain and three lockers along the wall on the right.

Opposite the lockers stood a china cabinet with all the accouterments on the counter for brewing coffee and an electric water kettle for making tea. Flanking the cabinet was a counter-high refrigerator and a miniature sink. The aroma of fresh-brewed coffee, no doubt Nina's handiwork, filled the crowded cubicle.

Misha ceremoniously removed his hat and coat and deposited them in his locker. He took out white sleeve protectors from a shelf and pulled them over his arms and elbows and donned an apron. He swept aside the curtain and revealed a space that was somewhat narrow but seemed to extend the full length of the building. It was jam-packed with equipment which, aside from several wide-screen *Apple* computer stations and a draftsman's table, was a total mystery to me.

"In recent years, technology significantly automated the processing of gemstones to the extent that true artisans like our own Isaac Leibovich are few and far in between," said Misha. "It also changed the emphasis of how we do business. No longer do we waste our time with marginal stones. There are factories in places such as India, China, Indonesia, and Thailand operating around the clock that produce thousands of cut diamonds daily and sell them in bulk at competitive prices. We concentrate on investment size stones. Isaac's reputation as an outstanding brillianteer keeps us occupied with challenges from all corners of the globe."

"What exactly is a brillianteer?" I asked.

"A brillianteer is the expert who polishes the final facets onto the diamond to bring out the maximum attainable brilliance in the crystal. A properly faceted diamond, depending on size, can possibly sell for double the price of an equivalent carat gem. Some people like Isaac have that extra sensory vision that people like me are not blessed with. The larger the raw stone, the more their services are sought."

Misha approached a workstation with dual computer screens positioned at convenient viewing angles on either side of a black oblong cylindrical machine imprinted in white letters *Sarine.* He opened the cover and exposed a layered turntable with a central post on top of which was mounted a roughly cut crystal.

"This is the heart of our operation," he explained. "It is the state-of-the-art gemstone evaluation system that provides a three-dimensional mapping of a stone using laser technology."

He sat down at the console and turned on the equipment. He motioned me to pull up a chair and sit next to him. An oblong vertically oriented stone resembling an oversized potato filled the left screen. The right screen displayed a cut crystal in an irregular shape similar to the one exposed in the machine but magnified to full-screen proportions.

"What does all of this mean?" he began his explanation. "We received the stone on the left screen a week ago from our contact in Tel Aviv. You can be sure that the stone was critically examined there in a similar manner. Because of its size and potential market value, they wanted Isaac's opinion of how to get the maximum yield from the specimen."

He manipulated the keyboard and switched the display to reveal the interior detail. There appeared to be a green vein on one side.

"The value of a diamond depends significantly on its clarity," said Misha. "Internal flaws devalue its worth. For example, a flawless one-carat diamond is worth much more than flawed two carats."

He took a pencil and pointed to the vein on the screen.

"You see this inclusion. It affects how the stone can be cut. The rest of the crystal appears clear and unblemished. The next several views are computer-derived possibilities of working around the imperfection. Notice that in every instance the computer recommendation is to extrude two individual but smaller, much less valuable round diamonds. Isaac and I blocked several single gem solutions."

He reacted to a puzzled expression on my face.

"Blocking is a term we use in the trade to mean possible layouts within a given stone to extract the best value from it. Every trade has its own jargon. You will become accustomed to it sooner than you think. Meanwhile, don't be embarrassed to ask . . . Isaac, with his keen eye and the aid of that microscope, managed to squeeze out several milligrams more than my solution. He conveyed his finding to the client in Israel and was authorized to process the diamond here rather than sending it back. He programmed the computer and the *Sarine* roughed out the crystal you see on the right screen.

"So that you don't get the wrong impression that we keep banker's hours"—he chuckled mischievously—"cutting the hardest substance in the world is a painfully slow process even with a laser. I turned on the Sarine yesterday morning to roughly cut the stone, and it completed the task only this afternoon. That is why I am so late . . . I will now transfer the crystal to that antique Orziv laser machine for two major cuts."

Asher appraised the *Orziv* with skepticism. Antique was a rather generous description—ancient would have been a more accurate description. It had the bulky old-Soviet execution of long-abandoned technology, including two CRT displays nested in its center.

Misha's quick eye read the apprehension on the face of his apprentice once again. He followed with a clarifying remark.

"Don't let the appearances fool you. That is the only equipment in our shop that is not up to date simply because it still works well, is reliable and we are used to it. The machine allows cuts at oblique angles that a diamond saw does not. Each cut should take about an hour. I will then return the crystal back to the *Sarine* to block the eight main pavilion facets before polishing the sixteen main facets. While that is in progression, it will give me time to familiarize you with the other tools that we use more frequently, especially the polishing wheels.

"I know all of this sounds confusing to you right now, but like I told you before, these terms will become second nature to you in time. It is the skill that is paramount."

12

Family

I would be hard-pressed to tell you who was more enthusiastic about my apprenticeship, whether it was I or my indefatigable bride-to-be. With all the demands of the medical curriculum—to boot, she chose advanced courses to accelerate earning her medical degree—she carved out time to scour the libraries and bookstores of the city for anything even remotely connected with gemology and diamonds.

Through the centuries, through epochs of greatness, invasions, serfdom, and subservience, one constant sustained the unconquerable Ukrainian state of mind. That constant was the insatiable thirst for knowledge and the love of the written word. It began with the modest chronicles of venerable monks to the patriotic romanticism of Nikolai Gogol of the *Taras Bulba* fame, to the inspiring, revolutionary poetry of the national bard Taras Shevchenko, even the semiliterate peasants, filled library shelves to capacity. Kyiv, the depository of the enormous creativity, had at least a dozen major libraries in addition to the volumes nurtured in the universities, monasteries, synagogues, and mosques. The National Library of Ukraine alone, perched on Holosivskyj Prospect and dominating the southern skyline of the city, boasted over sixteen million titles in its inventory. As such, the library is rated as one of the ten largest in the world.

Where Zina found the time to do the search I dared not ask or imagine. But the results of her effort were stacked high on my desk. I could picture her bouncing from site to site in her rusted relic, her Lada coupe. She loved to tool around alone in the Stalin-era eyesore without the need for a bodyguard. Who would be attracted to the rust and the dents and the beleaguered driver of the rolling deathtrap other than feeling pity for the downtrodden maiden? Despite the slovenly outward appearance, the coupe was mechanically brand new in every sense of the word. Under the hood was a turbo-charged V-6 that sprinted on a dime and would fly on the open road. The tires were brand new Michelins which were camouflaged with grease and soot. The interior was also brand new but upholstered in drab, nondescript cloth. The Lada was maintained at peak performance. It would easily give the best German sports car a run for its money.

And the textbooks—language did not appear to be a discriminator. Russian, English, German, Dutch, it did not matter as long as there was a hint of diamonds or gemology in the title. There was Alexander Zeitsev's *Optical Properties of Diamonds*; there was Peter Read's *Gemology*; there was even the Antwerp edition of Verena Pagel-Theisen's *Diamond Grading ABC*, written entirely in Flemish. Zina had actually the Russian translation on back order in a bookshop on Khreschatyk, the central thoroughfare of the city. The only saving grace for the language barrier in Pagel-Theisen's monumental reference volume was the four hundred plus photos and illustrations to which I turned whenever Zina and I studied together in the evenings, she, her medical assignments, and I, my gemology indoctrination.

This does not mean that I was not eager to learn or that I resented Zina's obsessive enthusiasm with my apprenticeship. On the contrary, her enthusiasm made me work harder not to cause her disappointment and to love her even more for it if indeed that was possible. We developed a routine on weekdays to which I looked forward daylong. After dinner at her mother's table, we retreated to my apartment for serious studies. More often than not, her father was not present. He was either on travel or doing what he enjoyed doing most. He would be downstairs in the shop conjuring a new jewelry design on the computer and refining it on the drafting table where it all began before the intrusion of technology or in the basement experimenting with the precious metals, configuring the delicate settings for his latest creation. There were no clocks in the work areas of the shop, and time did not exist when Isaac Leibovich was on the verge of a breakthrough.

We cleared the area in the living room in front of the windows and moved the dining room table into the vacated space. This became our improvised study hall. Zina occupied one end and I sat opposite her. Stacks of books and notepads were scattered on the elongated table, and a desktop computer faced each one of us. Once Zina began her homework, her concentration was on the material in front of her. I, on the other hand, was more of a daydreamer, frequently distracted by the maddeningly desirable creature across from me and wondering how in the heavens I landed in such unbelievable circumstances that I could not have ever dreamed of. My other source of distraction was the incredibly fascinating western sky at sunset, where wave after wave of reds, oranges, and bright yellows interspersed within the rippled pewter cirrus clouds slowly rolled over the horizon into the abyss.

In deference to Zina, I perused the books which she so obligingly supplied. But my real source was the internet. Between *Wikipedia*, YouTube, general information, and advertisements from around the world in every imaginable language, my notebook was filling from cover to cover with idioms, definitions, color reprints, and an extensive list of websites on specific topics to which I could refer at moment's notice.

My real hands-on education was in the capable hands of my good-humored mentor Misha. He took my apprenticeship very seriously to heart once he realized that it was not a mere whim or charade on my part. I was at his side every step of his daily activity from the cutting and polishing variety of precious stones, to molding Isaac Leibovich's imaginative designs, to setting the gems in rings, bracelets, pendants, earrings, and necklaces.

The *Sarine* system was the focal point of my training. Misha patiently led me through the process starting with the keyboard and the various elements of the software. He gave me the manuals that he knew inside out, which I studied whenever there was a free moment and in the evenings when I was not gazing at my beloved Zina. Eventually he permitted me to program the cutting of lesser quality stones. Like a seasoned teacher, he never embarrassed me by harping on my mistakes. Instead, he led me through the steps to discover the errors on my own. The interaction was always amicable and without reproach. He also taught me how to identify the crystalline structures of diamonds which dictated the type of cut that was optimum—the octahedron for brilliant round or square diamonds or the macles for other fancy cuts.

The polishing skills were initially honed by recutting older diamonds, a less demanding and less risky procedure, into more popular shapes as dictated by the desirability in the marketplace. Soon I was sufficiently proficient to polish the main facets of larger carat-weight gemstones.

My future father-in-law did the brillianteering on all the larger diamonds. He showed me his insights using the microscope to determine at what precise angle to impart the eight stars on a round diamond and how to apply the final polishing to the pavilion and crown halves.

I found a calmness and peace of mind behind the polishing wheel. Diamond cutting would be my profession. Above all, I also found a family that I never had.

By three o'clock on Friday afternoons, all activities in the shop were rapidly winding down in preparation for observing Shabbat. Toward sundown, when the candles were being lighted, my adopted family and I—all four of us—were seated at the dining room table for dinner. The aroma of freshly baked challah bread filled the air and stimulated the taste buds with anticipation of the sumptuous meal to follow. Isaac Leibovich solemnly recited the blessings of bread and wine in Hebrew, which I did not understand but by now knew the religious essence of the invocation. Learning Hebrew and my heritage was foremost on my to-do list.

I always wore the yarmulke for the occasion in remembrance of my mother, the same yarmulke I wore at her funeral for the very first time. It did not escape my notice that my future in-laws appreciated the gesture even though Rifka was more a traditionalist than a religious practitioner. Zina seemed to have followed her mother's example.

Isaac filled the glasses with wine and wished all of us a hearty appetite. The soup course followed.

"Mama, the roasted duck gets better every time you make it," Isaac complimented her on the main course. "Lately you seem to have developed a special liking for the fowl."

Sheepish glances and smiles floated around the table. It was a reference to my favorite dish and an unspoken acknowledgment of my acceptance.

"Asher, I am very pleased with your rapid progress," said Isaac. "Misha tells me you demonstrate a talent for our kind of work. And your dexterity on the *Serine* is excellent. I must admit you are a quick learner. He tells me you are qualified to work independently."

"I enjoy the work," I replied. "Making something worthwhile from a rough stone gives me a lot of satisfaction and a feeling of accomplishment."

Zina's expression signaled satisfaction as if my words poured honey on her heart as the saying went.

"Well, it is high time to get you out of the shop and broaden your horizons. I am scheduled to be in Tel Aviv in two weeks. My contacts acquired a sizable stone from South Africa. They want my opinion for the most profitable way to shape it. It's like having a doctor offer a second opinion before a major surgery. There is a fee and expenses, of course, and a possibility for us to process and sell the finished diamond here. I would like you to accompany me. I would have a chance to see how you would recommend cutting the stone. Do you have an international passport?"

"Never had the need for one."

"That is easily remedied. I have a contact who can expedite it. I will call him on Sunday. Unless he is not available, he will meet you at the Interior Ministry on Bohomolets Street at ten in the morning. If I am not mistaken, I believe the main entrance is at number ten. You can't miss it. He will walk you through the bureaucracy without issues. What documents do you have?"

"Documents? All I have is what is in my wallet."

"It's not that important. He will take care of everything, including the photos and the fee. It's not the first time he has done this. Just don't volunteer any information. He will speak on your behalf. That part is taken care of. Now, let's talk about what is really important. Have you youngsters decided on the plans for your wedding?"

"As a matter of fact we did, Papa," Zina spoke up. "According to my school schedule, I will have several weeks free toward the end of June. That would be the best time. It will also give us time for preparations."

"The end of June then it shall be."

13

Settling In

On Saturdays the business was closed and the display window remained dark. I had the day to myself unless there was a special request from known customers who happened to be in town, then I would receive them in the showroom in the daytime or Isaac would see them after sunset. Such appointments were discouraged and not part of the usual routine. It happened rarely. The enterprise did not cater to walk-in trade on weekends.

Zina had classes until noon. She was primarily occupied with laboratory work. I would meet her at the city center, most frequently on Khreschatyk near Independence Square, and spend the afternoon in an outdoor café or just strolling about and lunching on a park bench of a nearby park.

When the weather was doubtful, I rode my Harley, and she, of course, always drove her souped-up sardine can to school. But when the day was full of promise and I did not oversleep, I preferred a leisurely walk. My favorite path led through the *Andriyivskyj Uzviz*, Andrew's Descent, the national landmark that connects Kyiv's Upper Town with the Podil District.

For me the serpentine road was actually an ascent up the legendary *Uzviz*. According to the chronicles, Saint Andrew the apostle, who preached along the Black Sea and the river Dnipro, erected a cross on the site of the current church that bears his name. Perched on the hill, the church provides an unobstructed panoramic view of the entire Podil and well beyond the river of the outlying districts.

Conversely, looking up from Podil, the Baroque style edifice rises on white Corinthian columns interspersed with bright-blue stucco panels surrounding leaded windows and gold-trimmed ornamental decorations. The textured emerald dome is capped with an onion-shaped decorative spire and a golden cross. The dome is flanked by four lesser spires set on columns at each corner like a regimental honor guard. The incomparable image leaves one spiritually uplifted regardless of one's faith.

The cobblestone road is wide enough to accommodate automobile traffic as well as parking and a pedestrian walkway. The street is noted for its architectural history, many gift shops, and art galleries. A number of high-end restaurants are located along the busy tourist thoroughfare. For me of most interest were the outdoor vendors occupying every available space along the walkway. It was an open-air market from end to end. Kiosks were filled with locally grown produce and seasonal fruit. Some ambitious hawkers purveyed fruit from more tropical climates such as my favorite figs, which I indulged in season. They tasted freshly picked and reminded me of the fig tree in the backyard of my home in Mariupol. Recent art dazzled the eye, hanging from buildings, parapets, and on free-standing wooden stands, the creations of artists from the far reaches of the nation. Tables were filled with embroidery to suit every taste, from shirts, neckties, delicate blouses, dresses, skirts, and anything that resembled national craftsmanship in wood and metal. There were even stacks of genuine American jeans and running shoes flown directly from China for label-conscious customers.

Every time was a new adventure. Many of the street vendors were from out of town rotating the wares from week to week. All in all the street was a tourist destination as well as a pleasant diversion for the locals.

Thanks to Boris, my Harley was spared progressive decay from languishing in the bowels of the fortress. He was an ardent participant in a group of riders who regularly made day and overnight trips to the countryside on the weekends. The free spirits were very much like my biker friends in Mariupol. The rough-edged, rebellious individuals, comprised of laborers as well as professionals, were the type who would stand unwaveringly at your side at the slightest hint of need or difficulty.

When we traveled we owned the road. On the highways, which were maintained to some degree, we traveled four abreast. We raced like a fiery phalanx in an attack mode feeling exhilarated in the headwinds on our faces. Cars cleared the lanes on hearing the full-throttled roar of the streaming exhaust. Police cars monitoring traffic remained casually off-road in observance without impeding our momentum or giving us chase. Most of us were outfitted in leather from head to toe and wearing helmets, reclaimed World War II relics, adorned with aggressive insignia. No one displayed the dreaded swastika, no matter the fierceness of the rider. Skull and bones and the grim reaper were a favorite. Aside from me, a few displayed our national colors or the trident. Some riders, of course, wore no helmets but were capped in outrageously colorful pirate-like bandanas.

On country roads, the formations were abandoned because of countless potholes. The most treacherous were benign-looking puddles that would send the careless rider tumbling over the handlebars or rattle his teeth from the sudden high-speed impact. It became a challenging obstacle course through which we meandered with abandon and in the end, derived great satisfaction.

Destinations varied with the weather and the seasons. The day trips were to outlying farmlands and familiar rest areas along river banks. Fishing enthusiasts fashioned freshly cut tree limbs with twine and hooks and settled in for the afternoon absorbed in their hobby. Inevitably a concertina would fill the air accompanied with ribald Kozak refrains as a bonfire was started in anticipation of the fish fry. Local produce and seasonal fruit were plentiful at the festivities. The laid-back, rustic environment was no less satisfying than the high-speed dash through the brisk air stream. The bonhomie was also an opportunity for me to establish friendships in a new circle of friends.

The full weekend jaunts ventured further out from Kyiv toward the nearest sizable settlements such as Zhytomyr to the west, Sumy to the east, Chernihiv to the north, Bila Tserkva to the south, and points in between. We stayed at previously visited country inns at the outskirts of the cities that welcomed us and treated us royally having experienced our unrestrained spending sprees.

These were more communal outings; wives and girlfriends were invited. Zina accompanied me only once or twice as far as I can remember. She could ill afford to miss two days from her school workload.

Saturday evenings were the social events where camaraderie was the order of the day. Weather permitting, the innkeeper set out a barbecue pit and a variety of cozy seating arrangements. Tables were stacked with food and condiments and the drinking man's favorites—pickled cabbage dressed with onions and sunflower oil, dill pickles, and pickled tomatoes. On the pit was a piglet rotated slowly and periodically moistened with bacon fat. I must admit that I very much enjoyed the forbidden flesh, but this was before I embraced my faith and abstained for the rest of my days.

The innkeeper was glad to oblige. The drink flowed as if it poured from a faucet. Toast after toast and later without a toast mellowed my new companions. This was a hearty group that, at that point in the festivities, tended to see only black or white—you were either with them, or if you passed on a drink, you were against them. Fortunately I was no stranger to the custom. Once I filled up on the pickled fare and fatty food, I could hold up my end with the best of them. I suppose that was my inheritance given me by my father.

At an outing in the suburb of Zhytomyr, I noticed a new participant. He was a sturdy fellow, above-average height and no neck. He wore a cutaway shirt with the entire exposed skin covered in multicolored India ink. His shaven head moved back and forth while imbibing the fiery liquid and having a grand old time. He was in a state we refer to as "more yomy po kolina," the sea is merely up to his knees. Alternatively his state could also be described as "he was feeling no pain." Somehow I don't recall feeling much pain either.

I saw something troubling about him.

I approached Boris and said, pointing in his direction, "Boris, that skinhead over there, do you know him? Who is he?"

"You mean the one with all the tattoos?"

I nodded.

"First of all, he is not a skinhead, far from it. Despite his rugged appearance, he is actually one of the gentlest and most generous of men, that is until you cross him. Then he erupts like one of those raging freebooters from the pages of *Taras Bulba* who could raise a stallion in the air without breaking a sweat or tear apart a protagonist with his bare hands. He is a good man to know, to have as a friend. I assume he gets his strength from being a stevedore on the Dnipro working on merchant ships. His name is Yaroslav Pankratovich Bereza. His nickname is Slava."

"Is he easily provoked or enraged?"

"Why do you ask?"

"Oh, I don't know. I suppose it's one of his tattoos that is bothering me. Do you think he would start a fight if I approached him about it?"

"No, not at all. Just don't be belligerent or threaten him with your hands. If it really bothers you, then go on ahead and get it off your chest. I'll keep my eye on you."

"That's great. Thanks."

I poured myself two hundred grams and proceeded casually with a drink in hand in his direction.

"Pardon me," I said amicably, "I have not seen you before at our outings. I would like to make your acquaintance. My name is Asher. I recently moved to Kyiv from Mariupol."

"I am glad to meet you, Asher from Mariupol. My friends call me Slava. I raise my glass to your health. Nazdorovia!"

"And to your health, Slava!"

Both glasses emptied in one burning gulp without grimace followed by a robust exhaled breath "ahh . . ."

"Join me, Asher, in a bite of herring."

"Don't mind if I do."

"We should not let the herring dry out from thirst," he said as he refilled our glasses. "Nazdorovia!"

"Nazdorovia!"

"I hope you don't mind if I ask you a personal question," I said after a while.

"Why would I mind. I am an open book. Go ahead—shoot."

"I notice that you display the lightning bolt logo of the SS on your neck. Are you a NAZI sympathizer?"

Slava roared in a deep belly laugh.

"Asher . . . Asher, my friend . . . I want you to know that you are the very first to bring that atrocity on my neck to my attention and I appreciate it. When I realized that I had that odious emblem on my neck, I was furious and wanted to have it obliterated. I honestly forgot about it until you brought it up. No one else ever mentioned it. I guarantee you that next time you see me, it will be gone."

He continued sheepishly. "I was celebrating something or other with my friends and I tied one on. The last thing I remembered, I was sitting in a tattooer's chair surrounded by my buddies and telling him to scribe something intimidating and hideous. Then I passed out. I woke in my bed the next day with my neck defiled.

"I want you to know that this is the last thing in the world that I would honor. My grandfather fought the NAZIS in the Great War. He was in the 1st Ukrainian Front under Vatutin. He was killed by those bastards in 1943 in the second battle liberating Kyiv. Do you think I would defile his memory by honoring those bestial Huns?"

14

Wedded Bliss

"Good afternoon, Isaac Leibovich," said Yaakov Dov Bleish as he rose from his desk and hastened toward the entrance of his office with an outstretched hand in greeting. "Glad to see you. Do come in."

"Shalom Aleichem, Rabbi," replied my future father-in-law. "This is Asher, the young man I spoke to you about."

"I am pleased to meet you, Asher."

"Good day to you, Rabbi."

"Please be seated. Let's get better acquainted . . . Can I offer you a glass of tea?"

Hearing "no thank you" replies, he continued. "I've known Isaac Leibovich since I migrated to Kyiv some fifteen years ago. He is a prominent member of our community. So, Asher, consider yourself highly recommended."

The chief rabbi of the Great Choral Synagogue, as well as the chief rabbi of all Ukraine, displayed an affable, down-to-earth personality. Beneath the robust facial growth of alternating gray and black chest-long strands anchored beneath a black yarmulke was a round face and a disarming smile. He wore black-rimmed eyeglasses, an open-collared white shirt, and black trousers. He sat casually behind his document-laden desk affecting an air of informality.

"I understand that you hail from Mariupol. I have not had the pleasure of visiting that part of our nation. The climate must be delightful there."

"It is a popular resort city although the area is highly industrialized, lots of tall chimneys and black smoke."

"One day I must visit the famous southern shores, Mariupol, Odesa, and Crimea. I myself grew up in America—in Brooklyn, close enough to enjoy the sandy beaches in my youth . . . Sorry, I digress. Asher, tell me about yourself, about your family."

"There is not much to tell. Both of my parents are deceased. I was orphaned at the age of fourteen."

"Zichrono Livracha—may their memory be blessed. Do you have any siblings?"

"No, I was the only child."

"Were both your parents Jewish? Were they religious?"

"Yes, they were both Jewish. But they did not practice the faith. My mother and I celebrated the high holidays with our next-door neighbors who were devout Orthodox Jews. My father did not participate. He was a proletarian in every sense of the word, a communist through and through to his last breath. I don't think he was an atheist. But then, I was too young to know or care. When the Soviet Union fell apart, so did my father."

"Regrettably yours is an all too familiar story of our people that I hear literally day in and day out. The Soviets marginalized our heritage and declared the state their deity. The few that remained true to their faith languished in the shadows. Once independence was declared, many Jews, uncertain of their future, scattered throughout the free world. A large percentage, of course, migrated to Israel. Some have actually begun returning with the realization that their fears were unfounded.

"Our community, thanks to people like Isaac Leibovich, is flourishing and growing stronger every day. Personally I have not experienced any animosity toward me or witnessed any desecrations with the Star of David or swastikas like I have seen all too often back in the States. Recently there have been televised instances of anti-Semitic outbursts. I believe these are staged events coordinated by the Kremlin to create chaos in our society and undermine our desire to join the European Union. Keep in mind that most of the media in Ukraine is either owned or directly controlled by Moscow's propaganda and disinformation services. Tell me, Asher, have you encountered much discrimination in Mariupol?"

"Offhand I would say no—and that also includes some tough-minded bikers who befriended me."

"In any event, we must never get complacent. Now, let's get back to your state of affairs. While it may seem that your wedding is months away, it is prudent to book the facilities as soon as possible. Is it safe to assume that particular detail has been taken care of, Isaac Leibovich?"

"Indeed it has."

"Good, good. What is the date of the wedding so that I can reserve it on my calendar?"

"It is Sunday, the nineteenth of June, at four o'clock."

After a quick reference to the desk calendar, he said, "I see that the date is not committed. It will be my pleasure to officiate. And where will the nuptials take place?"

"We will have the Fairmont Atrium at our disposal."

"It's a very prestigious venue. I expected no less."

My father-in-law's chest thrust forward, and he straightened up in his seat. A hint of a smile lighted his face.

"We will meet several days prior to the ceremony to familiarize you and Zinaida with the details and the meaning of the ritual. Meanwhile, may I suggest that you, Asher, join our evening study group at the yeshiva? We have dozens of young men like you who are eager to rediscover their heritage and immerse themselves in their traditions and their faith. We deal with a variety of subjects, both religious in nature such as readings from the Talmud and the Torah and the contemporary environment."

"I would like that very much. But, except for the few phrases I heard at the dinner table, I don't speak Hebrew."

Dov Bleish chuckled. "And no one expects you to. All evening instructions are in your mother's tongue. Let's take a quick tour of our complex. I will introduce you to Rabbi Zelman. I will ask him to personally undertake your coursework."

The highly anticipated day penetrated my bedroom window with intensity and roused me from a restless twilight sleep. I greeted the glorious sunrise groggily with beads of perspiration on my brow, trepidation in my chest, and a painful quiver in my stomach—a fine start for the most significant day in my life.

It may have been last-minute jitters or that I had gone overboard with my preparedness. Since my introduction to Rabbi Zelman, I applied myself with a passion to the curriculum he had outlined. The soft-spoken rabbi was a walking encyclopedia on Talmudic themes which he would recite word for word from the scripture and then use the quotation as the basis of the discourse and its historic present-day significance. I was part of an enthusiastic group of professionals, all roughly my age, who thirsted to discover their heritage but perhaps more importantly to learn how to prosper in the new, independent society without shirking their own identity.

Rabbi Zelman was an enthusiastic, wiry cleric of average height and indeterminate age. Beneath the well-trimmed, salt-and-pepper facial growth that was accented with round wire-rimmed spectacles were the youthful features reminiscent of Pasha Antipov, the star-crossed revolutionary of the *Doctor Zhivago* film saga. He was dressed in the customary white shirt, black trousers, and black shoes, and with *tzitzit* tassels overhanging his belt.

Filled with renewed spirituality, self-esteem, and pride, I began wearing my yarmulke at all times like my yeshiva companions and embarked on cultivating a beard.

Hebrew was more of a challenge. My instructor was Yehuda, a young man who, I would have sworn, was yet to complete the first year of the gymnasium. He was a gracious, accommodating youth, a strict adherent to the orthodox traditions, including curly side locks proudly dangling over his ears down to his shoulders. I was so impressed with his knowledge and level of maturity for someone so young that I could not resist asking him his age. He replied with a sheepish smile to be barely eighteen years old.

Russian was the spoken word in Mariupol, including in our household. Once I became involved with the tourist trade, the preferred form of speech with visitors from the western regions of the nation was Ukrainian. Without exception, they were very patriotic and resented being addressed in the vulgar vernacular of their oppressors. On a number of occasions, I would bid them welcome in Russian, and they would respond to me indignantly in Ukrainian. I adapted quickly to the situation and at the same time, improved my earnings. With the similarities in the Cyrillic core of both languages, in short order, I could think and speak the language flawlessly. You would have sworn that I was born and bred in Lviv.

Hebrew, on the other hand, was on the opposite end of the phonetic spectrum. Before I could embark on learning the alphabet, vocabulary, and stitching together a simple thought, I needed immersion in the nuances of Semitic sounds, diction, and speech patterns. Yehuda, that clever young man, quickly assessed my needs and patiently led me step-by-step through the rudiments of the unfamiliar tongue. Perceiving my serious commitment, both my future father-in-law and Misha began mixing Hebrew phrases in our conversations. On my trips to Tel Aviv, which were frequent, first as a courier and later as a brillianteer, I insisted on speaking the local dialect. All in all, by year's end, I could stumble through a legible conversation. It seems I had a good ear for languages. When it came to English, it was no challenge at all.

A protracted shower and a bottomless mug of coffee somewhat mollified my nerves. I dressed in my work clothes and carefully made my way to the workshop down the back stairs to avoid accidentally running into Zina in the elevator. The showroom was closed for the day, allowing me to spend the morning in solitude. There was a backlog of rough-cut gems that needed polishing and brillianteering. Once I was at the wheel my mind cleared of all thoughts but for the task at hand.

By early afternoon I returned to my apartment, refreshed and donned my formal wedding attire. Boris was at the curb with the Mercedes and whisked me away to the Fairmont.

The Fairmont Grand, the stately residence executed in the luxurious style of its San Francisco cousin is located in the Kyiv Podil District overlooking the banks of the mighty Dnipro. The five-star hotel is renowned as one of the best in Western Europe and is frequented by demanding tourists and savvy business clientele.

I was warmly greeted at the main entrance by my weekend biker friends who were formally attired and accompanied by their ladies in eye-popping finery. Front and center was the devil-may-care stevedore Slava minus the offensive tattoo on his neck. At his side was a willowy, pint-sized, bleach-blonde beauty, beaming as if she, moments earlier. stepped down from the silver screen.

Surrounded by well-wishers, I was escorted with fanfare to the cocktail bar. I anticipated such a reception from the hearty crew with whom the prenuptial welcome had become a custom, and I expected no less. I fortified myself with a healthy measure of buckwheat gruel smothered with caramelized onions, which, according to the old wives' tale, would neutralize the effects of the fiery liquid. Even so, I tried to slow the toasts and preserve my wits. I wanted to be an active participant in the wedding ceremony and not embarrass myself and my future family. It was at my insistence that the ceremony be conducted entirely in Hebrew, and I memorized the entire service and the responses with the help of my instructor Yehuda. After all, it was now my tradition and all that went with it!

By the time my disposition was beginning to mellow, my imminent father-in-law gently tugged at my arm, saying, "Asher, it is time for you to go in. It will give me a chance to introduce you to some important guests along the way before the ceremony." He then addressed my companions, "Ladies and gentlemen, please come in. We are about to start."

The buzz of convivial chatter subsided momentarily as we entered the atrium. The ornate chamber was filled to capacity with guests. Elaborate sconces set on gilded pedestals lined the walls. Oversized bouquets bursting with exotic flowers elevated on crystal vases decorated each table. Late afternoon sunlight bathed the intricate leaded glass ceiling and the crystal candelabra suspended from the apex of the vaulted dome. The environment could not have been more opulent and festive.

I acknowledged several clients whose companions ostensibly displayed my handiwork. There were a number of familiar faces from the big and the little screens. Several jewelers came from Amsterdam and Tel Aviv. They wished me well with cheerful smiles and hearty handshakes.

We moved slowly through the throng. Near the head table, Isaac Leibovich introduced me to a stocky individual with a taut weightlifter's physique tapering down from the shoulders to a trim waist. He was impeccably dressed in the latest-style tuxedo hand-fitted to his frame. He congratulated me heartily, addressing me with familiarity by my patronymic and a firm handshake. His smile was pleasant enough. But there was something about his tanned facial features and vacuous eyes that left me with an impression of a scoundrel with dubious scruples.

"Asher, this is my long-time business associate Nikita Filipovich Grushev. I hope you will get to be good friends."

Business associates? Protection? Surged through my brain. But this was not the time to dwell on distasteful thoughts.

"I am pleased to meet you, Nikita Filipovich," I said. "Thank you for honoring our nuptials."

He responded with a squeeze of my hand, a nod, and best wishes for the future.

When we stepped away from the table, I said, "Isaac Leibovich, I seem to recognize some of the men at that table. Are any of them perchance deputies in the parliament?"

"Indeed they are. As a matter of fact, everyone at that table happens to be a deputy, including Grushev. They are powerful men. Most of them serve not from love of country or some patriotic idealism. They serve because they have immunity from prosecution as long as they hold that protected seat. That, I am afraid, is our sad present-day reality!"

We finally made our way to the front where the *Chuppah*, the white wedding canopy, stood, and beyond it was a free-standing *menorah*, its seven branches fully lighted.

Rabbi Bleish greeted us. At his side was the cantor.

"Are you ready, Asher?" he said. "Do you have the wedding bands?"

I showed him the bands.

"Good. You should step into the *Chuppah*. I see Zinaida is making her entrance. She is as punctual as ever."

It is customary for the groom's parents to escort their son to the wedding canopy. Similarly, the parents of the bride escort their daughter. Sadly, in my case, I had no relatives whatsoever. Isaac Leibovich, whom I would address with affection as Papa from that day forward, suggested the arrangement we were following. He escorted me and Rifka escorted Zinaida.

My beautiful bride approached the *Chuppah* and I beckoned her into "my tent." She walked around me three times and stood beside me on my right. I lifted her veil to keep with tradition to assure that it was indeed she and not the substitute described in the scriptures.

The cantor intoned his glorious baritone in Psalm 118:26, "*Blessed are you who come in the name of Adonai . . .*"

Our union was sanctified for a lifetime.

We consummated our wedding night in the presidential suite, no less. On Monday afternoon Boris picked us up in the limousine and took us to Borispol airport. Earlier in the week, he tried to convince me that I should highlight our honeymoon with a memorable adventure which we could fondly retell to our grandchildren. He would outfit his Harley with a sidecar and send us off in the lap of luxury on three wheels. While the suggestion had its possibilities, I nixed the idea offhand since it would be too strenuous on Zina, and we would waste too much time with a lengthy road trip. Zina had to resume classes in less than two weeks.

We flew to Mariupol in first class, of course, to my childhood stomping grounds. Yuri, my erstwhile driver and friend in need, picked us up at the airport in his battered taxi. He made a commitment to dedicate himself to our needs throughout our stay and make certain that we would have nothing less than an unforgettable honeymoon.

Our destination was the Poseidon, the magical seaside venue that assisted fate in bringing us together. Zina, the romantic soul that she was, even reserved the same room she stayed in the previous year.

The hotel manager and staff greeted us at the entrance as if we were royalty, bouquet in hand and welcoming smiles all around. I was returning home not as a destitute profligate, but as an accomplished person of substance with an enviable bride on my arm. We were honored guests and I made every effort to be reserved and congenial throughout our sojourn.

Once we settled in, I made the rounds from the top floor to the bowels of the hotel, making certain that I did not omit a single soul, no matter a chef, a chambermaid, or a floor cleaner. At one time or another, they were all good to me. I had every intention of returning in the future and being accepted as part of the family. All too often the lowliest clerk can prove more helpful than some self-important cog further up the food chain.

First and foremost Zina and I paid our respects to my mother's gravesite. A year's worth of neglect and weeds overgrew the plot and obscured the modest handmade marker. Yuri was thoughtful to bring some utensils and the three of us cleared the site. We stood with our heads bowed as I recited the *Kaddish* prayers in Hebrew to the best of my ability.

That evening we visited Avraam, the next-door neighbor who came to my aid at the most desperate time in my life. He and his wife Masha received us joyously as though we were their own children. Like all mothers, Masha doted on us with tea and homemade sweet bread while Avraam was ecstatic with my new circumstances and my adherence to the customs of my ancestral heritage as evidenced by my covered dome. I was not yet accustomed to wearing the *tallit*, but neither was he.

I asked Avraam to erect a proper monument for my mother and maintain her gravesite. I gave him a wad of American hundred-dollar bills and asked him not to spare the cost. I would send him more if needed.

As for my biker friends, I did not need to search them out—they found us on their own. We were in their custody around the clock to the point of exhaustion. It was a grand time. There was not a single nightspot in Mariupol that we did not close up at sunrise. Some of the places that I would not venture in alone even in daytime proved unforgettable with their workingman's ambiance and friendly, unpretentious, festive atmosphere.

We barely fell asleep on Saturday morning after a night of clubbing when a deafening roar rattled the windows, the wall sconces, and the glassware on the bedroom tray. I rolled out of bed bleary-eyed and made my way to the window. I opened a slit at the edge of the heavy night curtain not to wake Zina and peered out. The drive in front of the Poseidon was jam-packed with motorbikes, each rider seemingly trying to outgun their companions—the distressing wake-up call for us and the entire neighborhood.

Zina and I washed quickly, dressed, and with an overnight satchel that we prepared on the previous day, rushed downstairs to shut down the alarm. We exited the hotel to rowdy cheers and blaring horns. At the front stood a motorcycle with an attached sidecar. We mounted the ride. The mufflers growled. The armada launched westward along the Azov coastline for the weekend.

15

Orange Revolution

When I arrived in Kyiv, election fever overwhelmed the city media ahead of the presidential elections scheduled for October 31, 2004. The newsprint, wall posters, the airwaves, and the idiot tube flooded the citizenry with slogans, truths, half-truths, lies, propaganda, and credible disinformation concocted by our meddlesome neighbor behind the Kremlin walls. The candidates were Viktor Yanukovych, the prime minister in the outgoing Kuchma cabinet, and the leader of the opposing coalition Viktor Yushchenko. Broadly speaking, it became a tug-of-war between the Russophile east and the patriotic west.

The election was froth with massive corruption, voter intimidation, and widespread fraud. An attempted assassination of Yushchenko at a dinner with his so-called close friends failed and drew worldwide condemnation. His soup was spiked with deadly TCDD dioxin, which he barely survived. Eventually the perpetrators fled to Russia and were rewarded for their failed attempt with sanctuary and citizenship.

The initial ballot did not produce an outright winner and required a run-off vote. Rampant fraud by the government tilted the margin of victory to Yanukovych contrary to independent exit polls favoring Yushchenko by at least 11 percent. Outrage triggered massive nationwide protests, civil disobedience, sit-ins, and general strikes. What has become known as the Orange Revolution, derived from the color associated with the opposition, forced the election to rerun on December 26 and the eventual ascent of Yushchenko to the presidency.

Frankly speaking, my interest in political machinations was peripheral at best. My preoccupation was with fitting in with my new family and honing the skills that fell into my lap. All else was an unnecessary distraction. At one point I even stopped listening to the radio and turning on the television since they exclusively preached the Yanukovych propaganda as that media was obviously in Russian hands.

Although the demonstrations in Kyiv took place in the Upper Town of the central square commonly referred to as *Maidan*, it was impossible to be completely divorced from the action when the firebrand medical student dominated the dinner conversation with various aspects of the civil disobedience. Her primary color was orange. Her woolen scarf was orange with the national trident knitted in at both extremities. Her woolen hat was orange with the trident at its center. Her villains were the Kuchma gangsters and his thieving disciple Yanuk as she referred to him with distaste. She was an impassioned revolutionary in every sense of the word—she was ready to man the barricades.

I had little choice but to accompany her on the freezing December nights to join the massive peaceful gathering. We would motor her sardine can to the Postal Square and abandon the eyesore in the vicinity of the Riviera Hotel, to be picked up on the way back. Next door to the hotel was the Funicular station, a three-minute ride to the Upper Town exiting in the vicinity of St. Michael's Golden-Domed monastery. The popular tourist attraction was jam-packed with mostly young passengers liveried in orange. The entire cable car hummed with enthusiasm and excitement and dialects from all corners of the nation. Zina outfitted me in an orange woolen hat and a duplicate of her scarf. We were an intimate part of the protest.

We walked around the western wall of the monastery and passed the monument to the victims of the 1932–1933 famine at the front entrance then down Tr'ochsviatytelska Street—the street of three saints—in the direction of the main city square, the *Maidan*, where the main stage was erected. Toward the end of the street, there were tents set up with first aid and kettles of tea brewing on propane burners and sending clouds of steam into the frigid night. We could barely hear the loudspeakers in the distance except when the throng rang out, and us included at the top of our lungs, "Glory to Ukraine!," "Out with the Thieves!" The center city was clogged around the clock with over a million energized participants.

Zina moved with purpose through the crowd until we almost reached Khreschatyk, the central thoroughfare of the city where *Maidan* was the focal point. An oversized tent stood at the juncture with Red Cross patches on the exterior. Field beds were disposed of within the interior, and electric space heaters blazed at either end, barely keeping the chill at bay. It was manned with students from the medical school, many of them Zina's classmates. Zina's close friends Lena and Olia, whom I first met in Mariupol on that fateful summer, rushed to greet us and offered mugs of steaming tea. Lena was Zina's classmate; Olia studied accounting. There were minimal injuries to speak of other than relieving the onset of frostbite on the exposed surfaces of the face.

Fortunately the forces of evil caved into the popular uprising after only two weeks of protests, nullified previous results, and rescheduled a revote. Victor Yushchenko was sworn in as the third president of independent Ukraine.

16

Parenthood

Alas, the Orange Revolution, with all its promise, was ineffectual and short-lived. Mired with infighting within the coalition, rampant corruption from the street patrolman to the pinnacle of the governing pyramid and the blatant tight grip by the oligarchs on every aspect of the economy and national wealth drove the beleaguered citizenry into the thieving arms of the evil Yanuk.

I tried to remain apolitical and insulated from daily tribulations. Business was brisk with the inflow of new money. I was content to cut precious stones, enjoying the travel and building my reputation as a brillianteer.

Zina's education was on track. In less than a year of our marriage, her symptoms of pregnancy enlivened our household with anticipation and joy. Mother-to-be took her condition in stride. But after six months, as her womb became somewhat oversized and difficult to manage, we convinced her to refrain from driving the Lada. Boris would transport her in the Mercedes. The single-minded girl relented but insisted to be dropped off and picked up blocks away from school to avoid contemptuous glances and obsequious, preferential treatment from fellow students.

On approaching full term, she refused to stay at home. She maintained that she needed to be active to avoid doldrums and excessive cravings for unhealthy food. The best place for her was to carry on at the medical school. In the end, the proximity to the hospital and to her gynecologist swayed the argument. Sure enough, her insistence was on the mark. In the midst of an anatomy lecture, she felt that the time was at hand even though it was somewhat premature. She exited calmly from the lecture theater, retrieved the suitcase from her locker, and engaged a maintenance man to take her in a wheelchair to the hospital. The Kyiv City Clinical Hospital No. 18 was two short blocks away from the medical school. The hospital was noted for obstetrics and gynecology. Her doctor was a prominent physician. He was on the medical staff as well as on the governing board of the institution.

She made all the arrangements well in advance. Cell phone in hand, she alerted reception that she was on her way and was at once escorted into the delivery room on arrival.

The biggest surprise to her and to all of us, and presumably to her doctor, at least that was his claim, was that she gave birth not to one but to two healthy boys. The older son we named Asher and the younger son, the late arrival by all of two minutes, we named Isaac in honor of Zina's father.

Her convalescence overlapped the summer recess and minimized the downtime from her studies. She returned to school for the fall semester and eventually specialized in and practiced emergency medicine. Her mother Rifka gladly took care of the boys with the help of a very competent nurse.

The birth of the twins had a profound change in my outlook, which I did not anticipate. While my ambition to be a world-class brillianteer did not diminish, my desire to be the father I never had dominated my daily routine. From the very beginning, I arranged my workday around their schedule. Early in the morning, after breakfast, Zina and I changed the boys, dressed them, and fed them cradled in our arms. We carried them, still drowsily sucking on the formula, down to my in-laws for the day. Rifka waited for us at the door with anticipation and gently took the sleepy child into her arms from Zina and carried him to his crib. She knew that I preferred to complete the transfer myself. We alternated carrying the infants from day to day, not to ever show a preference for either one from the start.

The cribs were located in Zina's vacated bedroom. Painted in soothing light blue, the chamber was an oversized daycare playpen. The cribs were aligned along the far wall in tandem. A hand-painted mural covered the entire background depicting the adventures of Ivan Franko's *Lys Mykyta*, the sly fox, romping through a verdant meadow and reeds peppered with light-brown cattails, disguised in female embroidery and carrying a bewildered rooster in a satchel over his shoulder. Birds, exaggerated butterflies, and sunflowers embellished the scene with a hint of a rainbow in the distance. The colors were brilliant, Van Gogh-like. The artistry was highly professional. I wondered at times why the Franko fable was the choice instead of a scene from someone like Shalom Aleichem. Surely there was a wealth of rustic images from the *Shtetl* that could have been appropriate. I suspected the subject, on which I was not consulted, was Zina's choice. I did not deem it necessary to ever bring it up and cause unintended discomfort.

Other than a dressing table with a washbasin and a shelf with powder and ointments, the furnishings were sparse, awaiting to be augmented as the boys progressed. A scarce commodity for child hygiene, the highly absorbent American-made diapers were stacked on a stand adjacent to the dressing table, and white linens were folded on an adjacent sideboard. There was also a comfortable rocking chair planted on an intricate antique Heriz carpet and next to it a free-standing shaded lamp and an end table with reading material and a dos and don'ts volume on childcare.

A quick kiss goodbye in the elevator and I proceeded to the shop. Zina continued down to the basement and her indestructible Lada. The early start provided me ample time to plan the day's activity, timed for intervals to cuddle with the boys during their waking hours.

With the increased demand for one-of-a-kind jewelry, Isaac purchased a second *Sarine* workstation and somehow managed to wedge it into the overcrowded space. I became sufficiently adept with these latest high-tech devices at mapping rough gemstones and selecting the best options to fit the current requirements for mounting in a house-designed piece of jewelry or maximizing the value of the finished product for sale to mattress hoarders who preferred investing in flawless, multi-carat diamonds. With some complex internal crystalline structures, I consulted Isaac before programming the *Sarine.* Isaac, for his part, confidently left the daily labor to Misha and me while he dealt with out-of-country wholesalers and the demanding nouveau-riche. I tried to minimize my own travel to spend quality time with the boys.

Because the *Sarine* blocking procedure consumed many hours, I set up the machines toward midday with the expected completion of the grinding cycle by the following morning. I removed the faceted gems and placed them next to the polishing wheel on which I would finish the main facets and brillianteer the gems later in the afternoon. Then I inserted the next batch of stones, studied their internal 3D images, and programmed the computer.

To an observer, the aspects of polishing may seem tedious, highly repetitive, and unfulfilling. For me, it was a calming and very satisfying part and parcel of creating a unique piece of art from an otherwise rudimentary stone. That was all the motivation I ever needed.

None of us adhered to the clock in our daily routine. Like in any family-owned business, the end product was the norm. In my case, an early riser by nature, I was up at daybreak to enjoy breakfast with Zina and seeing her off to school. When the twins came, the waking hours were that much more pleasant. In the evening the clock stopped with Zina's return unless, of course, a quick touchup of a stone was needed after dinner.

Misha, on the other hand, displayed little appreciation for the clock with the exception of respecting the approaching sunset on Fridays. When he did appear late in midmorning, he never walked in empty-handed. A small container from a bakery brimmed with honey cakes or jelly ponchiks or cream puffs or a pastry that enticed his sweet tooth or whatever was the day special. It was also an indicator that he intended to work late into the night. Much of his endeavor was in the foundry one floor below in the basement where he executed Isaac's intricate jewelry designs in precious metals prior to the insertion of gems. For me it meant energizing the tea kettle and joining the paunchy munchkin in the delectable sweets.

More so than in the past, I rarely turned on the television or listened to the radio. The Babel of disinformation on the airwaves and in print, if anything, had gotten worse no matter what the source. My contact with the real world, the world of the beleaguered citizenry, was the chitchat at the dinner table through the outpouring of interpretations and grievances from my socially conscious spouse.

Toward the end of Yuschenko's term, the availability and price of gas held the center stage of discontent, especially in frigid weather when the power went out and there was no heat. The machinations between Yuschenko's robber-baron cronies and Yulia Timoshenko made the winter of 2009 a bitter pill to swallow.

With the ascent of Yanukovych to the presidency, the outrage turned from blackouts to the consolidation of power by his clique and the suppression of political opposition. This was not entirely a new phenomenon since it was preceded by the Kuchma administration and eventually spawned the Orange Revolution. But on this go-around, the corruption and the blatant grab of national assets were done with unrelenting, shameless impunity. Criminals came out of the shadows and gangsterism became the law of the land. A vengeful show trial was staged in the manner of another Soviet-era despot and was adjudicated with a harsh seven-year term imprisonment of Yulia Timoshenko, his former rival in the presidential election.

To draw attention from the malfeasance, the free-fall of the economy, the persistent unemployment, and the lack of opportunities for the next generation of highly educated university graduates, association with the European Union were floated as the remedy for what ailed the nation. True to form, Yanukovych cleverly played the charade orchestrated by his cunning, blue-eyed benefactor from the Kremlin. He publicly promoted some convoluted form of integration with Europe. When challenged about his dalliance with Putin's Eurasian Union, he dismissed it as a negotiating maneuver to get the best deal possible with the West.

Meanwhile, the propaganda machine from Moscow and the fifth column in Ukraine flooded the media favoring a deal with the Kremlin. Even Patriarch Kirill, the primate of russian orthodoxy, was dispatched with fanfare to convince his little russians that they had always been an integral part of the *russkii mir,* the russian world, and should maintain that historical bond. His efforts fizzled when the photo of his thirty thousand dollar Breguet timepiece drew worldwide attention and overshadowed his contrived spiritual message.

The nation was obsessed with the thought of embracing the West. In our household, the subject was such a frequent part of the dinner conversation that even our six-year-olds would parade around the table chanting the mantra, "Ukraina ye Ewropa!" Ukraine is Europe, to their mother's delight.

The long-overdue signing of the Association Agreement was scheduled for the summit to be held in Vilnius at the end of November. Yanukovych suddenly did an about-face. On November 21, 2013, his government suspended preparations for signing the agreement and to seek closer economic ties with Russia.

17

#euromaidan

On that fateful Thursday, the twenty-first of November in 2013, a message was posted on Facebook in the late afternoon by Mustafa Nayyem, the noted Ukrainian journalist and political activist of Afghan descent:

> Let's meet at 10:30 p.m. at the Independence monument. Dress warmly, bring umbrellas, tea, coffee, a good attitude, and friends. Re-post highly appreciated!

I received the first text message from Zina sometime toward sunset: "Betrayal!!! Shame!!! Yanuk-Azarov reneging on signing EU agreement!!!"

It was unusual for her to be texting. We always spoke on the phone and at length. As usual, the topic was the children and I related in great detail how they were spending the day. I assumed that she must have been too busy at the hospital to talk and overwrought with the shocking news to be shouting to the heavens with all those exclamations.

The second text message came at 10:00 p.m. after her emergency-room shift ended. The message was also terse. She forwarded the posting from Mustafa, the moniker with which he was known nationwide in social media, followed by "I'm on my way. We are going."

Winter nights in Kyiv are unpredictable, often at subzero temperatures and blanketed with snow. Zina and I bundled appropriately for the frigid weather and each of us carried a thermos of hot tea. I drove the Lada up the St. Andrews Descent, past the Funicular, around St. Michael's Monastery, and parked downhill on Mykhailivska Street, a brisk walk to *Maidan*, the Independence Square. Zina came prepared with an EU flag which she wrapped around her shoulders. She was not about to let me proceed undeclared. She proudly took out a blue and yellow banner from the back seat and draped it over me.

We walked at a comfortable pace, unimpeded almost to the Independence Column. A modest group of protesters was milling about—no more than several hundred strong. I could see the disappointment on Zina's face.

"Zinochka darling, it's barely past ten thirty." I tried to console her. "We came too soon. You know our people. They are rarely on time. You'll see. They are sure to come."

But in my heart, I had a sinking feeling that this call to arms, unlike the Orange Revolution, had little support and was destined to be short-lived.

Zina's cell phone chimed with a refrain from "Fűr Elise."

She engaged the speaker. "Hi, Lena, where are you?"

"We're coming out of the metro on Instytutska. We have a whole group with us. Come join us. We'll wait for you."

"Asher and I are in the square. We are on our way."

By the time we reached Lena's contingent, we could see a mass of people pouring out of the subway station as well as from across the square at the Khreschatyk station. A wave of banners was unfolded and raised fluttering in the light breeze high above their heads: the national sky-blue and yellow, the EU circle of white stars on a dark blue background, and the nationalist red and black colors of the Right Sector.

Within the hour, *Maidan* was crowded with protesters as far as the eye could see. There did not seem to be any organized agenda. Groups of friends clustered in an outdoor get-together enjoying each other's company, condemning the government's betrayal despite the freezing weather. What was notable to me was that the majority of the protesters were very young, at least a decade younger than Zina and me. This was the next generation of revolutionaries, and it made me feel, at the ripe age of twenty-eight, a relic of yesteryear. I was glad that I did not date myself by wearing my orange woolen hat and scarf.

The atmosphere felt like a live rock concert. Square patches of blue flashed on and off through the *Maidan* as if thousands of fireflies synchronized their glow with a popular tune. If there were speeches or handheld megaphones, they were somewhere in the distance and could not be heard. This was a spontaneous gathering of the iPhone generation. I, for one, was reconsidering my previous misgivings. This indeed appeared as the first step toward a new future, and I wanted to be a part of it.

I spotted my stevedore friend Slava and his beautiful girlfriend emerging from the underground both outfitted in camouflage winter hunting gear. I was surprised to see them as politics never came up in our outings. I rushed over to greet them. They were accompanied by a group of my weekend biker enthusiasts. I was even more surprised when Slava unfurled a nationalist red-and-black banner, attached an extension pole, and raised the banner into the air.

"Hi, everyone, so good to see all of you," I greeted them enthusiastically. "Anyone for a cup of hot tea? Slava, I did not realize you were partial to the Right Sector."

"I have you to thank for my conversion, my dear Asher. You made me realize where my heart belongs. I never considered myself a damned little russian—*a maloros.*"

As a spur-of-the-moment event, this turned out to be unexpectedly successful. Later I found out from Zina—who else?—that similar gatherings simultaneously took place nationwide from Lviv to Poltava to Kharkiv to Dnipropetrovsk to Odesa and major settlements in between.

From that day on, the umbilical cord that instantly connected us all from the shores of the Black and Azov seas to the snow-peaked Carpathian Mountains became ***#euromaidan***.

The next day began as one of those gloomy mornings when once you took one look out the window and saw the downpour, you wanted to roll back into bed, cover your head, and refuse to face reality. Freezing rain assaulted the city and rattled the window panes. Body aches appeared out of nowhere and multiplied the discomfort. It was not a very good omen for a peaceful demonstration.

On the previous evening, Zina promised her friends that she would come to Maidan early and stay with them until noon until her shift at the hospital would begin. I was persuaded by my biker friends to join them. They would be there in force. After breakfast, Zina and I brought the boys downstairs and drove the Lada to the city center. Our rain gear was of Chinese origin, the paper-thin hooded plastic wrap that every tourist in the world carries in their travel kit. We also wore the equally indispensable, waterproof hiking boots.

I was amazed to see the massive gathering despite the foul weather. There seemed to be many more people there than on the previous night. Some wore assorted foul weather outfits; some were wrapped in flimsy Chinese plastic-like ours; some stood in groups under construction tarps while others, teenagers in appearance, were soaking wet and proud of it. Eventually a sea of umbrellas covered the square. The ages in attendance ran the full gamut from school children to gray-haired octogenarians.

The skies cleared. Banners floated in the air. Columns of students paraded the grounds and up-and-down side streets. "Ukraine is Europe! Sign! Ukraine is Europe! Sign! Sign! Sign!"

I supported the mantra with the full capacity of my lungs as appropriate, "Glory to the heroes!"

Vitali Klitschko tweeted, "Friends! All those who came to *Maidan*, well done! Who has not done it yet—join us now!"

The former world heavyweight boxing champion planted his mayoral campaign truck on Khreschatyk facing the square where the reviewing stand for the annual parade in celebration of the national Independence Day is usually located. The vehicle was equipped with a speaker's platform and sound equipment. The peaceful protest now had a formal focal point.

He disembarked and waded into the sea of youthful enthusiasts. Towering over the eager protesters, he encouraged them to stand their ground. From my vantage, I could barely discern his massage which he delivered with a handheld megaphone. The passion and the tone of the boxer turned politician energized the crowd. Every now and then, "Glory to Ukraine!" rang out through the crowd, followed by "Glory to the heroes!" and the familiar mantras of Euromaidan.

A celebratory feeling permeated the gathering. Speakers, Mustafa included, mounted the elevated stage draped in the EU colors. Their message was blaring throughout the center city. Musical interludes fueled the crowd. Some danced to the sounds of traditional favorites while others shuffled their feet in rhythm to ward off the bone-chilling cold. In the land weaned on bathtub spirits, not a drop of alcohol in any form was evident. It was a sober social event dedicated to a bright future in a free European nation.

Every day the participation was reinforced, filling the entire square and spilling out into the adjoining streets. A tent city sprang up and barrels appeared ablaze to keep body and soul from succumbing to the frost. Makeshift burners warmed kettles of tea and soup. Samovars percolated round the clock. It was so crowded that I reverted to my Orange Revolution itinerary by motor biking to the Postal Square and taking the Funicular up the hill. I juggled my days between work and making my voice heard along with my compatriots.

A rock-concert stage replaced the Klitschko campaign truck. National artists took center stage entertaining with patriotic ballads. The most prominent among them, and highly outspoken, animated, and dynamic, was Ruslana, the winner of the prestigious Eurovision Song Contest and recognized internationally as the most influential female solo artist. Representatives of every political party appeared on the podium. Remnants of the communist party were the exception. They all exhorted the president to keep his word and sign the agreement. Prelates of every religious denomination, including Greek Catholics, Roman Catholics, Protestants, Jews, and Moslems, offered prayers for a successful outcome and bestowed blessings on the gathering. His Holiness Patriarch Filaret, the primate of the Ukrainian Orthodox

Church, delivered spiritually inspired homilies on brotherly love and unity and prayers for divine guidance for the nation's leaders at the most critical juncture on the path to the promising future for its people. Conspicuously absent was Putin's fifth column, the Moscow patriarchate, who preached from the pulpit support for Moscow's Eurasian Customs Union and to be honest, whose presence at these gatherings no one missed.

An enormous conical metallic scaffold was erected on the site which was referred to with affection as the *Euromaidan* Christmas tree in honor of the forthcoming Christmas holidays. The structure was draped in national and Euro colors. Placards representing every region were added daily. Eventually an oversized portrait of Yulia Timoshenko was posted with demands for her release from Yanuk's prison. Henceforth her fabricated incarceration became the driving motivation of the demonstrators.

Surrounded by the budding flower of the next generation, I was amazed by their openness, by their camaraderie, by their aspirations, by their zeal, by their love of country, but most of all, I was taken by their solidarity in their language. They sang and roared support exclusively in Ukrainian—united in their mother tongue. Yet among themselves, they would inevitably revert to the ingrained verbiage with which they were more comfortable.

It was barely two days of peaceful protest passed since Nayyem's call to action when the kleptocrats vented their displeasure.

I was in the midst of setting up the two *Sarines* for processing the next set of gemstones when my cell phone vibrated—text message from Slava, "Something's up. Can you come? Usual place."

I keyed, "On my way."

I asked Misha to keep an eye on things and headed to the basement for my Harley. I sprinted up St. Andrew's Descent, around St. Michaels, and down Tr'ochsviatytelska until the crowd was impassable. I abandoned the bike on the sidewalk adjacent to a Baroque apartment building and waded through the crowd until I reached Khreschatyk where my buddies were waiting for me.

"Slava, what's up?"

"There's trouble brewing on Instytutska. A phalanx of storm troopers, armored in helmeted riot gear, formed a barrier across the street and began advancing on unprotected students. With hotheads on both sides, it's bound to explode. We have to provide some sort of protection for those vulnerable young students."

The demonstrations were not yet formally organized and were merely gatherings motivated by the success of the previous action that ousted the corrupted Kuchma regime. However, the seeds of coordination were germinating with each passing day despite the hope of a peaceful conclusion to the protests on November 29, the scheduled date for signing the EU Association Agreement in Vilnius.

Sadly, the show of force was a harbinger of things to come. A cordon of tightly interlocked crowd-control shields was backed up by police ruffians, planted at least five deep. The troopers swung rubber batons indiscriminately at anyone within their reach and were launching tear gas grenades at the bewildered crowd. Wave after wave of unarmed protestors rammed the blockade with their shoulders, only to be beaten back—bloodied but not entirely discouraged. Some resourceful Kozak came with a bag full of assorted firecrackers. He was surrounded by a group of enthusiasts igniting a cocktail of explosives and hurling them across the divide, triggering a volley of threats and profanity from their tormentors. Others, with handkerchiefs covering their faces from the acrid fumes, were picking up the discharging grenades and throwing them back to their source.

A young man caught my eye in the midst of the mayhem. Something about him did not ring true. Lean, muscular, above-average height, and bareheaded, he wore a windbreaker, jeans, and Adidas sneakers. In contrast to everyone else, he was dressed too lightly for the weather. He was roaming among the forward ranks shouting slogans but stayed far enough away from the scull-cracking batons. He carried a sizable cloth bag across his chest. From time to time, he reached in, withdrew a small can, and tossed it at the opposition. Curiously, the objects that landed on the police helmets did not discharge or cause any visible damage. They merely bounced off and fell harmlessly to the ground.

The second variant that he was hurling appeared to be in the shape of the First World War grenades. They landed beyond the blockade and billowed a harmless grayish smoke without much effect.

I turned to Slava and said, "Take a look at that guy in the denim windbreaker that's making threatening gestures with his fists and throwing stuff at the police. What do you think?"

Slava was not in the best of moods. He had been struck with a baton on the side of his head. A trickle of blood was oozing from behind his right ear, which he was wiping with a handkerchief. He bent forward and braced his hands on his knees and concentrated on recharging his chest with oxygen in preparation for yet another run at the target. He and the others next to him also turned their heads and watched.

At that point, I myself was not in great shape. The tail end of a baton whacked my left shoulder blade on the previous encounter with the gendarmes. As I was calming down from the excitement, the aching pain was making its presence felt. I needed a surge of adrenalin or go home and apply some hot liniment. Next time I would be better prepared, including wearing my helmet.

"I see what you mean, Asher," said Slava. "Let's check him out."

We ambled over to our target. Slava casually placed his right hand on the young man's shoulder and addressed him in a friendly manner, "Zdorow bratok . . . Yak tu trumajeshsia? Yak tu na imya? Ya Slava [Good day, little brother . . . How are you holding up? What is your name? I am Slava]."

The young man was startled and seemed unnerved. "I am Dimitri," he replied in Russian, sending a healthy trail of bathtub spirits into the air with his reply.

"Glad to make your acquaintance, Dimitri! I see that you are taking an active part in the protest. That's good of you. And I see you came well prepared. What exactly do you have in that bag of yours?"

"Well . . . well, I don't exactly know what it is," he mumbled with a noticeable quiver in his reply. The onset of rosacea colored his cheeks.

"What do you mean you don't know?"

By this time we surrounded him—in a comradely manner of course. But the message was clear. The jig was up. He may as well come clean and avoid a pummeling.

"This guy approached me on the street and asked if I was interested in making five hundred hryvnias. All I had to do is make a lot of noise and throw these canisters at the police and the gas bombs way behind the line."

"Thanks for being forthright. Have no fear. You are with us. You're in good hands . . . Vitali, take the bag from our friend and let everyone have a handful of the smoke bombs. Throw them all on the first row of the troopers. We will then charge one more time . . . You, bratok, if you don't mind, you will join us. You will be in front of me and give it all you've got so that I should not be disappointed."

18

Re-vo-lu-tsi-ya!

To no one's surprise, November 29 had come and gone, and the Association Agreement was not signed. Meanwhile, the number of participants in the weeklong peaceful protests mushroomed in the vain hope that the government would relent and respond positively to their growing voices. Late into the night, Yanuk's henchmen, true to form, delivered the official reply to their demands with unbridled bestiality.

Independence Square was occupied to capacity with protesters, spilling the overflow into adjacent streets. Despite their disappointment, the mood was upbeat. The chorus of "Sign . . . Sign . . . Sign" and "Ukraine is Europe" migrated to "Shame . . . Shame . . . Shame" and "Away with the criminal!" Yet another slogan was fermenting in the air—"re-vo-liu-tsi-ya."

Music blared from the podium and reverberated from the surrounding buildings, creating a vibrant echo chamber. Idealistic students from every corner of the nation comprised the majority of the activists. Bundled in bulky winter clothing necessitated by subzero temperatures and wrapped in national and EU flags, they cheerfully gyrated every which way and bobbed up and down to the rhythm of familiar sounds to ward off the chill without apprehension or apparent care in the world.

Helmeted militia, dressed in assault regalia, disembarked police transports and without fanfare, encircled the perimeter. Their ranks were reinforced with the dreaded storm troopers wearing camouflage and the ominous opaque body armor that was stenciled across their backs "**БЕРКУТ—BERKUT.**" Emulating the close-combat tactics of the Roman Legion, they were equipped with body-length shields and instead of the ancient short swords, each one was issued a truncheon—not the customary rubber police baton, but a metallic weapon that was meant to inflict considerable bodily injury.

After the collapse of the Soviet Empire, the remnants of the paramilitary militia in the Ministry of the Interior were reconstituted under the blue and yellow banner and was rechristened Berkut, embracing the insignia and the predatory attributes of its namesake, the golden eagle. The semiautonomous contingent harbored the dredges of society. These defenders of the state became notorious for racketeering, terrorism, torture, and deep-seated anti-Ukrainian sentiment. Their viciousness was permanently etched in the tapestry of the emerging nation in mid-summer of 1995 when they rammed mercilessly into the funeral procession of Patriarch Volodymyr, the deceased prelate of the independent Ukrainian church. Berkut rushed headlong into the column with rapid-fire truncheons, indiscriminately bashing heads of the clergy as well as the faithful. Like the martyrs of old, the mourners continued defenseless along the thoroughfare to the Saint Sofia compound and laid to rest their pastor in a hastily dug grave at the entrance gate because the thugs would not allow them into the cemetery located behind the sanctuary walls. The bloody attack was televised nationwide and shocked the beleaguered population. From then on the mere thought of encountering Berkut aroused fear and sent chills up one's spine.

The signal was given and the attack ensued from all sides of the square. A barrage of stun grenades rained in at the bewildered innocents. Confusion, disbelief, and panic overtook them. The shielded phalanx pressed onward and broke down any attempts at resistance. They cleared the lanes for the shock troops who battered their way forward at running pace without losing a step. The assailants deployed in waves. The victims who were not sufficiently swift to get out of the way or who stumbled and fell were left for further defilement by the next line of persecutors. Those who fell to the ground, despite assuming submissive fetal positions, were kicked time and again with steel-capped military boots and imparted hurried blows with the truncheons across the shoulders. The ground was splattered with patches of crimson. The injured sat dumbfounded on the cobblestones pressing bits of cloth against their wounds in an attempt to contain the hemorrhaging.

Our group gathered at the intersection of Mykhailivska and Khreschatyk, close enough to participate in the protest but far enough from the ear-piercing music to carry on a conversation. That does not say that we did not vigorously join in bellowing the slogans or bobbing up and down in synchrony with the crowd. I must admit that several couples danced to the folk favorites and to my amazement, Slava and his blonde beauty let loose every time a hopak filled the air. For a man of his bulk, he was surprisingly nimble and light on his feet and quite an entertainer to boot. We were in a celebratory mood just like the rest of the gathering despite the chill and the absence of stimulants.

We were about to call it a night. Suddenly explosions erupted from the far side of the square. The music stopped abruptly; a din of screams overtook the merriment. People were running past us uphill on Mykhailivska. Panicked mothers propelled strollers ahead of them while holding on to their young. Boys and girls ran in groups not looking back at the pursuit. Older men, frightened and out of breath, clung to buildings clear from the path of the chase.

We moved back from the street and to the rear of the walkway and surrounded the women, resolutely facing the mayhem. We stood firm, arm-in-arm and were ready to return blow for blow. Better judgment prevailed on our protagonists. Some ran toward us, stopped in confusion, had second thoughts, and bolted past us. Others, sensing danger from the distance, veered to the left and continued past us.

The entire episode was surreal and seemed to end as quickly as it began. *Maidan* was vacated except for the litter abandoned in haste: torn placards, flags, woolen hats, and scarves. Ambulances appeared on the main thoroughfare. They administered first aid, mostly to those bleeding from blows to their heads.

My cell phone pinged. “Where are you? Are you hurt?”

Zina was working the night shift. She knew I was going to *Maidan* where half-million were expected.

“I’m all right. On my way home. Tell you all in the morning.”

Slava burst out through clenched teeth, expressing his disdain, “Those bloody bastards. They attacked defenseless women and children. Women pushing baby carriages for Christ’s sake! We’ll show those devils the next time. And there will be a next time. And we’ll be ready.”

We dispersed for the night in anger. I walked up the street to my Harley and rode uphill. When I was passing the gates to Saint Michael’s, I saw that the courtyard was humming with people. I parked the bike and approached the entrance.

“Glory to Ukraine!” I said to the men standing guard. There was a heavy padlock on the latch and a solid bench propped across the entrance. “What’s going on?”

“Bishop Agapit opened the gates and gave us refuge.”

I could see a smear of dried blood behind the ear of the speaker.

“Are there many seriously hurt?”

“Yes, they are being attended to in the infirmary. But there is not enough medication and bandages to go around. Some wounds require stitches. We are waiting for doctors to come. The injured can’t go to a hospital. They are likely to be arrested.”

“I see. I’ll try to get help.”

I sent a text message to Zina, “Trauma at St. Michael’s. Bring meds, bandages, need to stitch wounds.”

“Will do and bring others. Don’t wait for me.”

The outrage expressed by Slava was multiplied by a thousand voices later in the day. The shock troops violated civil norms and touched a raw nerve. Saint Michael’s Square roared its outrage to the heavens. The beating of the women and the young was unforgivable. Speaker after speaker decried the atrocity. The day ended with a call for a massive demonstration on the following day as a sign of unity and defiance.

Students, parents, grandparents, invalids, mothers pushing strollers, the very young and the very old, over a million strong, descended on Independence Square. Hand-drawn placards representing every corner of the nation fluttered high about the tumult. European engagement, freedom, and human dignity were demanded by speaker after speaker on a wave of "Зека Геть [Away with the criminal]!"

Patience for peaceful demonstrations ran out with the barbaric brutality of the previous night. The call for a march on the seat of the government spread like wildfire, especially among young extremists. Placards proclaiming the end to the police state took on urgency. The mantra, "They give us corruption . . . We give them revolution!" guided the procession down Instytutska Street.

We barely turned the corner onto Bankova Street on the way to the Presidential Administration where we come upon a makeshift barrier planted across the roadway. Behind the barrier was a line of storm troopers with their shields poised at the ready. They were backed up by black helmets as far as the eye could see. They seemed to be frozen in place with vacuous expressions on their faces, anticipating orders to strike.

None of us were prepared for another encounter with the metallic truncheons. Some urged for composure and not provoking an incident. Others ran up face-to-face with the militia, begging them to break ranks and join the people. Stoic young faces peered at them through their visors, confused and devoid of all emotion. Yet others were mustering their courage to charge the blockade.

At this stage, the activity was spontaneous, not organized, and without a definitive plan. Moreover, fighting was breaking out among the protesters. There were men masked in balaclavas accosting those milling about, shoving, and lambasting them with foul threats. Decidedly something was not making sense.

I tried to size up what was going on. Lo and behold, as I live and breathe, there he was again, our erstwhile friend Dimitri in the denim windbreaker. But this time he was dressed for the weather and hiding his face behind a balaclava. On his sleeve, he wore an armband with the insignia of the Right Sector, similar to those of several other masked ruffians. He was ridiculing a young man and pushing him with both hands in his chest trying to provoke retaliation.

"Bratok, perchance, is that you, Dimitri?" barked Slava gruffly as we drifted to his side. "What gives? And why are you wearing that ridiculous mask? Take it off when I'm speaking to you!"

The street-tough, by now commonly referred to as a *titushky*, reluctantly removed his woolen cap and the mask and stood bareheaded in panic with his hands at his side.

"Now what is this all about, Mitia?" Slava demanded. "Why are you here starting trouble? Who the hell sent you here? And why are you wearing that armband? Is it to give the Right Sector a bad name?"

He replied meekly, "A bunch of us were given these armbands and balaclavas and told to start a brawl so that the militia would rush in and scatter the protesters. You can see for yourself. The troopers are just itching for any excuse."

Slava pointed his forefinger in his face. "First of all, give me that armband. Consider this your lucky day. I will let you off one last time. But I don't ever want to see you again. Never! Do you understand? Because if I do, you will not walk away in one piece. Now, who is this provocateur that hired you? Is he here? I would like to have a serious word or two with him."

"He is over there in a leather jacket . . . He's gone."

"Looks like he's not that committed. Neither should you be. Now get going!"

The other masked *titushky* also appeared to be neutralized. We proceeded to the front lines to support the attempts at breaching the roadblock.

Futile attempts were repelled time and again. The night was upon us when the shields swung open and the flood of black helmets poured into the crowd. Like unrelenting locust, they executed the assault at a run with the ferocity of the previous night. Bleeding bodies were strewn about randomly.

It was another exhausting night for Zina at Saint Michael's infirmary.

19

Dignity

The massive bloody skirmishes could not be sustained for long without seriously undercutting the protests even possibly bringing the entire movement to a screeching halt. The obvious thrust of the administration was to cut off the opposition at its roots before the resistance could be solidified. Rumors circulated that Berkut reinforcements were arriving daily for a decisive dismantling of *Maidan*. Also, convicts and street toughs, the infamous *titushky*, were being recruited on mass to infiltrate the demonstrators and cause turmoil from within.

Late in the day of December 11, the belfry at Saint Michael's rang out—not with a single bell that tolled the call to evening prayers, but with the entire belfry peeling with urgency, warning of imminent danger. According to Fr. Ivan Sydor, the monastery bell ringer, this had last occurred in 1240 when the Mongol-Tatar horde was approaching the gates of Kyiv.

The response to the alarm was overwhelming. Men, thousands of men, descended on the square wearing hard hats and heavy coats to soften the blows from the deadly batons and confronted the Berkut cordon. I opted for my bike helmet cushioned by a woolen cap and a quilted winter coat.

The face-to-face proximity constrained the mobility of the tightly packed belligerents. They could not break out and attack at a run as they did in the past; they could not even raise their truncheons. Their attempts at breaching the human wall failed time and again. The night ended in a stalemate.

Emboldened by the standoff, sunrise was greeted with renewed enthusiasm and vigor. Self-organized groups spontaneously began fortifying *Maidan*. The first line of defense was a barricade across Khreschatyk, the city's central thoroughfare. Park benches, railings, discarded furniture, tree stumps, lumber, oil drums, and even old mattresses were piled high. Ingenuity dominated the task. Even the freezing weather was used to advantage. Sacks were filled with snow and buttressed the structure. Water solidified the contents and hardened them overnight. Bulldozers would face a challenge breaking through.

I made good use of Zina's Lada. After driving her either to the hospital or more often to Saint Michael's infirmary, I scoured the city for supplies. Vendors were more than happy to oblige. Grain sacks and old tires were my initial thrust. One of my finds was a spool of barbed wire, which was immediately stretched across the barrier. Later my attention turned to offense and the poor man's petrol bomb, the Molotov cocktail. I commandeered empty bottles, gasoline, motor oil, and other flammables like methanol, which I passed along to eager hands that assembled them for an eventual counterattack.

The tent city expanded and grew self-sufficient. Grandmothers stood at long tables recounting tall tales while chopping vegetables in preparation for the national sustenance, the Ukrainian borsch. While it would not be exactly the way Mother would prepare at home where a spoon could be stood vertically in the center of the dish without tipping over, the liquid beet and cabbage concoction was not lacking in nutrition and kept body and soul rejuvenated. Oversized cauldrons steamed at their side, mounted on modified oil drums adapted for outdoor cooking. Samovars and coffee urns percolated round the clock, energized through a massive electrical cable connected uphill to the monastery. Not only did the electric light the area through the night, but it provided a vital link to the outside world. A heated tent was dedicated to keeping the out-of-towners in communication with home. Cell phone charging stations and Wi-Fi were available to disseminate the news that was censored in the media.

Defensive patrols were formed to oversee the encampment. The units were organized in brigades of one hundred, modeled on the Kozak cavalry formations designated as *Sotni* and commanded by a colonel. Slava was our commander assigned to secure the streets leading from the monastery to *Maidan* and the sprawling tent city. The patrols were deployed in shifts round the clock. Nighttime was the most critical period for mischief; *titushky* continuously made attempts at sabotage. Their most obvious target was the electrical cable.

I roamed the area on my Harley, appraising the troops of what was happening and fortifying them with coffee and hot soup. Both the monastery and the tent area maintained a low level of activity, mostly occupied by students who could not find lodgings. They huddled around bonfires, nurturing new friendships and passing the time singing folk songs. The fortunate ones squeezed into Saint Michael's Cathedral, which was made available for their use. They slept shoulder to shoulder in the heated sanctuary on the carpeted floor.

The nights were bitterly cold and battered intermittently by bursts of snow. Heavily bundled shapes moved about with only their eyes exposed. One would think that these were the ideal conditions for infiltrating our ranks and causing serious damage. Fortunately, the *titushky* were not very ambitious nor very crafty. Inevitably they wore jeans and preferred Adidas sneakers to winter footwear. Without exception, despite the covered faces, they gave off a foul stench of rot-gut spirits. By choice, the *Maidan* protest was entirely alcohol free.

The numerous incursions by the vandals were usually diffused without incident. Once identified, we surrounded the saboteurs, forced them to remove their face masks, photographed them and their documents, and warned them sternly in colloquial terms that if they dared show their faces again, they would be recognized and severely beaten. Usually their home addresses were outside Kyiv; some were from as far away as Crimea. One inebriated hero, who was apprehended near the cable, reacted with unusual nervousness. During our friendly tête-à-tête, an ax slipped to the ground from beneath his coat. He was also photographed and sent running unharmed, but our vigilance on protecting the vital lifeline intensified.

My activities beyond *Maidan* were not out of the ordinary, other than having to adjust my day to the scheduled tour of duty posted by Slava. I did not participate much in the rallies, which were held on every Sunday. Hundreds of thousands attended them passionately decrying the brutality and betrayal of the regime. To be honest, milling about aimlessly and shouting slogans was not exactly my cup of tea. Instead, I used the day to help my father-in-law and Misha in filling the holiday jewelry orders which increased dramatically. Although during this particular season, the demand shifted from decorative finished pieces to a quantity of easily transportable, high-quality precious stones.

Whenever possible I enjoyed spending time with my sons; they were otherwise in the care of Zina's mother. Boris was also of great help when I was on duty. He drove the boys to nearby parks and frolicked with them in the snow to their heart's content.

Zina divided her days between the hospital and Saint Michael's infirmary. As time progressed and skirmishes with the riot police intensified, I drove her directly to the monastery. There were nights when the workload was too demanding that she remained at the post overnight with her girlfriend Lena who also practiced emergency medicine even though I was a phone call away.

We welcomed the new year with our friends in the open air on *Maidan*. It was the grandest outdoor party the capital had ever experienced. The square, resplendent in national colors, swayed and bobbed to the sounds of national artists. It was emceed by Ruslana, the figurative patroness of the protests. I too danced and bobbed up and down, not necessarily to keep the frost from numbing my feet since my boots were insulated for the arctic but socializing in solidarity with my comrades. Zina and I felt like uninhibited teenagers absorbed in the festive atmosphere. During the musical interludes, we responded to the *Maidan* mantras at the full capacity of our lungs. When the clock struck midnight, the entire gathering rang out the national anthem, "Sche ne wmerla Ukraini" in one defiant, passionate voice.

Like Herod, the biblical tormentor of innocents, the merciless criminal Yanuk, overanxious to quash the growing unrest, unleashed his venom in the decrees of January 16 known as the Dictatorship Laws. And like Herod, he seriously miscalculated his subjects.

The group of ten laws restricted the basic freedoms of an open society and provided total immunity to security and law enforcement forces. In effect, the legislation was aimed directly at anything connected with the anti-government protests and decreed martial law. Among some two dozen provisions, the ones that captured the imagination of the public were the anti-mask and anti-hardhat laws.

The very next morning *Maidan* was inundated with every type of mask that could be imagined, including papier-mâché caricatures of the demon Yanuk, rubber masks, and scarves of their nationalist heroes Stepan Bandera and Taras Shevchenko, and an inexhaustible variety of feathered, new-year novelties. I and the less frivolous demonstrators wore balaclavas. While I stuck with my intimidating biker helmet, many mocked the hardhat prohibition with pots, pans, and metallic strainers covering their heads.

The *Sotni* were instructed to maintain the gathering peaceful and incident free and to simmer down the hotheads and provocateurs. By this time there were many defense units. Some units were ethnically grouped including Jews, Moslems, Tatars, nationalists, and veterans, and others identified themselves with painted insignia on their hardhats from cities like Lviv or Kharkiv or Lutsk.

The outrage over the draconian laws blared over the square from speaker after speaker at the podium. The patience of the protesters for inaction was running thin. Finally the leadership recognized the futility of their rhetoric. The only choice left to them was to take action. They decided to proceed peacefully to picket the parliament until the laws were rescinded.

The throng intermingled with baby carriages and vehicles decorated in national flags moved leisurely eastward along Khreschatyk toward the European Square, then turned right on Hrushevsky Street where the parliament was located. As we passed the columns at the entrance to the Dynamo Stadium, a line of Berkut shields cut across the roadway, ready and waiting. Our entreaties for clear passage went on deaf ears and was followed in reply with salvos of the foulest derisive language.

There were too many provocateurs planted in the crowd to evade our vigilance. In short order, fighting broke out on the left flank. Any semblance of a peaceful protest ended with "Зека Геть! [Convict out!]." A barrage of Molotov cocktails rained on the internal troops and their transports. By nightfall the Hrushevsky Street barricade went up, anchored on burned-out carcasses of toppled buses. One way or another, the beginning of the end had begun.

Our weapons were the incendiary cocktails, cobblestones excavated from the roadway, and the acrid irritant and dense black smoke from burning tires. The opposition countered with tear gas, stun grenades, water cannon, and for the first time, with rubber bullets, shotgun shells filled with screws and bolts and buckshot.

The carnage was bloody and one-sided. But you could not tell from the government-controlled media. The commentary and broadcast videos highlighted the brave militiamen being defenselessly chased, collapsing, and being clubbed on the pavement or on the bewildered faces of Berkut nursing injuries inflicted by fragmented cobblestones or on uniforms retreating to safety in panic, their posterior ablaze from fiery cocktails. This was textbook Soviet-style disinformation justifying the ferocious assault on the citizenry.

The truth, however, is difficult to hide in the age of social media. The gory details were simultaneously streamed on cell phones from every angle of the battleground and viewed worldwide and in every household of the nation. Massive bloody injuries were inflicted on the demonstrators, so much so that ambulances transported to hospitals only the critically injured in need of life-saving surgery. Minor injuries were attended to on-site by medics or in the makeshift clinic of a close-at-hand sushi restaurant. Saint Michael's infirmary was overrunning capacity; Zina remained in place oblivious to time, mending the wounded, herself on the verge of exhaustion.

The barricade was active day and night, illuminated by bonfires and burning tires. I continued patrolling on my bike and distributing thermos bottles of hot liquids, especially during the frigid subzero nights. The atmosphere remained very friendly. It continued to be more like a social gathering rather than an intense revolutionary struggle against tyranny. I enjoyed meeting a variety of professionals: doctors in red vests and displaying the Red Cross insignia, lawyers, university professors, scientists, and hard-working laborers. Everyone seemed to be in a talkative mood. When passing time over a hot cup of tea, not one expressed qualms about hurling cobblestones or a lighted cocktail at the government enforcers. Most striking was their commitment and their lack of fear despite seeing their injured compatriots. In between catnaps, I sent videos to friends in Mariupol who constantly prodded me for updates.

Less than a week later, in the twilight hours of Wednesday, January 22, a shockwave devastated our encampment. Serhij Nihoyan was mortally wounded by an assassin's bullets fired at close range. He died by daybreak. I was stunned and stood frozen in disbelief at hearing the news. Only hours earlier I brought the youthful Armenian, which was his preferred nickname, a thermos of black coffee that we leisurely shared. He was part of the security detail policing the night. He became the first fatality of the protests killed by a firearm.

Serhij was barely twenty years old. He was the most affable fellow you could encounter. He greeted you with a welcoming, infectious smile outlined by dense black facial growth that would disarm even the most threatening assailant. He was the only child of Armenian parents who fled the violence in their ancestral home and settled in the Dnipropetrovsk region where Serhij was born. He cherished his heritage but equally professed his love for his adopted country. His motivation for participating in the *Euromaidan* was in reaction to the brutal beating of the students by Berkut—a sentiment shared by countless *Maidan* participants. In the quiet moments of the night when the chitchat was depleted, Serhij would sit back and recite with passion his favorite poems, especially the patriotic creations of Taras Shevchenko.

I raced to the clinic to pay homage to my revolutionary compatriot. A somber crowd had gathered and stood in silence. As the stretcher was brought out with Serhij's remains covered with a blanket, the spontaneous choral rendition of the national anthem bid farewell to the fallen hero. The hymn had evolved as an expression of defiance, strength, and the activist's prayer of last resort.

The administration goons, sensing exhaustion on the part of the protesters after six nights of uninterrupted rioting, launched a violent assault on the barricade. They charged in waves. Berkut led the onslaught with their full arsenal of weapons including live ammunition. They were followed by the militia and then by the recently recruited criminals, the *titushky*. They dispersed the Hrushevsky blockade and left behind enormous human carnage in their wake.

Heartbroken and barely keeping the slits of my eyes open, I rode up Mykhailivska at a walking pace to avoid running into anyone and turned into the monastery to see how Zina was fairing. My attempts at calling her through the night went directly to her mailbox, which was full. She remained at the makeshift trauma center for days as well, attending to the continuous flow of injured. The medical volunteers were provided sleeping accommodations. Like her girlfriend Lena, Zina decided to forgo the comforts of home to be on-site in case of emergency. The Kyiv citizenry poured out their generosity with food, blankets, and daily necessities. The entire encampment was self-sufficient with basic medical supplies included.

Zina was completely absorbed in treating a nasty head wound. I waited patiently at the door until she would notice me. Once we made eye contact, she smiled and signaled me to wait as she proceeded to bandage the wound.

She made her way toward me at a lead-footed pace, absentmindedly shedding her surgical gloves. I sensed a weariness in her eyes. Her face was drawn and free of makeup. Her head was covered with a medical bonnet. Her white apron was smudged with bloodstains.

We embraced and whispered our intimacies.

"Darling, you look exhausted," I said. "You need a hot bath and a good night's sleep."

"It's been a strenuous night. We worked late. By the time I fell asleep, the casualties from Hrushevsky began arriving in large numbers. What is worse, now only life-threatening injuries are being taken to the hospitals. Everything else comes to us. The titushky backed by the militia have been posted at the hospital entrances and are arresting the injured. In some cases, the unwitting escorts are themselves detained. Stepan Pavlovich called and told me not to go near the hospital. The staff is staying put, afraid of stepping outside and also either being beaten or arrested. Rumors are that the titushky are kidnapping patients from hospitals, some even from the ER beds."

"The entire protest has taken a devastating turn. The goons are using live ammunition," I said. "I just paid my respects to Serhij Nihoyan, the young man I had spoken to you about. He was shot point-blank."

My voice began to break. I had to stop and regain my composure.

"He was a gentle soul. He meant no harm to anyone. Why did they have to single him out? And single him out they did. You can be sure of that! They can't demoralize us. We will pay them their due!"

My thoughts flashed to the weapon I had hidden beneath the saddlebag of my Harley. I would need more ammunition for it to be of any use. One spare clip was just not enough. The time had passed for fighting bullets with cobblestones and cocktails.

"Asher, darling, don't work yourself into a frenzy. I am saddened that this tragic sacrifice had to happen. But it may be a sign that Yanuk is getting desperate and the end is near. The truth is on our side. We will stay the course and overcome this tyranny once and for all."

"How can I not be upset? Only hours earlier I whiled away the night with Serhij over mugs of hot chocolate. He was optimistic about the future. He was at ease and entertained me wistfully, reciting his favorite poems."

My cell phone buzzed. It was Slava.

"Asher, where are you?" burst the excited voice, impatient for a reply.

"I'm at the monastery. I just stopped here after bidding farewell to Nihoyan. He died from gunshot wounds fired at close range."

"I am aware of it. May he rest in peace! Stay where you are. We are trapped on Instytutska. We're trying to get everyone out to safety. Rubber bullets and stun grenades are battering us. I'll call you once I clear this entrapment."

"I need to get back," Zina said. "It sounds like another long night."

"Zinochka, I will head home. I need a few hours of sleep. Why don't you call me when you see a break, and I will bring you home?"

"I feel fine. I would like to see the boys, but another day won't matter. As it is, I'm on the phone with them throughout the day. They are doing just fine . . . Make sure to thank Boris for his help. Now go and get some rest."

I watched my darling Zinochka slowly drift to her station. My chest swelled with pride and my thoughts, once again, blessed by the good fortune that smiled on me.

Four nights of burned tire residue on the neck, face, and hands took lots of soap and serious scrubbing in the hot shower. Future excursions to the barricades would be in a balaclava, goggles, and heavy gloves.

My mother-in-law Rifka plied me with piping-hot chicken soup, the household remedy for whatever ails us, and a generous slice of rye bread. I wolfed down the food with glutinous fervor. Rifka smiled at me benevolently and left quietly without engaging me in unnecessary banter.

The cell phone buzzed.

"Yes, Slava."

"Are you still at the monastery?"

"No, I'm at home. I need a few hours of sound sleep."

"It's a good idea. I might do the same . . . They overwhelmed us, shooting rubber bullets at will down from the overpass on Instytutska. Lots of casualties. We finally managed a full withdrawal . . . I have some more unsettling news for you. Mikhail Zhyznevky, the Belarusian, was shot in the chest this morning and died in the hospital. He too was part of security, just like Serhij . . . Two assassinations of security is not a coincidence . . . We will have to regroup. But you, Asher, do not go to the barricades on your bike anymore and become the next target. Also, cover up your helmet with some kind of scarf. Better yet, I will get you a construction helmet . . . Call me when you wake. We should have a plan of action by then. Stay strong!"

Anger, indignation, hopelessness—an avalanche of emotions increased my heartbeat, numbed my knees, and constricted my throat.

I pushed away the soup and retreated to my bed in anguish. Had our efforts come to a screeching, innocuous end ran through the nagging cerebral stream. Mercifully, as soon as my head touched the pillow, I flamed out.

I awoke groggily in confusion to midday sunlight thinking the brief sleep was not much of a recovery. I still felt tired and emotionally drained.

I switched on the electrical teapot and proceeded to the bathroom to wash up. With a steaming cup of linden tea and a slice of buttered bread in hand, I plunked down in front of the television and flicked it on the news on channel 5. The banner read 23 January 2014. My eyes popped. *The twenty-third?* I hit the sack on the twenty-second! I shivered.

The news was not what I wanted to hear. But there it was, the depressing reality in challenging ruthless demagogues: killings, mass arrests, kidnappings, disappearances, beheadings—the full gamut of inhumanity that only man can inflict on each other. Then followed the images that my mind had difficulty assimilating. Despite the brutal cold, a young man, Mychailo Havryliuk, was stripped naked down to his bare feet which were tucked into open, unlaced high-top shoes. He was paraded in front of a militia bus, ridiculed and prodded along with a Dragunov muzzle like a defenseless beast of burden. He seemed to be in a trance. His eyes were wide open and transfixed at a point in the distance. He moved without resistance in response to the humiliating prodding.

Clusters of winterized uniforms stood about socializing, smoking casually and mocking the anatomy of their captive, and launching the foulest indecencies at his ancestry and his sexual prowess. Each outrageous profane volley shouted in guttural Russian drew outbursts of side-splitting laughter. Clearly the enforcers were passing the day in grand celebratory style.

The victim was Oleg Albashian, a patriot of Armenian descent and an ardent *Maidan* participant. He stood erect, stoic in his demeanor and not in the least intimidated by his tormentors. He bore himself with an air of dignity and defiance.

The episode made my blood boil. Instinctively I reached for my cell phone.

"Zdorow, Slava. How goes it?" My voice was still somewhat agitated. "I just woke up."

"Good day to you, Asher. You just woke up? You must be well-rested. I was beginning to be concerned when I did not hear from you last night."

"I can't believe how exhausted I must have been . . . Have you seen the latest atrocity?"

"You mean Albashian? Yes, I have and so has the entire nation. Those mongrels will live to regret it. The social media is ablaze with indignation. The Nihoyan and Zhyznevky killings and the Albashian barbarism decidedly crossed a line and stuck a sensitive nerve. Rather than demoralizing us, they managed to strengthen our resolve. Busloads of men will be streaming to the rally on Sunday. A requiem will take place for Zhyznevky and live-streamed nationwide. The remains of Nihoyan were shipped to his parents for burial in his native village Bereznuvativka.

"For now we must hold firm our positions, especially the occupied government buildings. I understand negotiations are ongoing regarding our demands. Klitschko and others represent our side. But so far, it's only hot air. It will need more pressure and not only with slogans and bricks . . . by the way, I got you an old German helmet. We'll have to think about getting maiki, bulletproof vests. Your father-in-law may have contacts in Poland. See what you can do. Our stuff is crap. And finally, don't ride your bike on *Maidan* and become a target . . . See you later tonight."

20

Reinforcements

The glittering pigments of the spectrum shimmered across the window panes of the capital. The highly anticipated Sochi Olympics, launched with fanfare on February 7, captivated every screen in the realm, including active billboard displays as well as the laptops on the *Maidan*. The harsh winter finally exhausted its fury. Balmy spring temperatures eased the bitter daytime chill, but warm clothing was still in order, especially during the anxious nights saturated with acrid, charred smoke from burning tires on the barricades.

I shed my heavy quilt for a camouflage jacket, no longer concerned about receiving a debilitating blow from a metal truncheon across my unprotected spine. As soon as live ammunition was unleashed on the protesters, my father-in-law Isaac, seemingly overnight, provided me with a half-dozen Kevlar vests. The vests were lightweight and durable and would withstand any aggressive pummeling. The possibility of neutralizing a stray bullet did not cross my mind at that time. I did not ask where or how he was able to obtain them. He found a way on his own initiative, and I appreciated the thought. All I knew was that they were hand-carried from Poland. Body armor was not available outside the NATO military and was strictly controlled and prohibited from export. It would have been confiscated at the border and the smuggler would be arrested and dispatched to prison for transporting contraband. I would have been least surprised that the vests were commandeered directly from a NATO armory and were of the latest American design.

I dutifully passed on the remaining five vests to Slava for his use and his crew.

The intransigence and duplicity of the ruling class and the televised wanton abuse of basic civil rights eventually convinced the citizenry that the widespread protests in the major cities of the nation merely amounted to venting their indignation and expressing their moral support of the *Maidan*. The revolution had to be won on the streets of Kyiv and in the chambers of the government. Busloads of volunteers converged on the capitol despite roadblocks and harassment by the militia and flooded *Maidan* beyond its boundaries.

On Sunday, February 26, four days after the assassinations of Nihoyan and Zhyznevky, a massive gathering bid farewell to the popular, devil-may-care Belarusian. His open casket was borne in a somber procession on the shoulders of his Right Sector comrades, symbolically dressed in camouflage and balaclavas, to the center of Independence Square. Flowers enveloped his youthful round face. He was clad in a white shirt, knotted tie, and a dark suit, a formality he shunned on the *Maidan*. His remains were draped with a red-and-black banner emblazoned with nationalist insignia.

I made an infrequent trek to the Sunday rally to pay my respects to our fallen hero. In a tribute to Serhij Nihoyan, who was being interred at the time in his native village, I bought an oversized cotton T-shirt stenciled with his familiar cheerful depiction, which I wore over my insulated jacket. I was not surprised to see the haunting image duplicated among the mourners as well as that of Mikhail Zhyznevky.

A reverential hush permeated the gathering at the first sound of the invocation, the initial prayers of the Requiem. Bowed heads, sobbing, and chanted responses to the funeral ritual underscored the solemnity. Memory Eternal culminated the religious service. The national anthem rang out the farewell in one emotional voice.

The influx of additional protesters enabled us to expand the barricades, increase and formalize the ranks of self-defense brigades, and reinforce the occupation of civic buildings. The Trade Unions House, a sprawling office complex generously disposed along the Khreschatyk and facing Independence Square, morphed into the vibrant heartbeat of the revolution. Not only did the building maintain the organizational and political headquarters, but it also accommodated the security center, the press center, a trauma center, and, no less important, a place to shelter, socialize, and enjoy a hearty meal available around the clock.

My days and nights became much more hectic than before. I heeded Slava's warning about supplying too obvious a target for snipers by moving about on my Harley. I resorted to using Zina's Lada instead. She was totally committed to the Saint Michael's infirmary and had no need for the car. Most of the time I staged from the courtyard of the monastery and would be there if she needed me.

I also became a registered member of the *Automaidan* contingent. It comprised volunteers who owned automobiles and were on call to transport the more seriously injured to the hospitals. The task was not as simple as it sounds. Once outside the protected perimeter, the driver was at the mercy of the militia and could be harassed or arrested at their whim. Worse yet, on arrival to nearby hospitals, they would most likely encounter *titushky* who were posted at the entrances. Depending on their disposition and their level of sobriety, the drivers could be waved off, dragged out of the vehicle and beaten, or in some instances, kidnapped and their vehicles confiscated.

By no means was the Lada well suited for transporting the seriously wounded; it was too compact. Despite the temporary discomfort, the rusty tin can was ideal for the task. The militia hardly gave it a second look, and on the rare occasion that they did, I would outrun them even if I had to jump a curb or two and zip along the sidewalk. After a quick look at the city emergency entrances for signs of danger, I was off to the safety of the hospitals in the western suburbs. When not engaged in an emergency, I did not remain idle. I scoured tires and ingredients for Molotov cocktails which were in peak demand.

I was in daily phone contact with my erstwhile chum Yuri, the Mariupol taxi driver, and Zakhar, the bartender at the *Poseidon* from the very beginning of the protests. I also plied them with videos of the blazing ramparts that protected *Maidan*. The nighttime pyrotechnics piercing the night in charred crimson bursts never failed to stir the imagination, including my own. Their continuous interest and the outrage after the two assassinations inflamed their anger beyond the boiling point. They and half-dozen bikers could not forgo taking part in the patriotic battle and avenge the senseless killings. Slava took them under the wing of his *Sotnia* and deployed them in his assigned sector.

My apartment was converted into a temporary bivouac. We moved the boy's bedroom furniture down to my in-laws and filled the space with air mattresses. My mother-in-law fussed with the bedding, the toiletries, and continuous flow of hearty sustenance. Zina remained for the duration at the infirmary, which expanded and was staffed to perform minor surgeries. On less hectic days, I brought her home for a deserved respite, spending time with the boys and replenishing her laundry.

I cannot say that the atmosphere in the apartment was overly somber. But we were all at the point of exhaustion, and after the initial jovial reunion, we were more interested in a warm bath and sound sleep than reminiscing over a drink or two. After the welcoming celebration, in deference to the abstinence on *Maidan,* no one went to the cupboard, which was well stocked with liquor. Each of us was nominally on a staggered twelve-hour shift. But no one adhered to the clock and the shifts often drifted unnoticeably until the eyes refused to unglue.

Diamond cutting temporarily took a back seat not because I could not carve out a few hours in the day but because I felt uneasy about damaging a valuable stone in my physically overstrained condition. I spoke about this concern with Isaac and he agreed with me. He and Misha would carry the load. The reality was that most of the trade during the upheaval shifted to reselling imported finished products, which mostly consisted of easily disposable quality diamonds.

21

Heavenly Hundred

Three months of rallies, protests, riots, bloody skirmishes, arrests, killings, kidnappings, disappearances, and beheadings, all enveloped in the shroud of deceitful negotiations with Yanuk's regime absolutely yielded no tangible results. As a last resort, the protest organizers appealed to the parliament with three basic demands:

1. release of political prisoners
2. establish equality of power between the parliament and the president
3. schedule new presidential elections

On February 18, a working Tuesday for the legislators, an endless procession of men, women, and clergy set out from *Maidan* uphill on Instytutska Street to Mariinsky Park where the parliament was in session. A peaceful rally was planned in support of the discussions which presumably were taking place. The march was peaceful, without fanfare, and filled with hope despite the earlier setbacks.

When the column turned left on Shovkovychna Street, an alarm surged through the supplicants as if the gates of hell burst wide open in front of their eyes. Facing them was a blockade reminiscent of an extraterrestrial nightmare. Government shock troops were planted shoulder to shoulder, shield to shield and outfitted in antiriot regalia with their blank faces concealed behind bulging gas masks. The fiends were prepared for us in force and were eagerly anticipating the signal to launch a decisive onslaught.

Flash grenades exploded; tear gas saturated the air. The police charged forward with flailing metallic batons. Behind them, similarly equipped Berkut joined the fray. At their heels were the intoxicated, scum-of-the-earth mercenaries, the blood-thirsty *titushky.*

Clearly, no one anticipated the brutal attack. Our *Sotnia* had been assigned to protect the rear flank and prevent provocateurs from disrupting the peaceful initiative. Explosions and gray smoke emanating from the Mariinsky complex alerted us that something had gone terribly wrong, and we immediately initiated a hasty withdrawal to the *Maidan.*

The violence escalated in an instant. The protesters were being clubbed on the run. The slower ones, and the ones who had fallen, were beaten and kicked by the marauders that followed in waves. Some men stood their ground and fought back, but they could not stem the assault. Shotgun discharges packed with shrapnel spotted the roadway in pools of blood.

The Performing Arts Center, nostalgically referred to as the October Palace, is situated on a rise overlooking Instytutska Street, and adjacent to it is an elevated footbridge connecting to a multilevel staircase. The site could not be avoided in the disoriented retreat. Berkut was positioned there with rifles, as well as with snipers on the roofs of nearby buildings.

The vantage point created a shooting gallery below. The panicked civilians dispersed in every direction. Gunfire felled them at will. The barrage of gunfire intermingled with desperate entreaties for ambulances and medics became soul-wrenching.

Our brigade attempted to move the crowd out of harm's way as expeditiously as possible. Some picked up the more seriously wounded and hastened them to Hotel Ukraina. The hotel lobby had become the central trauma center of the revolution. It was fully staffed with top surgeons, medics, and even veterinarians from all corners of the realm.

Slava ran up to me and hurriedly said, "They are slaughtering us. I don't see any ambulances. There are too many serious casualties to be hand-carried. We need stretchers. We need wheels. Where is your Lada?"

"Up at the monastery," I blurted.

"Get it as quickly as you can. We'll load it with the injured, as many as will fit on the hood, the rooftop, in the trunk—any which way possible. Meanwhile, I'll make some calls for additional help. Now go and be quick."

Under such dire circumstances, my sardine can would have to do. Quick access to first aid by any means was paramount.

As we spoke, I felt a jolt on my back and then another.

Bless you, Father-in-law, for your foresight. Without you, I would surely have been a goner, I kept repeating to myself as I ran with abandon.

Burning tires, irritating black smoke, and a favorable wind temporarily held back the ferocious pursuit.

Yanuk's janissaries were intent on clearing *Maidan*. Water cannon combined with bulldozers and armored vehicles rammed the ramparts, only to be repelled and set ablaze with Molotov cocktails. The revolutionaries did not disperse but committed to stand firm in defiance.

By nightfall, the entire encampment was in flames. But this time the petrol bombs flew in both directions. The opposition targeted the tents. One by one the temporary shelters were destroyed, littering the square with piles of soot, ash, and charred rubble.

And then in the twilight hours, the unthinkable happened. Without warning, the police ascended the roof of the Trade Unions Building and set it on fire with flash grenades. Other than the sanctuary provided by Saint Michael's Golden-Domed Monastery, the symbolic headquarters of the revolution was the last major facility still at the disposal of the demonstrators. All others were reclaimed by the government.

Absent firefighting equipment, the sprawling edifice was instantly engulfed in flames. The protesters' reaction could at best be described as desperate. They burst into the blazing inferno and rescued the occupants from the lower floors, many of whom were wounded and could not manage the exit on their own. The interior stairwells were in flames, saturated with smoke, and not passable. The residents on the upper floors were trapped with no way out, except through the windows. Someone commandeered a tall ladder, but it only reached the third-story windows. Ropes and knotted bed sheets were the only means of escape. Once they reached the limit of the lanyards, the victims had to drop down to awaiting arms. The less fortunate jumped in panic, barely surviving with broken limbs. They were the lucky ones; the others perished on impact.

At daylight the *Maidan* landscape resembled the carnage of a devastated war zone. The previous night's catastrophe claimed over fifty innocent lives. Their remains were beyond recognition. They were charred, faceless corpses whose identity was relegated to the book of the righteous and more likely to parents who looked forward in vain to a cell phone call from their beloved offspring. All other identification evaporated in the all-consuming conflagration.

Rather than wallowing in defeat, a renewed sense of urgency, driven by anger over the previous night's treachery, dominated the activity on the square. A push against Yanuk's gangsters with clubs, petrol bombs, crushed cobblestones, fireworks, slingshots, and unrestrained courage cleared the square. The ramparts were reinforced with the scorched litter while a massive flow of tires was hand-carried by new volunteers.

But sticks and stones are no match against an armed belligerent. The leadership decided to regroup and launch a decisive armed confrontation on the following morning on February 20. One way or another, the insurrection could not be sustained much longer.

Our *Sotnia*, including my buddies from Mariupol, gathered early next morning in force on Instytutska Street with the intention of pushing back the aggressor and breaking through to the parliament. Another group would take the route along Hrushevsky Street with the same objective.

By this time our arsenal was more substantial, mainly from the armaments abandoned by our not-so-fearless tormentors. Militia riot shields, truncheons, and even a few rifles augmented the less-formidable homemade equivalents.

I myself expropriated a shield and truncheon on an earlier counterattack. I clubbed an overzealous Berkut on the neck and stopped him in his tracks. He dropped his shield and raised his arm to prevent yet another blow. I was angry. I was agitated. I was reckless and unstoppable. I struck him repeatedly at the back of his legs until he was about to collapse. I wanted to tear off his helmet and spit in his murderous face, but I saw his companions heading in my direction. So I grabbed his shield and truncheon and made a dash to safety.

The rat-a-tat of machinegun fire and more powerful explosives than were evidenced in earlier skirmishes evoked an ominous feeling that military weapons more suitable for mass killing were now being deployed. And yet another more lethal weapon was introduced to the battlefield. It manifested itself as a distinctive single-shot click, recognized by veterans of the Afghan War as the Dragunov sniper rifle that can discharge armor-penetrating ammunition at long range. By then, the possibility of martial law and deployment of army troops no longer seemed that far-fetched.

Undaunted by the dire implications, we were determined to strike even if need be, at the cost of our lives. The commitment was that pervasive. It was now or never.

The security forces maintained the elevated positions from the previous day. As much as we tried to avoid their line of fire, casualties mounted, including serious injuries to the rescuers. Sadly, a number of our fighters were felled by lethal shots to the head. They were beyond rescue and had to be temporarily left where they had fallen.

Toward noon the gunfire, except for a few random potshots, unexpectedly came to a halt. Berkut did an about-face and pulled back from their positions.

We cheered their departure and were eager to give chase eventually all the way to Mariinsky Palace where the debate on the agreements reached with the regime on the previous night was in progress. Fortunately, the more experienced heads, mainly retired military officers, held us back and stressed caution. Scouts were dispatched ahead before advancing in full force.

"It's a trap!" was the unequivocal report. Snipers with long guns were positioned on hillocks and rooftops. Riflemen were hiding behind buildings and concrete barriers. It was a deadly trap indeed.

It is daunting to describe the emotions at the point of spearheading into the jaws of certain death. But we were not the first to face such a dilemma. The three hundred inexperienced cadets and students who withstood overwhelming Bolshevik forces at the Kruty rail terminal in 1918 came to mind. Their sacrifice on behalf of the motherland saved the nation's capital and the survival of the nascent Ukrainian National Republic.

Now or never was the unanimous consensus.

Slava addressed our regiment with last-minute instructions. We would attack in groups of two and not more than three. With the shields canted at an angle, we would dash in a crouched posture from protected position to protected position and avoid moving in predictable straight lines. Those without shields and with Red Cross bibs would attend to the wounded and rescue them from the field of battle.

"Glory to Ukraine!" Slava bellowed the *Maidan* battle cry as he pointed his truncheon forward.

"Glory to the heroes!" rang out the full-throated response.

I thrust my shield forward in anticipation of my turn to proceed. The image of Serhij Nihoyan was stenciled on my shield. His remembrance would carry the day. I also had my peashooter in my pocket, in the vain hope that I would be close enough to avenge his execution.

Zigzag, fall, and duck behind a tree trunk, the initial advance seemed swift and painless until my shield shook on impact from a bolt and then from a bullet—two dents and no penetration. A false sense of security propelled me forward. Another hit, this one peeled back the metal and left a large hole in the shield. I looked down and saw a hole in my quilt jacket. I explored the hole with my forefinger. A bullet was lodged against my Kevlar vest. I wondered if the vest would survive a direct hit—this one had to be from a lethal weapon.

Chaos reigned the battlefield. Intermingled with gunshots and grenade explosions were cries for medics, stretchers, and declarations, "I'm hit!" The wounded were being dragged by their coat collars out of the firing range and then carried to the clinic. Dead bodies were scattered in pools of blood seemingly everywhere. But we advanced deliberately and the opposition was receding back.

I was running on adrenalin, looking for the next reasonably protected spot. I was also aware of where my cohorts were in case they needed help. Then I saw Slava collapse to the ground. I ran to him and covered him with my shield.

"Be careful," he shouted. "The sniper is over there." He pointed.

"I see him. Where are you hit?"

"In my left leg."

I dragged him behind a tree trunk and slit the pant at the oozing red stain with my knife. Blood was surging above the knee.

I took off my belt and bound it as tight as I could above the wound. The bleeding diminished.

Several others ran up to us to help. There were no medics in sight. We laid him on my shield and dashed at quickstep to Hotel Ukraina.

The hotel lobby was a beehive of activity with the wounded streaming in from every direction. We brought Slava inside and set him down on the carpet at the entrance. There were no available surgical tables, gurneys, or stretchers.

A medic approached us and took a close look at the wound.

"Remove his coat," he said as he reached for an IV.

One of the men held up the solution as the medic sterilized the arm and inserted the needle into his vein. He then took a rubber tourniquet and applied it above my belt. He removed the belt and gave it to me. The bleeding stopped.

He then sanitized the wound and applied a dressing. He pressed his fingers around the wound and said, "Does not feel like the bone is damaged. The bullet tore an artery. Your quick thinking saved him from bleeding out. He will be alright until a surgeon can see him. Just be patient and wait. Slava Ukraini!"

"Thanks. Heroyam Slava!"

I turned to Slava and said, "Are you feeling much pain? I can ask if they can give you a pain killer."

"I'm okay for now. I'm just angry this puts me out of action. The bullet ricocheted from the edge of my shield. Had it been a direct hit, it would probably have torn up my entire leg."

"That is a bit of good luck," I commented. "I had a close one myself. The bullet went through my shield and into my chest. It stopped at my vest." I stuck my forefinger into the hole for emphasis. "I'll have a souvenir once this is all over. Now close your eyes and rest. By the looks of things, we'll be here a while."

I reached for the bag of liquid and addressed the volunteer, "Let me have that. I'll stay with him until he is taken care of. By the way, what is your name? I am Asher."

"I am Pavlo Honchar. I am with the Grigorenko Sotnia," he said with a tinge of pride in his voice.

He seemed awfully young and rather handsome. His soft features, unspoiled by facial growth, placed him in the final year of the gymnasium or the freshman year of university. He was dressed in camouflage, wore an orange hardhat, and an oversized, woven red-and-black-striped scarf with Stepan Bandera's image around his neck.

"I am glad to meet you, Pavlo Honchar. Thank you and your companions for your help. Slava Ukraini!"

"Heroyam Slava!" he replied vigorously and left.

The subject on everyone's mind in the impromptu infirmary was the source of the unprecedented killing spree—the snipers. Berkut was not known for such deadly weapons. Bits and pieces of hearsay and facts were stitched together to form a devastating picture.

In early February, well past midnight, an unscheduled, unmarked transport landed at the Hostomel Airport. The airport, located in the northwestern suburb of Kyiv, was once a secret Soviet military test site for the Antonov aircraft company. In recent years it also functioned as a cargo facility.

The airplane discharged about two dozen men dressed in opaque uniforms. Each carried a dark duffle bag and a hard-shell case. They appeared to be clones in every respect. Their attire had no insignia whatsoever.

They were met by men similarly dressed and were whisked away in unmarked vehicles without license plates. They bypassed customs and the airport security and left the airport for parts unknown.

They reappeared on the fateful day of February 20 in predetermined critical locations, planted behind Dragunov sniper rifles with their identities secreted with balaclavas. They communicated among themselves only with walkie-talkies. No cell phones vulnerable to signal intercepts were evident. The overheard conversations were brief, to the point, and highly professional. The combatants were later identified to be with the Alfa Group of Spetsnaz, the Russian FSB Special Forces. Their dialect was not recognizable; they were most likely a team from the hinterlands.

All activity in the lobby suddenly came to a halt. The sound of an invocation could be heard from the rear of the lobby. The benediction concluded, followed by the singing of the national anthem by everyone with their right hands securely placed over their hearts—the de facto prayer of *Maidan*. Stretcher after stretcher, bodies covered with blankets, were solemnly carried past us on the way to their eternal resting place. "Slava Ukraini! Heroyam Slava!" was a defiant farewell to the fallen heroes.

Well into the night, two medics approached us, transferred Slava onto a gurney, and relieved me of the IV fluid that I was holding.

"You can come with us if you wish," said one medic.

They wheeled the gurney into the interior where a middle-aged mustachioed doctor was waiting. He removed the bandages and put on fresh surgical gloves. He then removed the dressing and began probing around the wound.

Slava screamed a painful "oy" at the touch.

"Did anyone give him a pain shot?" the doctor asked.

"He did not want one," answered one medic.

"Well, it's too late now. Put him on the table and strap him in. We'll have to do the procedure under narcosis."

He removed his gloves and placed his hand on Slava's shoulder. "You are a brave Kozak," he said with confidence. "I will see what internal damage was done, repair the artery, and remove the bullet. You will be up and about in no time."

He then turned to me and said, "Rest assured your friend will be all right. Once he is fully sedated, there is no need for you to remain. We don't want to disturb him until morning. You can come then and take him home. I will arrange for an ambulance. I will be back once he is sound asleep. See you tomorrow, but not too early."

He then left to examine another victim who was just brought in.

I picked up the Lada at Saint Michael's, drove home, and crashed.

On the following morning, my Mariupol buddies and I had a leisurely breakfast which my mother-in-law prepared. There was no hurry since the first item on the day's agenda was to bring Slava safely home. The doctor said not to rush. Later in the day we would return to the barricades and select a new leader of our *Sotnia*.

My cell phone was overloaded with messages. Zina was dominant among the many callers. The messages simply stated, agreement signed, security goons vanished. Slava Ukraini!

We piled into the Lada and I drove uphill on Andrew's Ascent. As usual, I turned into the courtyard of Saint Michael's where I intended to park and walk down to the *Maidan* after a brief visit with Zina in the infirmary.

Zina was sitting in the vestibule nursing a hot cup of chocolate. She greeted me with a weary smile.

"Zinochka, my love," I said. "I got your messages. I apologize for not replying. I was exhausted and slept soundly like I never slept before."

"I quite understand. After three tries, I called Mother to see if you were home. I was afraid you may have been hurt. She checked with Boris. You left the Lada with him. So I assumed you were sound asleep."

"It's been a long, trying day. I am sure you heard about the slaughter on Instytutska. Slava caught a sniper's bullet in his leg. Luckily it was not a direct hit, otherwise he would have lost his leg. I was with him late into the night at the hotel until a surgeon attended to him. I am on my way to bring him home with the fellows."

"He was fortunate indeed. They massacred seventy-seven protesters just on Instytutska. Most died from sniper shots to the head through their hardhats and helmets. These were highly trained killers . . . I am just about finished for the day. Once I clean up here, I want to go home and scrub out all the grime in a steaming hot tub. Call me when you have Slava settled in, and you can pick me up. I am also nearly exhausted."

"Darling, I should not be long. I'll call if something unexpected happens."

After the mayhem of the previous day, the eerie silence and the absence of the irritating soot from burning tires evoked an ominous feeling on the drive to Hotel Ukraina. *Maidan* seemed almost deserted. The few protesters that were there seemed to be wandering about aimlessly, waiting for what was to come next. Some were huddling around the cauldrons, waiting for the next cup of hot soup. Others were milling about the burned-out carcass of the Trade Union in disbelief, pointing up and shaking their heads. Some were just sitting on tires that still remained intact, exchanging anecdotes of the battle and the abrupt disappearance of the blood-thirsty enforcers.

Several ambulances were parked at the main entrance to the hotel. Medics, wearing bibs and hardhats hand-painted with red crosses, stood to the side, enjoying the break in the action and saturating their lungs with nicotine.

"Slava Ukraini!" I greeted them.

They all replied with the *Maidan* mantra.

Slava was awake although a bit groggy. He was still strapped to the table. His entire leg was encased in a soft cast.

"Zdorow Slava, I've come to take you home. Are you ready for travel?"

"Can't wait to be out of here and get back into the fight. How's the battle going? It seems awfully quiet."

A young man approached us. "I am Dr. Nahirny. Are you here to take Yaroslav home?"

"Yes, we are."

"I assisted Dr. Koval with the surgery. He left moments ago and asked me to speak to you. The procedure was successful. Fortunately the bullet was spent and did not damage the bone. But it tore the artery which Dr. Koval had to repair. In a week or two, Yaroslav will be good as new. But the wound needs time to heal, especially the grafted artery. He must stay in bed for at least a week and minimize walking, otherwise he may tear the stitches. You can take these crutches with you.

"We entered Dr. Koval's private number into Yaroslav's phone before he left. He should call him in three or four days unless he experiences severe pain. Here is a packet of pills for pain. I don't recommend taking them for more than two, three days. After that, two aspirins should do. Do you have any questions? If not, you can be on your way."

He motioned to the attendants, "We are ready."

They transferred Slava onto a gurney and wheeled him to an ambulance.

Toward sunset, a massive rally filled the square and the adjoining streets. Open caskets of the nation's gallant heroes weaved somberly through the throng on the shoulders of the honor guard toward the stage. The mourners murmured with reverence, "Rest in peace . . . Memory eternal" in homage to the martyrs.

On stage was the leadership that negotiated the peace agreement with Yanukovych. Vitali Klitschko held the stage as the spokesman for the group. As he enumerated the points of the agreement, he concluded that new elections would take place in December, some ten months away. The crowd erupted their dissatisfaction, "Shame! Shame!"

A youthful warrior, Volodymyr Parasiuk, took to the stage and passionately addressed the gathering. He was the leader of the *Sotnia* from Lviv who lost several fighters in his regiment. He argued that leaving a sadistic murderer in office for almost a year would result in total dismemberment of the revolution and probable death to the leadership. He concluded with the ultimatum that if Yanukovych did not resign by 10:00 a.m. the next morning, he would be forcibly removed with weapons.

Maidan responded with a resounding, "Зека Геть! [Convict out!]"

Yanuk's reply was swift. Under the cover of night, he and his mistress mounted a helicopter with suitcases of stolen currency and fled to the welcoming arms of his KGB puppet master. By next afternoon, February 28, the parliament voted him out of the office and scheduled elections for May 25. The revolution achieved its goals overnight.

In honor of the patriots who sacrificed their lives, their memory was immortalized in the history of Ukraine as the Heavenly Hundred

22

Little Green Men

The two bosom buddies were sitting in the privileged seats, chuckling contently at private jokes and cheering on their national hokey team. Viktor Medvedchuk and the godfather of his daughter, the lord potentate—Vladimir Putin, did not seem to have a care in the world even though their Russian team was not playing up to par in the Sochi Olympic competition. Putin's surrogate, Viktor Yanukovych, escaped Ukraine safely and was on his way to Moscow. The affairs of the state were set in motion; the payback for the insolence was given the go-ahead. The glory of the Soviet Empire would be restored step by underhanded step under the *Novorossia* banner.

I sent off my buddies back to Mariupol with a banquet befitting the gallant warriors that they were. I spared no expense. I booked the Fairmont Atrium where my life had its second beginning. My darling Zinochka and the in-laws were there. Our entire *Sotnia* was invited with their wives and companions. Slava was there in a wheelchair along with his petite, dazzling beauty at his side. I even invited my weekend biker friends who technically did not fight with our contingent but supplied us on the barricades with life-saving medicines, food, tires, Molotov cocktails, and yes, cobblestone fragments.

An eye-popping buffet was staged like only the Fairmont chefs could conjure and an open bar was stocked with high-quality spirits. Tall cocktail tables were scattered throughout with hors d'oeuvres, leaving lots of space for mingling, lively conversations, and tall tales. Waiters circulated, barely keeping up with the demand for refills.

Toast followed toast. We toasted ourselves. We toasted each other. Time and again, we toasted our illustrious leader and his bride-to-be. We toasted his quick recovery. We bowed our heads and raised our glasses to the memory of the *Heavenly Hundred*. We toasted the rebirth of our homeland. We toasted the European Union. Fortunately, we were spared acknowledging any martyrs from our *Sotnia* because the only casualty of the warfare was our own leader Slava. On his insistence, while manning the barricades, we had undergone weeks of training by retired army officers until the tactics of proper battle engagement became second nature.

After three months of total abstinence, each one-hundred-gram dose rapidly elevated the decibel level of the festivities. The conversations became louder; the laughter became contagious. Peace and prosperity in the fold of the European Union were on everyone's lips. The camaraderie would be long remembered and many friendships would be solidified for life.

Two days later, when my head barely cleared from the tumultuous merriment, I returned to work and applied myself to rudimentary tasks but stayed away from brillianteeing until the cobwebs completely evaporated from my brain. I never brought my cell phone with me to avoid unnecessary distractions. There was a telephone line in the workshop for emergencies.

Zina came down all excited. She rarely did that, so something serious must have happened and could not wait.

"Asher," she said, showing me the screen, "look at this. The social media is abuzz with these strange men assembling in the center of Simferopol."

Like her friends, Zina spent much of her free time either text messaging or on Facebook. In fact, without the social media, the Revolution of Dignity may have been short-lived. The airwaves were in the hands of the Fifth Column and was not trusted for their all-too-often misleading reporting.

I took the cellphone and looked closely at the display. There was something familiar about the image dressed in green fatigues with the face hidden behind a ski mask and the headgear that triggered recent memory.

"Zinochka, are there more such photos?"

"Yes, several."

"I am finished for the day. Let's go upstairs and take a closer look on the big screen. There is something familiar about this figure."

The magnified images were much more revealing. The resemblance to the sniper uniforms on Instytutska Street was clearly evident. Except for the green color, the uniforms, including the black knee pads, were replicas of those worn by the FSB snipers. There was no identifying insignia on the apparel, just like there were none on the killers in Kyiv. Most likely, they were the Spetsnaz forces either of the FSB or the GRU.

Other views were more ominous. They showed masked soldiers with Kalashnikov assault rifles slung either across their chests or across their backs, blocking the entrance to the Crimean Parliament building in the center of the capital city, Simferopol.

YouTube videos unraveled the mystery in short order even though the shameless puppet master assured the world with a sincere KGB expression on his face that the masked invaders were not at all Russian troops.

The most humiliating episodes for the interim Ukrainian government occurred at the gates to the Crimean military garrisons and erased any doubts about Putin's big lie. Typically, an arrogant, gun-toting strongman, backed up by an armed contingent, strutted toward the locked gates with contempt and planted his feet squarely across from the bewildered Ukrainian soldiers. He barked at them in guttural Muscovite jargon, issuing an ultimatum to unlock the gates, lay down their arms, and surrender. This occurred at the Perevalne military base on the outskirts of the capital while attack helicopters hovered menacingly overhead. This occurred at the Belbek military base and airport outside of Sevastopol where the peninsula's fighter jet fleet was located. This occurred at every major military and naval installation like Balaclava, Evpatoria, and others.

The commercial airports were taken over without a whimper. Military armored personnel carriers roamed at will, clogging the roadways and preventing any attempts at resistance. The border with the mainland was sealed off with barricades and checkpoints manned by armed thugs.

In the face of the overwhelming force, the repeated response from Kyiv to stand down demoralized the defenders on land and sea. The peninsula was surrendered without the firing of a single shot in a matter of days. The invasion was complete but for the formalities.

The disinformation machine spewed venom unabashedly against the government in Kyiv, accusing it of promoting fascism and being staffed with Nazi sympathizers. The Fifth Column penetrated every aspect of life—the parliament, the military, and the broadcast media—to the extent that no one could be certain to whom one's loyalties were pledged. The most flagrant sedition, however, streamed from none other than the Russian church. Cloaked in its Ukrainian mantle like the proverbial wolf in sheep's clothing, the clerics shamelessly preached Moscow's mantra *Russkii Mir*, Russian world, from the pulpit.

The media was saturated with staged pleas to Moscow of Crimeans for protection from the fascist tyranny and for their acceptance into the fold of Mother Russia. How could his benevolence not respond to such passionate and aggrieved supplicants? How could he not bow to the people's will? Of course acceptance was a given. But the universal backlash, which ensued when Russia swallowed Ossetia and Abkhazia from Georgia, had to be avoided. This needed a touch of KGB finesse. A referendum would do the trick and be implemented as soon as it could be organized.

Billboards went up overnight announcing the referendum on March 16 with the simple statement in boldface: "WE ARE CHOOSING ON MARCH 16." Two images were rendered side by side. The one on the left was the Crimean peninsula dyed in red and overlaid with a barbed wire grid and a black swastika. On the right was the peninsula liveried in fluttering Russian colors. Binding the two images together was a single word "ИЛИ", meaning OR—a simple powerful message, a simple powerful yes or no choice.

The vote was televised live with exuberant fanfare. Smiling eager faces lined up to register for their ballots and symbolically deposited them into transparent containers. There was nothing dishonest or irregular with the exercise of democracy for the world to see. It was picture-perfect, in full compliance with democratic procedures and international norms. In true Soviet tradition, 96 percent of the vote was in favor of joining the Russian Federation; a hundred percent would appear too contrived. All that remained was for the Federal Assembly to rubber-stamp the annexation and follow with an ostentatious parade in honor of the victorious supreme ruler.

The predictable lame reaction from the West was condemnation and token sanctions. Most notable was the hot air and lack of action from the guarantors of Ukraine's territorial integrity, which they signed in Budapest in 1994 when Ukraine surrendered its nuclear arsenal and became a nuclear-free state. So much for Western guarantees!

The tepid reaction from the West wet Putin's appetite for further incursion into Ukrainian territory. In the southwest, his surrogates, reinforced by "volunteers" from Transnistria, affected a deadly insurrection in the port city of Odesa. In the southeast, Kharkiv, Donbas, and Mariupol were besieged by "volunteers" from the breakaway regions LNR and DNR. Most of the insurgents, however, were Russian troops in civilian clothes.

I followed the events in Mariupol with daily updates from my buddies. Many of them had joined the paramilitary Mnipro-1 Battalion, which was instrumental in liberating the port city.

23

The Worst of Times

To parody the immortal words of Charles Dickens, it was not the best of times, but it was certainly the worst of times. These were truly the heart-wrenching times that tried a man's soul.

Emboldened by the bloodless annexation of Crimea, the vulture seized the opportunity to further cannibalize the wounded prey. The little green men, muscophile surrogates and remnants of Yanuk's enforcers, swarmed like locust over Southern and Eastern Ukraine.

In the port city of Odesa, clashes between *Maidan* sympathizers and the separatists began in earnest toward the final days of January. The clashes intensified at Yanukovych's ouster. A flood of disinformation and an alternative reality was being created in the social media, the airwaves, and the YouTube, Russia Today channels, characterizing the conflict as an existential struggle between the fascism of the West and the altruism of Mother Russia.

The protagonists demonstrated under Putin's tricolor, armed with baseball bats, axes, stones, petrol bombs, and eventually, with firearms. Instead of green uniforms, however, the little men wore camouflaged combat fatigues without identifying insignia, face masks, and red armbands. They were military contingents, "volunteers" and "vacationers" from Transnistria, the neighboring breakaway region of

Moldova, which, for all practical purposes, was an outpost of the Russian Federation. These troops were reinforced and guided by Moscow's seasoned mercenaries and agitators.

Their demands and those of the local Russophobes, in the early stages, were all too familiar: economic and political integration with Russia and entry into the Customs Union, rather than choosing a future united with Europe. With the demise of Yanukovych's Party of Regions, a referendum on establishing an Odesa Autonomous Republic became their immediate demand. The notion of *Novorossia* was once again resurrected.

The tragic events of May 2 temporarily diffused the hostilities. A unification rally was announced on the social media for 1400 on that fateful Friday in Soborna Square, prior to the scheduled football match between *FC Chornomorets Odesa* and *FC Metalist Kharkiv*. The well-attended gathering included many fans of both teams. As the spirited gathering marched toward Shevchenko Park and the *Chornomorets* stadium, they were singing patriotic songs, as well as chanting such unifying slogans as "Odesa, Kharkiv, Ukraine." From time to time, outbursts rang out of derogatory references to their nemesis, Vladimir Putin. A pro-Russian mob attacked the column with bats, petrol bombs, and firearms. Among the many serious injuries, there was also one fatality.

When the word spread that Igor Ivanov, a pro-*Maidan* activist, was assassinated with an AK-47 assault rifle, the social network exploded with cell phone videos of the killing and a call to root out and destroy the anti-*Maidan* encampment bivouacked outside the Trade Unions House building in the center of the city. The pro-Russian crowd was overwhelmed by the onslaught and some militants retreated to the five-story building. They tossed rocks and petrol bombs from the roof at their pursuers.

In the mayhem, the Molotov cocktail became the weapon of choice for both sides. Sooner or later, disaster had to ensue. The building went up in flames and many of the occupants were trapped. By the time the fire was brought under control, forty-two victims perished in the blaze.

The entire nation was witness to the atrocity. Two days of national mourning were declared by the government. Finger-pointing aside, significant outbreaks of violence diminished. Putin's invasion faltered, and Odesa was saved.

Kharkiv, the second-largest city in the nation, was the capital of Soviet Ukraine after the revolution until 1934 when the seat of the government was transferred to Kyiv. The highly industrialized city commanded a labor force that far exceeded the local supply of manpower. The neighbor to the east readily filled the void and thereby, constituted a significant segment of the population. Russian was the dominant language.

At Yanukovych's demise, it was not clear what course the city and the Kharkiv region would embrace. On February 22, the *Euromaidan* adherents made the initial move. They occupied the regional administration building, the RSA. Several thousand protesters also attempted to topple the Lenin monument towering over the city in the Freedom Square across from the RSA like it was done in Kyiv and other enclaves of the nation. The action was thwarted by the city administration. By year's end, however, the despised symbol of communist tyranny was pulled down unceremoniously and shattered to bits on the surrounding cobblestones.

The occupation of the RSA building by the protesters was short-lived. On March 1, a mere week later, a pro-Russian mob took possession of the building and raised the tricolor banner. Among the separatist attackers were several thousand "peace-seeking volunteers" who were later identified as Russians. Curiously, they were not betrayed by their appearance or their coarse vernacular, but by the Russian license plates on the buses with which they had come.

Freedom Square became the focal point of the conflict in the region. The RSA changed hands several times until the city administration took firm control and deployed the riot police. Clashes escalated in violence that included killings by the extremists. The calls for a referendum on establishing a "Kharkiv People's Republic" died out as rapidly as they were voiced. The Odesa tragedy in May dampened the zeal of the protests, except for occasional outbursts of violence. The city managed to remain under the blue and yellow standard.

During this turbulent time, my hometown, Mariupol, was foremost on my mind. I was in daily contact with Yuri, my erstwhile driver, and several of my biker friends who manned the barricades with me on *Maidan*.

The situation in Mariupol was chaotic. The seaport was Putin's strategic target for gaining a direct coastline land route to his recent seizure of Crimea. The familiar barrage of disinformation, accusations of a fascist junta governing in Kyiv, and appeal to Russian patriotism dominated the airwaves.

The successful Crimean scenario was played out once again by masked separatists in camouflaged fatigues. They were heavily armed and spoke with distinct Muscovite accents. They occupied the city council building and hoisted the tricolor above it. This was followed in short order with a night assault on a Ukrainian military base with petrol bombs. The assault was rebuffed with force in contrast to the lackluster response and eventual surrender by the disoriented military in Crimea and resulted in the killing of several insurgents.

I was proud to learn that the city council building was recaptured a month later by a mixed contingent of the National Guard, police, and members of the Right Sector. Among the liberators were many of my biker friends. Subsequently, when the government declared the anti-terrorist operation, the more aggressive ultra-nationalists joined the Azov Paramilitary battalion. Yuri, Zachar, the bartender at the *Poseidon*, and many of my buddies took up the cause in the ranks of the Dnipro Battalion.

The invading surrogates were military units of the self-proclaimed Donetsk People's Republic, significantly augmented with seasoned Russian warfighters. They were equipped with RPG rocket launchers, AK-47 assault weapons, and armored military personnel carriers. Their targets were government facilities, which changed hands with every major bloody encounter. During the lethal clashes, several buildings were set on fire, including the municipal police headquarters, which was completely destroyed.

Surreal reality, reminiscent of the calm before a violent storm, hovered over life in the city. Rumors circulated that a tank brigade was approaching from Novoazovsk, a neighboring breakaway town along the eastern shore, and in excess of 5,000 Russian troops were on the march for an attack on the city. This threat was ever present despite the repeated cease-fires, which the insurgents violated with impunity. Distant artillery bombardment periodically rattled windows and kept the citizenry on edge.

Yet, the *Poseidon*, like other resort hotels, was fully occupied. The restaurants, the bar, and the beachside café's hummed with convivial banter. War correspondents and observers from abroad flocked to the city in anticipation of the imminent disaster. Meanwhile, the sun worshipers crowded the seashore with every hint of a cease-fire, enjoying the waning days of summer.

In the end, the city defenses held and life resumed a measure of normalcy.

The Muscovites deployed on mass throughout southeastern Ukraine, led by a three-star general commanding army, GRU, and FSB regiments exceeding 50,000 fighters, 500 tanks, artillery, and mobile missile batteries. To further demoralize his embattled quarry, the KGB colonel staged major maneuvers along the porous border.

The revamped Ukrainian army, replenished with eager volunteer battalions, resorted to guerilla tactics and grudgingly fought with second-rate weapons for town after town, for village after village, for hovel after hovel and for every handful of its precious, bountiful soil. Rather than being intimidated, Putin's saber rattling ignited patriotic fervor that swept through a generation of passionate recruits.

The Western Powers embraced Neville Chamberlain's playbook in responding to Putin's belligerence—appease, don't jeopardize the supply of Russian gas, and at all cost, avoid involvement in a costly, unproductive war. They huffed and they puffed. They demonstrated outrage and threatened sanctions. They also dispatched ineffectual observers to the war zone from the OSCE, Europe's Organization of Security and Cooperation as if their presence would prevent the atrocities.

The conniving puppet master, in the aftermath of their inaction to the massacres in Chechnya and the bloody annexation of Ossetia, learned how to deal with the diffident, well-meaning international community. As far as he was concerned, the issue with Crimea was permanently settled; the peninsula was his. In the east, the self-proclaimed republics, DNR and LNR, for all practical purposes, were part of the Federation. What remained was to seize as much territory as possible and continue the hybrid warfare before acknowledging the stalemate and negotiating a truce on his terms.

The fatal blunder of shooting down the Malaysia Airlines Flight 17 on July 17, 2014, and killing 283 passengers and 15 crew with a Buk surface-to-air missile, which arrived from Russia to the separatist-controlled territory earlier on the very same day, was spun in the shopworn blanket denial and finger-pointing at Kyiv with endless conspiracy theories. Fact-finding, commissions of inquiry, and stalling tactics were geared at deflecting and manipulating public opinion. By no means did the tragedy pause Russia's military intervention.

At long last, the principal signatory of the 1994 Budapest Memorandum guaranteeing to *"respect the independence and sovereignty and existing borders of Ukraine"* that persuaded Ukraine to be nuclear-free and to hand over its 1,900 strategic nuclear weapons, relented and provided desperately needed nonlethal military assistance. They called it foreign military aid. The aid constituted the ultimate in defensive weapons—blankets and expired K rations. That assistance led Brzezinski to quip, "They would have to defeat Moscow's terrorists by throwing pancakes at them." True to form, the Americans followed up with Vietnam-era Jeeps that sported thread-bare tires, shattered windshields, inoperative engines, and broken axles—tons of obsolete military equipment from the scrap heap and lots of self-congratulatory fanfare.

Putin, another guarantor and recipient of the uranium-rich weapon, broke his pledge even before the ink dried on that infamous document.

The demand for investment gems seemed even greater than it was during the turbulent days of the revolution. There was little demand for ornate jewelry; basic stones, mostly diamonds, which could be secreted in a satchel for emergencies, were the preference. Isaac traveled much of the time to Rotterdam, Antwerp, and Amsterdam, personally selecting the highest quality merchandise. Currier deliveries arrived daily.

I put my nose to the grind partly to offset the work I neglected while protesting on the *Maidan* and partly to help my father-in-law while Misha's health kept him bedridden. I applied my brillianteering acumen to selected diamonds, which significantly increased their resale value. The intense concentration on the manual effort also helped suppress my anger at the senseless killings in the East, which seemed to escalate day by day. Sadly, the massive remembrances and requiems on Independence Square were becoming too commonplace.

Many of my chums had joined the volunteer battalions at first call. Several training camps spontaneously sprang up at the outskirts of the city teaching the recruits the rudiments of weaponry and tactics before dispatching them to the battlefront. Slava enlisted in the more aggressive Donbas Battalion, whose boot camp emphasized guerrilla tactics and door-to-door street fighting. As I bid him farewell at the central train station, I assured him that I would be at his side in short order as soon as Misha returned to work. At that time he was somewhere in the thick of the battle.

It was not enough that the mysterious "little green men" invaded Crimea, and like the plague were wreaking havoc on life in Eastern Ukraine, Kremlin launched yet another ploy in early August to facilitate the invasion of its less-formidable neighbor. The compassionate KGB colonel could not in good conscience let his beleaguered comrades in Luhansk suffer alone the ravages of civil war. What better way to ease their suffering and at the same time reward their loyalty than to send them humanitarian aid in their desperate hour of need. Yes, humanitarian aid was the right answer under the circumstances and flaunt the largess on a grand scale for the world to take notice.

Two hundred sixty heavy-duty trucks were assembled at the outskirts of Moscow. Each one was liveried entirely in white, the symbol of innocence, and draped with signs large enough to be seen from satellites: "HUMANITARIAN AID" in bold Cyrillic lettering. Tricolor and double-eagle banners fluttered above the vehicles. Later, the insignia of the Red Cross was also prominently displayed. Food, medicines, and electrical generators were the advertised cargo. International news media was invited to witness the spectacle from start to finish. The drawn-out, two mile long convoy rumbled across Russia on the morning of August 12 toward Ukraine. The motorcade was halted at the border until Kyiv permitted entry on its territory.

The stunt was greeted with universal condemnation, "Trojan horse," "wolf in sheep's clothing," "provocation," "blatant violation of sovereignty," "invasion." Moscow's propaganda machine fired back on all cylinders, "Humanitarian crisis," "starvation," "babies dying without milk."

The Western appeasers initially raised objections in the United Nations, in the halls of the European Union, in the pronouncements of the US State Department. But after all the empty rhetoric, pressure was applied on Kyiv behind the scenes on the presidential level and permission was grudgingly exacted for the convoy to cross the border after a perfunctory inspection of the contents.

The capacity of the Russian fleet could have easily fit half the food supply of Moscow. On border inspection, however, a large number of trucks had sacks of grain piled at the tailgate while the interior was empty. One glaring example of the deceit was a cavernous hulk that contained a single pallet of bottled water and nothing else.

Once the spotlight faded from the incursion, the charade paved the way to transporting troops and supplying the separatists with heavy weaponry at will. While casualties mounted on both sides of the conflict, the losses of Russian troops were purposely obscured—not so much in avoidance of admitting to the presence of Russian elite units on Ukrainian soil, which was common knowledge, but in keeping its citizenry from publicly lamenting the loss of their sons in Putin's hybrid war. Truckloads of cadavers were eventually secreted to Chechnya and the Russian hinterlands from where many of them originated.

The convoy humiliation barely exhausted the news cycle when the horrific Ilovaisk massacre flashed across the mass media.

To stem the tide of insurgent activity, the government committed significant manpower and weapons in an attempt to cut off the rebel supply lines between the breakaway enclaves of Donetsk and Luhansk. Capturing the city of Ilovaisk was a key objective of the initiative. In addition to a half-dozen mechanized and airborne brigades, the Donbas, Dnipro, and Azov Battalions were dispatched to reclaim the rebel-dominated sector. Through the summer months, one bloody battle after another, the army inched closer to the target. Finally, during the night of August 18, the Donbas Battalion broke through the defenses and occupied the city.

Slava filled in our biker crew regularly with terse text messages. He was not disposed to long-winded discourse, not in speaking and especially in writing. A typical message would be "Popasna, 3 killed" or "Ilovaisk, bloody fight, 22 brothers dead." I would go to the map on receipt and trace the progress of his unit. The Ilovaisk dispirited message came on August 10. It was the first attack on the city, which was repelled, sacrificing way too many fighters.

He never complained about the dire circumstances, except once. That text read, "Traveling in war zone on crowded rickety school bus!" That, in a nutshell, said everything about the readiness and equipment of the Ukrainian army—traveling not in a secure military personnel vehicle but in an old, battered school bus.

Voice conversations were, of course, a no-no and never used. Not only were the cell phones monitored by Russian intelligence, but the signal also could pinpoint the coordinates of the call.

While the troops were clearing insurgent pockets of resistance and dodging a barrage of artillery, mortar shelling, and Grad missiles launched from across the border, the Russian forces surrounded Ilovaisk in a maneuver commonly referred to as kettling. The metaphor is attributed to an encircled army that is about to be annihilated by a vastly superior force from a distance without endangering its own personnel in a direct engagement. Sometimes the maneuver is also described as a cauldron that is expected to be "boiling" from the kindling of enormous combat firepower.

The failure of military intelligence to track the Russian regular army divisions streaming from Rostov, equipped with the latest T-72B3 tanks and armored personnel carriers, APCs, and the failure to detect the massive Russian troop buildup that was encircling the city, were yet more examples of poor preparedness, gross negligence, and incompetence at the highest levels.

After suffering days of interminable bombardment and significant loss of life, the defeated commanders appealed to the Russian government for relief. Putin himself declared that on August 29 a "humanitarian corridor for besieged Ukrainian soldiers" should be established, allowing the trapped soldiers to leave Ilovaisk safely under a white flag. This directive was agreed to by Russian battlefield generals as well as the "prime minister" of the Donetsk People's Republic.

The Ukrainian forces evacuated Ilovaisk at sunrise, moving southward toward the village of Mnohopillya, where, as demanded by the Russians, they would follow a bifurcated route through the assigned corridors. They separated into two columns. The northern convoy comprised over 1,000 troops, armaments, and truckloads of wounded and the dead; the Southern convoy was some 600 strong and was similarly equipped.

The southern column was ambushed in a kill zone a mere five kilometers from their starting point. They answered fire with fire, destroying two tanks and capturing several fighters. They held their position into the night. With more than half the soldiers seriously wounded and facing an overwhelming Russian onslaught on the next day, they negotiated with the Russian commanders to surrender their weapons and leave the battlefield under the protection of the Red Cross.

Under the cover of night, able-bodied men scattered into nearby woods. Several infantry fighting vehicles, IFVs broke through the encirclement and vanished into the night.

The northern convoy hardly advanced ten kilometers when it was also waylaid by Russian troops. They were dug in with mortars and heavy machineguns nervously anticipating the go-ahead to begin the duck shoot. A bloody clash ensued. The leading half of the column broke through the encirclement and headed south with their tanks, armored trucks, and IFVs. The trailing half was trapped and mercilessly massacred, except for the few who managed to break ranks and disappear during the chaos.

The surviving regiments trudged through wide-open terrain of knee-high wild grasses while being pummeled by Russian howitzers. The armored spearhead reached the main kill zone at Novokaterynivka, which was manned by tanks, howitzers, and IFVs. The unimaginable devastation was described by several survivors as "a real meat grinder" and "like [being suspended] in a shooting range."

The KGB treachery proved to be an unequivocal success. Of the 15,000 fighters who withdrew from Ilovaisk, only 42 fighters ultimately managed to reach the Ukrainian positions. The carnage littered the steppe with over 500 bullet-ridden bodies, abandoned weapons of every kind, and empty helmets. Tanks, their turrets welded in place and their crews dispatched to eternity, sunk lamely on broken tracks. Trucks and military vehicles exploded one by one and billowed black smoke and ash into the air.

So much for Putin's guarantees.

* * *

The final message from Slava on that fateful day was all in capital letters, "DISGRACE RETREAT BETRAYAL SLAUGHTER." Rest in peace, my dear friend, I am on my way.

24

Volunteer

The bike roared along the open road at full throttle. Boris prepared my vintage Harley for the trip, for which I thanked him profusely. The HOG responded to my demands like a fine-tuned instrument. Early September breeze washed my face and kept me alert for the never-ending potholes. Slava's ominous parting words and his most likely demise were vivid in my thoughts. I was not about to shirk my civic duty and renege on my solemn promise to him.

I wore my trusty Kevlar vest beneath a studded Brando jacket and the patriotic scull-and-crossbones helmet. Anticipating the scarcity of good equipment at my destination, I bought myself rugged, all-terrain boots and wraparound goggles. Other than toiletries and several pairs of undergarments, I brought with me little else. I would buy appropriate clothes as the need arose.

I had spoken at length to Yuri several days earlier. He called me from Mariupol, disregarding the security protocol of keeping voice communications to a minimum. I supposed it no longer mattered since he was away from the active battlefield even though the city was on continuous assault from the east. Still, he chose his words carefully, aware that the vultures were listening.

He filled me in on the events somberly, frequently stopping to regain his composure.

"Our brigade was dispatched to Ilovaisk to reinforce the embattled troops, which were severely short-handed both in manpower and armaments. We fought every step of the way. When we finally got there, the situation seemed desperate. Pockets of rebel resistance caused havoc from within and incessant bombardment from without. Then, the BM-21 Grad rockets, launched from Russian territory, tore us to shreds. Countless wounded hobbled about seeking shelter and the dead—the dead lay scattered in the streets.

"I was assigned to a cleanup detail, to put it delicately. Our task was to clear the streets of the deceased warriors with respect. The task sort of reminded me of the movie clips of the oxen carts being piled with cadavers by the NKVD henchmen in the villages during the Soviet artificial famine of the thirties. Anyway, the streets were treacherous. Often we had to drop everything and run for cover. After a while, you could judge by the sound of what was incoming and decide whether to run or to carry on.

"But judgments under stress are not always one hundred percent accurate. An incoming fragmented mortar round appeared to land at a safe distance, at least so I thought. Somehow dispersed shrapnel pierced my right calf and I collapsed. My comrades carried me to the curb. They slit open my blood-soaked pants and attempted to minimize the bleeding. Fortunately, it did not sever an artery nor penetrate the bone.

"Medics were overwhelmed and were forced to patch the wounded on the run. Mine was rather young, but he treated me with confidence. He gave me two pills to swallow. One was an antibiotic and the other was a pain pill. He then injected the leg, sanitized the area, applied antiseptic, and closed the wound with suture tape.

"The medic spoke as he gently probed the injured area and observed my reaction. 'There is little more that I can do here. A surgeon will have to remove the shrapnel . . . The injury is not life-threatening—you'll live . . . I am applying a strong dressing and will bandage your leg up to the knee and down to the ankle for additional support. Stay off the leg so that the wound does not open and get infected. A medivac will pick you up and take you to a shelter. Tell them you need crutches. These should ease the pain. Take one only when you can't stand the pain. They are very strong . . . Good luck!'

"He speed-dialed someone on the cell phone as he moved on."

"How is your leg?" I said hesitantly, hoping that the reply was not negative, and he did not lose his limb.

"It could have been much worse. I am recovering at the city hospital in Mariupol. On our escape from the killing fields, I burst open my wound and got seriously infected. The shrapnel is gone, but the infection lingers. I'll be bedridden for a while."

"How did you escape the massacre?"

"By a miracle, no less, and the quick thinking of our medivac driver. Our convoy headed south in formation at a snail's pace, anticipating some kind of a trap. No one trusted the KGB guarantee. Something was bound to happen, especially when the withdrawal corridor was spelled out in great detail, and our force had to be separated into two columns. When our column approached Chervonosilske, all hell broke loose. Heavy gunfire erupted from every direction.

"Our medivac was positioned toward the rear of the convoy. Without a second thought, the driver veered off to the left and dashed across the steppe. Bullets came flying and several grazed the rear of the vehicle, but thankfully, no one was injured. After a while, the jarring ride came to an abrupt halt. It turned out that the gas tank was punctured, and the fuel drained out. We continued on foot. I was not used to walking with crutches and kept stepping with my injured leg. The pain medicine and adrenalin masked the impact. Most likely that's when the wound opened up, and I was infected. The bloodstain on the bandage kept spreading wider and wider.

"The driver was familiar with the area and was constantly surveying the horizon with his binoculars. He spotted our flag in the distance and told us that our checkpoint was ahead. He told us to sit and rest while he would go for help. I must have passed out while we roasted in the sun because the next thing I remember I was on a gurney being wheeled into surgery."

"Was the Donbas contingent part of your column?"

"I believe it was. They must have been way ahead of us and were probably one of the first to draw fire."

"Do you remember Slava, our Sotnia commander on Maidan?"

"Yes—that fearless, no-nonsense guy."

"That's the one. Did you perchance run into him at any time? He texted me from Ilovaisk in early morning of the 29, just as the convoy was moving out. His message was heart-wrenching . . . That's the last I heard from him,"

"No, I did not . . . It pains me to tell you this, and by now, you are aware of it yourself, most of the column was slaughtered. Close to five hundred fighters lost their lives. Except for the lucky few like me, several hundred were taken prisoner and are rotting now in some godforsaken cellar. In all, over a thousand brave souls were dispatched to their maker on that bloody Friday. Damn those two-faced KGB executioners to hell!"

"Kyiv, and I am sure, the whole world is in shock!"

"Shock? What is their shock worth? They will talk. They will commiserate. They will point fingers. In the end—nothing! We'll pay them back tenfold. I guarantee you that! What about you? What are you up to?"

"I am getting ready to join you in a few days."

"Do you intend to sign up?"

"Indeed I am. It's high time I did."

"Well, if you are, then don't come here straight of way. Our battalion has a boot camp outside of Dnipropetrovsk. You should start there and learn the basics. They'll figure out how you can best fit in."

"How do I find this camp?"

"It's at the outskirts of the city. Just stop any policeman and ask for Kolomoysky's camp, and he will direct you. By the way, are you traveling by train?"

"No, I will take my bike."

"A word of caution, keep to the main roads. There are too many hotheads who may use you for target practice. These are strange times . . . See you in a few. Keep in touch and stay safe!"

Yuri's advice was sound but not very much to my liking. After my experience with Yanuk's enforcers on *Maidan*, I avoided the police like the plague. As I entered the city, I hesitantly approached a parked police car, not knowing what to expect. At the mention of Kolomoysky's camp, the officer exited the vehicle and in a polite tone, pointed me in the right direction. The next patrolman down the line was equally pleasant and tried to chitchat whether I was intending to join and was the recipient of an affirmative yes. The last was a motorcycle cop who actually escorted me so that I would not get lost on unmarked country roads. He saluted me in the end, turned around, and left. The name Kolomoysky certainly evoked a magical response in Dnepropetrovsk.

Ihor Valeriyovych Kolomoysky—regional governor with three passports, unscrupulous oligarch, warlord with a private army, gangster—the attributes were too many to enumerate or contend with. But at the time of national peril, he was an unwavering defender of his motherland, a patriot in every sense of the word.

Two symbols greeted me on arrival at the camp. The first was a large blue and yellow banner, the proud colors of independent Ukraine. The second was a smaller black placard emblazoned with a trident, the Ukrainian national emblem executed in red within the framework of a menorah, and below it, the word *Zhidobandera*, also printed in red. The symbolism was inescapable. The red-and-black theme represented the Right Sector. More specifically, these were the colors of the Ukrainian Insurgent Army (*UPA*) under the leadership of Stepan Bandera. The word *Zhid* had become a derogatory word under the Soviets, loosely translated as kike or yid. The present-day reference to a Jew was *Yewrei*. Thus *Zhidobandera* would mean a *Jewish-Banderite*.

Later I would see photos of Kolomoysky smiling without a care, dressed in a black T-shirt with the *Zhidobandera* symbolism in red across his chest or sometimes a black T-shirt stenciled Right Sector. The image portrayed a resolute nationalist despite paying homage to Stepan Bandera, whom the Soviets vilified as a fascist and an anti-Semite.

The mission of the ultra-nationalist resistance leader had been to avenge the ruthless repression and rape of Western Ukraine during the Soviet invasion in the summer of 1939. When the war broke out, he sided with the Germans in his quest and on the vague promises of Ukrainian independence. When he issued the Proclamation of Ukrainian Statehood in Lviv, the Gestapo placed him under house arrest and eventually sent him to the Sachsenhausen concentration camp, where he was imprisoned almost to the end of the conflict. After the war, he oversaw the partisan warfare against the Bolsheviks and cooperated with the British MI6 at the onset of the Cold War. He was assassinated with cyanide gas by a KGB agent on October 15, 1959, on the orders of Nikita Khrushchev.

The public embrace of Bandera's nationalism was a strong statement that Gentile and Jew must overlook their past history and unite under one banner in the struggle to retain their independence. To this end, Kolomoysky funded the volunteer battalions in excess of ten million dollars. He supplied them with uniforms, flak jackets, helmets, boots, and arms. The boot camp and provisions were all under his care.

"Slava Ukraini!" a young woman dressed in camouflaged fatigues bid me the patriotic greeting. "Are you here to join us?" She spoke in Russian as did the policemen who helped me with directions. Dnepropetrovsk and most of southern Ukraine spoke Russian.

"Heroyam Slava!" I replied. "Yes, I am."

"Happy to make your acquaintance. I am Kvitka, Flower, the camp coordinator. Please sign the ledger. As you can see, we try to maintain minimum information on our volunteers for safety reasons. I will introduce you to captain Wowk, Wolf, who will be your instructor . . . And your name is?"

"Asher."

A middle-aged man in military fatigues walked in from an adjacent cubicle. His face covering was lowered below his chin.

"Wowk, this is Asher. He would like to join us in the fight."

"Asher, welcome." We shook hands. "Where do you hail from?"

"I live in Kyiv. But I was born in Mariupol and spent my youth there."

"Have you had any military experience?"

"None to speak of. I was in a self-defense Sotnia on Maidan during the revolution and used a rifle with some success in the final stages of the conflict."

"That's good. You seem somewhat older than most of our volunteers. Would you consider helping us in an administrative capacity?"

"I am volunteering for active duty. I have close friends in Mariupol who are in the Dnipro Battalion. I would like to join them."

"Very well then. We'll see how well we can prepare you with the basics starting bright and early tomorrow morning . . . I see you are a jeweler by profession. We do not use names for security reasons to protect not only you but also your relatives. How does a pseudonym Jewel sit with you?"

"When I was a young man, I used the nickname Ruslan. It brought me good luck. Would that be suitable?"

"It is more than suitable. That's settled. You will be Ruslan for the duration . . . Kvitka will settle you in. Our facility is rather Spartan to prepare you for the conditions on the battlefield. We'll start first thing in the morning. Slava Ukraini!"

The boot camp regimen did not leave a single centimeter of my body free of aches and pain. Calisthenics, pushups, jogging, and weightlifting at the crack of dawn began the daily routine. After breakfast, it was training on the gun range.

Every trainee, myself included, was outfitted in military uniforms displaying a patch of the national flag and the shoulder sleeve chevron of the Dnipro-1 Battalion. Boots, camouflage flack jackets, helmets, and balaclavas rounded out the full battlefield compliment. I opted to keep my own boots, which were outwardly similar to those that were issued but of higher quality and comfort. My Kevlar vest was always close to my heart cushioned by a T-shirt.

Wowk was similarly dressed as the recruits. Only his eyes were visible through the slit in the balaclava. He earned his spurs during the Soviet war in Afghanistan. He received distinction as a Hero of the Soviet Union for courage under fire, was wounded, and was eventually promoted to captain on the battlefield. He served in the army until his retirement. Now, he volunteered his expertise to the defense of his nation.

The reason for the anonymity was because correspondents had access to the camp and relentlessly photographed everything in sight. They also attempted interviews with anyone who would speak. Without question, some of the footage flowed directly to Kremlin's surrogates.

The armaments were the remnants from the Soviet army, all manufactured by the Kalashnikov Concern. The AK-47 was the foot soldier's most common assault rifle. Before bringing the students to the firing range, *Wowk* explained the intricacies of the weapon, especially the tendency of the older models to jam under heavy discharge and how to cope with it. On the target range, the drill included the proper standing, kneeling, and prone positions.

After four days the instruction shifted to the PKM machine gun. The general-purpose gun that could be deployed to the frontline infantry or as a vehicle-mounted weapon. It used a 100-round ammunition box and was provided with optional sights.

The one-week training session concluded, and *Wowk's* group was preparing to be transported to Mariupol.

Wowk approached me and said, "Ruslan, I have been observing your dexterity with the weapons. You showed excellent skill with both the AK-47 and the PMK. I would like to try you on a sniper rifle. We need snipers. It will take several days here and also additional training when you are in Mariupol. Would you consider it?"

"If that is where I can be most useful, then of course, I will try."

25

Sniper

The Armored Personnel Carrier, APC, traveled southward from Dnepropetrovsk at normal speed through the government-controlled territory until it reached the outskirts of Donetsk. At that point, the driver turned to his cell phone for guidance, because the situation on the ground was very fluid and could have changed overnight.

I felt reasonably secure in the APC. It was protected from small arms fire and stray shrapnel. The driver trekked this route on a weekly basis and was sensitive to the vagaries of the road. Initially, I wanted to go on my Harley, but I was persuaded that it was not safe. The Hog was strapped for the trip at the rear of the transport.

My emotions were jumbled. I looked forward to revisiting my home grounds, yet I was haunted by the loss of my close friends, especially the images of Slava. My training with the Dragunov sniper rifle went reasonably well. I was accurate at a kilometer distance most of the time. But to become highly proficient on the squad-support weapon, I needed further instruction and lots of practice with understanding the effects on the accuracy not only of the wind and the weather but also the time of day and the compensation for gravitational influence at extended distances.

On arrival, we were asked to sign a two-month commitment. This was standard practice. More often than not, the commitment became open-ended. A volunteer would serve beyond the term or remain until a critical mission would be completed. The oath would be administered on the weekend with a formal welcoming ceremony.

The clerk, seeing my signature, said to me, "Are you Ruslan?"

"Yes, I am."

"Please remain here. Before I show you to your quarters, Orel, Eagle, would like to have a word with you."

In short order, a senior officer with a grayish mane and thick, flowing mustaches approached me.

"You are Ruslan?" He extended his hand for a handshake. "Welcome. I was looking forward to meeting you. I am Orel. I was informed by Wowk of your prowess with the Dragunov rifle. I would like to take you under my wing for further instruction. We have a need for proficient snipers. You demonstrated abilities that few men have. I will help you to put them to practice. Why don't you settle in and we will start in the morning. Meet me here after breakfast. See you then."

The Dnipro-1 Battalion was a special volunteer militia under the auspices of the Ministry of Internal Affairs. The primary duties of the unit were manning the checkpoints in the southeastern part of Ukraine. They also augmented the military in major battles such as the ill-fated encounter at Ilovaisk.

While Mariupol was under firm control by the government, the population languished in an environment of a city under siege. This was despite a significant buildup of infantry, the presence of Donbas, Azov, and Dnipro Battalions, and an influx of howitzers and tanks. The major attacks in early September on the strategic port city left the impression that another assault by the separatists was just a matter of time. The nightly thunder of ordinance and visible flashes of light from weapon discharges reinforced the uneasiness.

At the first opportunity, I went on my bike to the cemetery to pay my respects to my mother as I had always done whenever I visited Mariupol. The gravesite was maintained by my former neighbor Avraam. The monument was spotless unlike the rest of the neglected memorial park. I donned my yarmulke and devoutly recited the mourner's *Kaddish* in her memory.

My attempts to connect with Yuri were not successful. I found out later that he was on duty at a vulnerable checkpoint and did not activate his cell phone. The checkpoint was east at the outskirts of town facing Novoazovsk, where the separatists and over five thousand regular Russian troops were positioned for an imminent assault. Heavy artillery, tanks, and even a Grad missile launcher comprised the arsenal of the aggressors.

The first line of defense was massive trenches dug in haste to prevent tanks from surging across the divide unabated and paving the way for the ground insurgency. The trenches were far enough from the city so that the damage from shelling would be minimized. However, sporadic shelling continued despite numerous declarations of a cease-fire.

Next, I headed to the second home of my youth, the Poseidon hotel. Seasonal guests had departed with the onset of the October chill. All that seemed to remain in the somber scene were foreign war correspondents. Several familiar faces dear to me were conspicuously absent. Among them were my accommodating concierge, the easygoing bartender, and several kitchen helpers who, all too often, fed me off the cuff. They all disappeared in the battle of Ilovaisk, and no one knew for certain whether they were still alive rotting in some separatist dungeon or whether they were at peace with their maker. I swallowed hard and returned to the barracks.

At the start of the training, *Orel* patiently reviewed the rudiments of the Dragunov and the necessity of thoroughly cleaning the barrel after a day's engagement. He emphasized that the rifle needed to become an integral part of me, an extension of my arms. Clearing my mind of all distractions and focusing on the target was vital. For me, distraction was never an issue. When I was brillianting without a steady hand and total concentration, the task would easily turn into a costly disaster.

Because no two guns were identical, I was issued a weapon which only I would use for the entire deployment.

The training on the firing range was exhaustive. The prone position was exploited first using both the weapon sight and the telescopic option. This was followed by exercising the bipod. Kneeling, standing, bracing on a tree trunk and inclement weather were all in the mix. The biggest challenge was instruction in the middle of the night. The target, at first, was a flickering light and then the ultimate, a barely visible dot simulating a smoldering cigarette.

I was deemed ready to be sent into the field as ready as could be expected from a crash course.

I was assigned to a squad of replacements and accompanied them in an APC to an eastern blockpost along the shoreline. This crew was to be my team for a number of weeks. The block post was important since it protected against a Russian incursion from the Azov Sea in an attempt to circumvent the impenetrable trenches.

The squad was an amalgam of volunteers from every corner of the nation. The youngest in the contingent was Ostap, a university student from Lviv. He was a bright, happy-go-lucky youth, barely beyond his teens. He was one of the thousands who responded to the Revolution of Dignity and came by busloads to *Maidan*. He lingered in Kyiv after Yanukovych's demise until the call to action came to confront Putin's aggression. He headed north of the city to the National Guard training facility in Novi Petrivtsi and joined the Donbas Battalion, the so-called "little black men" in contrast to Moscow's "little green men" because of their black uniforms. He was a seasoned combatant having fought in numerous battles including Ilovaisk, where good fortune smiled at him and enabled him to escape the debacle in one piece.

Another standout in the group was Professor, his nom de guerre. He was a bit taller than me with distinct Romanov facial features including the fastidiously nurtured facial growth—a sophisticated man in every sense of the word yet not at all standoffish. He was just a bit younger than me. He was a highly educated man with a doctorate in mathematics. He was on the faculty of the Kharkiv National Technical Institute lecturing calculus. During the civil upheaval, he marched shoulder to shoulder with his students in the Kharkiv protests in solidarity with *Maidan*.

And then there was Artem, the divinity student from St. Michael's Seminary. During the *Maidan* uprising, he proved to be an enthusiastic Johnny-on-the-spot as the monastery became a refuge from abuse by the Berkut thugs. Young out-of-town protesters flooded St. Michael's compound, seeking first aid, nourishment, and a warm corner to sleep in. Artem was the Good Samaritan day and night, fulfilling the needs wherever necessary. He extended that protective calling to his motherland under the banner of the Donbas Battalion and donned the uniform of the "little black men."

Quite often I would see him stretched out on the ground in solitude with his back propped on a tree trunk, absorbed in the book of scriptures which he carried in his backpack. His weapon lay at his feet. I wondered whether he ever discharged it in combat or when he did, whether he aimed the shot overhead into the air. Regardless, he was in the thick of things, performing his civic duty at the time of national crisis.

The group, including the army regulars, was a friendly bunch. We socialized on watch and ate all the meals together. Lively conversation and frequent vulgar references to our opposition were a welcome break from boredom as real action seemed to elude us. Surprisingly, anecdotes of recent battles were seldom recounted. Yet everyone at the table, except for me, was a seasoned veteran. The one topic that always tested the bonhomie was Crimea. Inevitably, one of the soldiers would bring up the disgraceful surrender of the armed forces without firing a single shot and an argument would ensue. The more combative veterans insisted that the troops should have fought, if need be, to an honorable death. These were the sentiments of the Right Sector memorialized in the national anthem, "We will lay down our souls and bodies for our freedom." Usually, when the disagreement was gaining momentum, we left the table to avoid ill feelings.

My mission was to harass the enemy day and night. I surveyed the Russian encampment with the telescopic sight and concluded that the distance precluded even a nuisance shot. I had to reduce the range significantly. The only answer was to find the path through the network of trenches, which fortunately were not continuous. Another consideration was how to get in position in the no man's land and not get spotted or worse yet, not get killed.

Somewhere in the recesses of my mind were stored the images of Soviet propaganda glorifying the guerrilla tactics deployed during the Great War. Those images were vivid in my mind's eye and formulated the course of my actions. I borrowed black fatigues from my Donbas comrades. One of the soldiers commandeered for me an ankle long greatcoat and winter underwear. After sundown, I transformed myself into a ghostly shadow, ready to test my skills. I had with me a thermos of hot tea and my rifle wrapped in burlap. Under the cover of night, I set out to be in position to cause havoc at daybreak. I outlined my route to the night watch, not to be victimized by friendly fire.

The night was overcast, obscuring the moonlight in waves. I moved swiftly through the maze and fell to the ground whenever the moon was on the verge of reappearing. Once in position, I lay prostrated behind an outcropping, had a cup of tea, and tried to sleep. My heart pounded to a heavy drumbeat. My thoughts were random and frequently made little sense. I dared not falter on my initial outing. I grew impatient waiting for the first signs of a new day. I kept anxiously aligning the telescope sight and repositioning the bipod.

I fired three shots in succession as soon as I could detect movement through the early morning mist. I moved down the line and hit another three moving targets. I felt confident—no doubts, no jitters, hands steady. As I crawled to a new location, I sensed a cluster of fire whiz by me and felt a bump in my lower back. The Kevlar did not yield. Three more rounds and I was done for the day. Bullets sputtered aimlessly about me as I withdrew.

I was not aware of the damage I had inflicted until I was greeted by the men of the night watch, pats on the back and a cheerful "well done."

One of the men quipped, "What's this? There is a big hole in your overcoat." He poked around, dug out a two-inch slug, and held it up to me between his thumb and forefinger. "Dragunov sniper bullet," he said. He then ceremoniously displayed it to his colleagues.

Apparently I caused quite a stir behind the enemy lines, the men were telling me. As soon as they heard the first volley of shots, all binoculars were fixed across the divide. They witnessed shock, confusion, and a frantic scramble to arms. The second volley gave them a sense of direction and rapid firing erupted. The last volley sent a barrage of led in my direction. And there had to be casualties, evidenced by the appearance of ambulates on the scene.

I thanked the men for their approval and left to get something warm to eat. A pot with gruel was simmering on a field stove. I shed my overcoat and ladled a bowlful of cereal and filled a mug with hot tea.

The men were gathering for breakfast. My nocturnal exploits were the topic of conversation. Pats on the back, expressions of well done, and questions about how I actually did it rambled on. What pleased me most was that my name, Ruslan, was spoken with new respect. I had truly become a warfighter and part of the team.

My thoughts dwelled on the comments of the night watch that they were alerted to my activity by the sound of the discharges from my rifle. Under the circumstances, my ability for a future meaningful attack would be limited, and my safety would be severely compromised. As it was, I dodged a serious wound had the bullet struck just a few centimeters lower.

I needed a silencer. I would call Orel after I cleaned the rifle and ask him to send me, as soon as possible, a silencer and two ten-round magazines.

By the time I woke up in the late afternoon, my request was on-site, including a wooden crate of ammunition. I attached the silencer and moved to an open area where I could evaluate the effects of the addition on the shooting accuracy and the maximum range.

My tactics had to change. Toward sunset I scouted with binoculars the disposition of forces in the enemy encampment that I would attack sometime during the night. I would rapidly discharge ten rounds at a time and reposition, firing the three magazines at my disposal.

When our replacements arrived, the team was given a three-day leave. It did not make sense for me to travel home for such a short period, most of which would be spent on travel even if I flew. Zina and I decided that I remain in Mariupol and get well-rested.

I left my gear at the barracks and took a suite at the Poseidon. I rented a laptop from the hotel and called Zina. We set the time to Skype in the evening. I filled the tub and scrubbed out weeks' worth of grime from my pores.

I called Yuri. He was back in town. We would meet at the hotel lounge for dinner after my Skype session. I then went out to exercise the power of my plastic. I ate a solid lunch, bought presentable clothes and shoes, and stocked up on the usual refreshments.

I dropped by the kitchen in the afternoon and asked the chef to prepare my favorite lamb dish for two. He knew, like the entire staff, that the curly-haired urchin of old was now a privileged guest of the hotel.

On seeing the entire family on the screen, I realized how homesick I had been after an absence of a mere month. In my business travels, I had rarely been away for more than a week. Life in the family and as a matter of fact, in Kyiv had not changed. There was no news of Slava's whereabouts. The Revolution of Dignity, other than tributes to the *Heavenly Hundred*, was viewed in the rearview mirror, politics as usual, the fifth column active openly.

My seven-year-old twins had the battlefront on their minds. They persisted on asking which battles I had been in and how many bad guys I killed. I dared not admit that I served as a sniper or the hazards I had undertaken. As far as the family was concerned, I was deployed on an uneventful guard post on the outskirts of the city. With the heralded declarations of truce, there was little to do but drink hot tea to ward off the autumn chill and the boredom of doing nothing. Everyone was satisfied with the explanation and ended with declarations of their love.

Yuri was seated comfortably at a corner table nursing a tall drink. He rose when he saw me enter and rushed to embrace me in the traditional way.

"Asher, my brother, I am so glad to see you. You have done yourself proud," he almost shouted. "When I first heard the exploits of Ruslan, I knew it had to be you. On that fateful day on Maidan, you were fearless under fire. That image will forever be etched in my memory. It could not have been anyone else."

"Zdorov, Yura. I am glad to see you up and about. Let's go sit down in the dining room, and we can catch up on our recent adventures."

"I'll be with you in a minute. I have to settle my tab."

"Oh, never mind that. They can add it to my bill."

"Then, at least, let me leave a tip for the waitress."

There were few patrons in the restaurant. The tourist season was over and the wealthier residents left the city in fear of an imminent invasion from the east. We settled at a table that gave us some privacy. I ordered a hundred grams each of Poseidon's best, and we proceeded to the appetizer, *zakuski*, and buffet.

"Asher, I thought I knew you well, but you are certainly full of surprises," Yuri said when we returned to the table with full plates. He then said as he raised his glass, "May you prosper for a hundred years! And may your life be full of pleasant surprises."

"To your health, my dear friend."

Glasses clicked and emptied in one swift motion, *zakuski* consumed, glasses refilled.

"How have you been fairing since I spoke to you last?" I asked.

"Except for a small souvenir in my calf, I recovered well enough to rejoin the battlefield. But first, tell me. of all things, how the hell did you ever wind up being a sniper? For a while, I thought you had your fill of violence on Maidan and would avoid future involvement in combat."

"There is little to tell. When the anti-terrorist action began, Slava and the guys from our Sotnia volunteered to the Donbas Battalion, which had a training camp at the outskirts of Kyiv. My predicament at that time did not allow me to join with them. I am sure I had mentioned to you that my father-in-law needed help because Misha, his long-time helper, had taken ill. I promised Slava that I would join the team as soon as Misha was back on his feet. Slava's last communication from Ilovaisk ignited in me a sense of urgency. I could not delay any longer. I had to make my move. After I spoke to you, I followed your instructions to the letter and wound up in the Kolomoysky boot camp."

"But why a sniper of all things?"

"Why a sniper? That's a good question. I had undergone the basic training with the assault rifle and machine gun. An instructor noticed something in my performance that he suggested I try the sniper rifle. I liked the challenge and he convinced me that being a sniper would be my best contribution to our cause. As far as the heroics attributed to me are concerned, I just focused on what was expected of me and nothing more. Heroics? Far from it. Running scared is more like it."

The waitress brought out a tray with the dinner and served it. She was accompanied by the chef.

"Braised lamb shank," he said with a satisfied smile on his face. "Just as you like it, Asher. I remember when you and Zinaida were here last summer, both of you enjoyed the brazed shank . . . I am glad that you gave me enough warning today. We no longer have it on our menu. It takes too long to prepare properly. Everyone nowadays is in such a hurry."

"I do appreciate it, Victor Sergeyevich. It does bring back so many good memories . . . The dish looks out of this world . . . And the aroma—you certainly outdid yourself."

"Enjoy it in good health. I left a portion for myself in the kitchen, which I will now delight in."

"May I send you a bit of refreshment to embellish your meal?"

"Thank you. I will raise the glass to your health. Bon appétit."

The festive dish called for another hundred grams to stimulate the digestion as the saying goes.

After another traditional toast, I said, "Yuri, which part of the police action were you engaged in?"

The cheerful expression on Yuri's face turned dour. He spoke with a deflated voice.

"For weeks we were repelling Russian attacks on Donetsk City. They came at us with Grad rocket launches hidden behind apartment buildings. Every time we would push them back, heavy artillery shelling and self-propelled grenades would light up the night. While the politicians quibbled about peace and cease-fires, their side maintained an inexhaustible supply of armaments and manpower. Those so-called humanitarian convoys crisscrossed the border at will resupplying the battlefront and removing the dead on the return trip.

"It is so demoralizing to defend every scrap of motherland one day and two days later, be attacked in the same sector but by a reinforced enemy. Perhaps the most unnerving feeling is to hear the inhuman screams, 'Allahu Akbar' prior to a barrage of missiles and artillery. It literally sent chills down your spine."

"Were there many casualties?"

"Our squad was very fortunate. There were casualties from shrapnel and flying debris. The wounds were not life-threatening. The same cannot be said for other teams who suffered fatalities . . . What is your next assignment, Asher? Are you returning to your previous block post?"

"No, we will be sent to the western outpost to protect the M14 highway, the so-called Black Sea Economic Association transportation corridor. The Russians are attempting to gain control of the route which connects Transnistria, Crimea, Donbas, and Russia along the southern border of Ukraine. It also gives the insurgents access to Mariupol."

26

Cyborg

The subsequent rotations took our squad westward to more vulnerable block posts that protected Mariupol. The insurgent onslaught was intensifying with an inexhaustible supply of manpower and the latest Russian weaponry. They unleashed on our positions multiple rocket launchers, howitzer salvos, Grad rockets, self-propelled grenades and mortars, and eventually, tear-gas grenades.

My response to the belligerents was with an unexpected and most likely, foolhardy outpouring of aggression. I roamed as close to the enemy lines as possible within my firing range under the cover of darkness and discharged the Dragunov at anything that moved. The nightly raids earned me the nickname Night Stalker. My facial growth took on biblical proportions, hidden beneath a black balaclava. My flak jacket, which I wore on my watch like a badge of honor, was riddled with oversized holes. The Kevlar vest absorbed the impact. But the black-and-blue souvenirs throbbed and blemished my torso for days.

Donetsk City and its airport bore the brunt of the Russian attack. As Yuri observed, the assaults came in waves, each one more violent and penetrating than the last. The fighting in the city was on the street level with the invading tanks using the citizens and apartment buildings as shields. A barrage of relentless firepower was similarly directed at the airport.

The Donetsk International Airport, or what was left of it, was a sprawling complex situated northwest of the city. It was built in the Soviet era and named in honor of the local favorite son, composer Sergei Procofiev. In preparation for the Euro 2012 football tournament, a new terminal was constructed and the old terminal was upgraded to modern standards.

In May 2014, the separatists, with heavy reinforcements of Russian mercenaries, seized the airport. The newly elected president Petro Poroshenko sent in the military and the priority target was once again restored to government control. The tug-of-war continued despite negotiations and declarations of cease-fires, which were violated by the insurgents before they were even officially announced.

By year's end, a skeletal framework remained of what was once the pride of Donbas. The airport was under siege and whatever was still standing with the exception of the control tower was time and again shelled with impunity. A small contingent of diehard defenders clustered at the center of the ruins determined to fight the enemy to the death. Their unrelenting stoicism, inhuman persistence, obstinacy, and heroism earned them the designation as Cyborgs by their fellow combatants as well as by Kremlin's surrogates.

The squad was a ramshackle band of volunteers from both the military and the battalions. The army, marines, and air force contributed battle-hardened fighters. The Cyborgs from the battalions, under the flagship of the Interior Ministry, were mostly drawn from the Right Sector and nationalist units.

Kremlin's propaganda and disinformation machine flooded the airwaves with accusations that the "Kyivan junta" deployed foreign mercenaries to destroy the peace-loving people of Donbas. Their malicious slander claimed that the airport was controlled by "a Fascist-Banderite punitive force." The daily televised programming on both sides of the border highlighted the battle for the airport and the bravery of the local citizenry without even a hint of Russian participation or the death toll of the insurgents.

The orders to the Cyborgs from Kyiv were simple—stand fast and don't surrender.

On my return to the barracks from the latest rotation, Orel sought me out.

"Zdrastvuj, Ruslan [Good day, Ruslan]! How was your outing? Any new souvenirs in your flak jacket?" He chuckled with a friendly smile and a paternal pat on my shoulder.

"Zdrastvuj, Orel—not this time. But this time the shelling was more intense. Their arsenal seems to be inexhaustible . . . I could have done more damage if I had a thermal imaging scope. They seemed most vulnerable at the crack of dawn and in the twilight hours before renewing the bombardment. A clear view would have made a difference."

"I may be able to help you with a thermal scope. But first, let me tell you what is on my mind. We have a serious situation at the Donetsk Airport. Our men are under siege and are asked to defend their position no matter the circumstances. I am sure you are aware of their predicament."

"That's the scuttlebutt in the ranks."

"They need all the support we can give them. They are all volunteers and are willing to do what is necessary. The fight is at close quarters—at times at meter distances. They are in need of experienced snipers. Have you given any thought to giving them a helping hand?"

"As a matter of fact, the thought crossed my mind. I want to contribute more than maintaining a block post."

"Give it somber consideration. This would be the most dangerous mission in the war. There are all too many casualties in that damned rat trap. Rest for a few days and we'll talk again. I'll have the scope for you tomorrow. You should practice at distances shorter than five hundred meters. That would most likely be the range you would encounter . . . Until tomorrow then . . . Slava Ukraini!"

The APC, scarred from previous near-death encounters, was stuffed beyond capacity. The replacements were squeezed together shoulder to shoulder without the slightest wiggle room. Boxes of ammunition, rations, white bundles stenciled with red crosses, and cases of liquid gold filled every remaining space. Bulging duffle bags were tied at the rear of the transport.

I was layered like a *matryoshka*—a Russian nesting doll—with heavy woolen undergarments, my Kevlar vest and flak jacket, winter overcoat, and a quilted greatcoat. One could have thought I was on my way to the artic. In addition to the sniper rifle and the two telescopic sights, I brought with me a PKM machine gun and lots of ammunition. Before my departure, I soaked in a hot tub, registering in my memory the decadent pleasure of a prolonged bath. That would have been the last such extravagance for the duration. Potable water was at such a premium that merely washing your hands or face would be considered sacrilegious. Hygiene was relegated to hand wipes.

We all sat silently in our knitted skullcaps and camouflaged helmets with our eyes closed, listening for the distant boom of heavy weapon discharge. We were about to enter the final and deadly stretch of the trip. The experienced driver made this journey on a regular basis and survived. Other APCs were not so fortunate. Their charred shells lay scattered in the field.

The key to survival was in the timing. Russian artillery had a predictable cycle. In between, the hazard was from small arms fire or land mines on frequented paths. So the method was to stagger the travel time and never use the same route twice. The final step was a dash across the unsheltered tarmac and hope for minimum injury.

The APC backed into the docking area under a barrage of bullets pelting the steel armor plate. At that point, rapid firing was returned from the terminal to give cover for the new arrivals.

The docking area was at the first Jet way of the new terminal, which precluded gunfire from the rear. Still, the hazard remained from the frontal attack. The external baggage was rapidly removed and the hatch was opened. The interior was emptied in a matter of minutes. The returning fighters, who completed their rotations, occupied the transport and were ready to depart. Finally, two body bags of fallen comrades were placed into the vehicle. The hatch was closed and the engine roared. The Cyborgs launched smoke bombs, turning the airfield visibility into the dead of night.

"Welcome to the asshole of the world, as the men will tell you," the commander addressed the new arrivals. "I am Sokil, the commanding officer of this godforsaken outpost. I have only one demand of you, you might say it's an inviolate commandment—don't foolishly succumb to heroics and whatever you do, stay alive! This may be the most treacherous rotation you will have encountered . . . One careless smoke, one unguarded, curious peek, and you'll find yourself in the crosshairs of a sniper's sight. Our fight here is at close quarters with seasoned Russian combatants. So don't take anything for granted . . . The boys will show you the ropes and where you can bunk. We'll meet later in the day to review your assignments . . . Good hunting!"

Sokil presented a formidable, no-nonsense image. He stood a head taller than his charges and spoke with authority, not in the commonplace Russian but in Ukrainian tinged with a noticeable Galician dialect. His broad shoulders and matching physique reminded me of Slava—a fearless warrior straight from the pages of the Taras Bulba epic. In contrast to his band of patriots, his round face was clean-shaven and his hair was closely trimmed.

"Which one of you is Ruslan?" he said as the others were slowly dispersing.

"I am," I spoke up.

"We are glad to have you with us and your special skills, Ruslan. You will be teamed with Artem." He patted the soldier standing next to him on the shoulder.

"Happy to meet you, Ruslan. I am Artem," said the soft-spoken young man and proffered his right hand.

Artem seemed to be a pleasant fellow of average height and a friendly smile on his lips. His freckled face was peppered with a rotation worth of stubble. His curly mane spread every which way as if it had a mind of its own.

"Let me give you a hand with your gear. We'll get better acquainted over a mug of tea."

Artem spoke as we descended into the basement. “You must be very careful when you negotiate any stairwell. This place is riddled with passageways, stairwells, and tunnels. The Orcs, as we call the bloody Muscovites, booby trap and mine the passages during the night, and by the way, we do the same to them. If you ask me, it’s a waste of time. But once in a while, you hear a loud bang followed by a terrified outcry. So don’t go exploring in the dark.”

We entered a smoke-filled room. Fighters were huddled around a makeshift table. Some were sitting on wooden ammunition boxes with their backs propped against the wall; some were sprawled on the floor warming their hands on enameled aluminum mugs and sipping the contents. The work day was at an end. It was time to unwind from another stressful cycle. Scattered on the table were open tins of food, slices of rye bread on plates, and mugs of steaming tea. A field stove stood in a corner percolating a kettle of water.

A soldier was fiddling with a shortwave receiver, but all he was hearing were annoying bursts of high-pitched static as he turned the dial.

All attention was on an animated storyteller who was acting out a recent encounter with an Orc, which, from the response of his audience, had been rendered previously more than once. In between uncontrolled laughter, the enthusiasts interrupted the hilarity with quips like “what did he say?” and “what did he do?” and “what did you say then?” The entertainer was in top form, going back and forth in reply to the listeners and repeating what he said earlier with more exaggeration. His hands were flailing; his fists were emphasizing his point by pounding on the table. And every sentence was punctuated with the foulest profanity to everyone’s delight.

Artem said, “Let’s put away your gear in an adjacent room where we will be sleeping. We’ll come back and have tea and something to eat. Our day starts here well before sunrise. So this banter will die out very soon.”

A bright, irritating light shining into my eyes startled me at an ungodly hour in the pitch-black room. Artem shook my shoulder and whispered, "Ruslan, it's time to get started."

I was not quite certain whether I slept or daydreamed through the frigid night. First-time-engagement anxiety churned my innards and raced my mind through gruesome encounters. This was an unexpected experience and was never my reaction to previous postings. I had plopped on a mattress in my entire wardrobe that I arrived in, the greatcoat and balaclava included, in anticipation of the bitter cold, but all it did was intensify my discomfort. Now I woke up stiff, tired, and aching in every joint of my body.

The communal room was already active. Several men were at the table having breakfast which consisted of canned gruel, black bread, and mugs of tea. The kettle on the field stove was steaming and a deep skillet filled with canned food was bubbling next to it. All food and water in the facility were frozen and needed to be thawed.

Artem said, "Ruslan, you better eat heartily because we have a long day ahead of us. Fish out a couple of cans from the skillet. Take some gruel and some meat. You will need the energy."

We ate, then stuffed our backpacks with ammunition. Artem filled two thermos bottles with tea and handed one to me. He stuffed a walkie-talkie in his overcoat pocket and we left.

Early morning mist hovered over the tarmac. Artem moved swiftly in the darkness avoiding the scattered debris to a crater that he selected on the previous day. The airfield was riddled with craters on all sides of the terminal. It struck me that the Russians had inexhaustible ordnance to waste.

We slid into a deep hole.

"Now we sit and wait," said Artem. "The attack usually starts on the ground level from over there and from the third level. The Orcs swarm down the stairwells to the second level, which we control, where the fighting takes place face-to-face. They move within the steel framework, which makes them vulnerable from our position since there are only a few walls standing that would give them cover . . . When the shooting starts, don't stay in one place. Move about. They have snipers who will blow your head off in a flash. They also have spotters who will direct heavy artillery at us. So be careful. Stay low."

"Allahu Akbar . . . Allahu Akbar . . . Allahu Akbar."

"Here we go," said Artem. "Those fanatical Chechens. They scream as they charge at the guns with abandon. By the looks of things, today many of them will surely be joining Allah in paradise."

I removed the silencer from the Dragunov and emptied the ten-round magazine, one after another. Adrenalin suppressed the cold. I felt like I was at a carnival shooting gallery.

The entire encounter was over in a blink of an eye. Artem sat down and told me to do the same. We both drank our tea.

He said, "This is a dangerous time for you and me if we were spotted. They have heavy artillery in Krasnokamensk that can pulverize us. All we can do now is sit and wait. If you hear any whistling sound, ball up against the wall and pray for the best.

"Right now Sokil is most likely speaking on the shortwave radio with his Russian counterpart. They are negotiating a temporary cease-fire so that both sides can remove the wounded and the dead. In the past, the fighters, who were not removed quickly from the field, were set upon by roving dog packs and were torn to shreds . . . Before his call, he was in touch with the commander in Pisky to send a medivac at once. He had to make certain that both vehicles would be in dock simultaneously. Once, true to form, our ambulance was late. The Muscovites destroyed it, and the driver was killed. You can see the burned-out frame on the tarmac . . . Sokil will call us. If necessary, you and I may have to provide cover."

The evacuation occurred without incident. Again, we cooled our heels in the well of the crater waiting *Sokil's* signal to return. It was a good time to get acquainted.

Artem was from Kharkiv. He took an active part in the local *Maidan* protests and after the Crimean invasion, he joined the *Aidar* Battalion. He had no need for a pseudonym since he was an orphan and preferred to be known by his given name. As a teenager, he was sent to a trade school and became a machinist. He worked in the Antonov Aircraft Plant until he volunteered and was given a leave of absence.

The walkie-talkie buzzed. *Sokil* signaled. Smoke bombs obscured visibility. We scurried to safety. Well done and handshakes were given by our commander. Our side only had non-life-threatening wounds. Conversely, I scoped from the crater many lifeless bodies being loaded into two Russian ambulances.

For the following number of days, there were no direct assaults by the enemy other than from random bombardment by Grad rockets and roving tanks. If only our ally sent us Javelin anti-tank missiles, for which we were begging on bent knee, instead of blankets and expired K rations, what a difference it would have made! But the Russians had to be more restrained with their shelling since their encirclement within the terminal was getting tighter, and they could easily be killing their own in the process.

Our task was to defend our territory within the terminal, which every day diminished from nightly detonations in the tunnels and the piecemeal destruction of the second level. In the interim, I was assigned to sentry duty like everyone else. One night I was guarding a stairwell that connected to a tunnel. I was sitting on a stair in pitch-black darkness intently listening for any sound whatsoever. I was armed with an AK-47 assault rifle and four thirty-round clips.

A flicker of light and a faint metallic scrape on the concrete nearby, followed by another somewhat louder scrape, alerted me to an intruder.

I said softly, "Grisha, eto ti [Grisha, is that you]?"

"Eto Sasha [It is Sasha]!"

I sprayed the space with bullets without hesitation. A violent shriek and the vilest profanity echoed through the cavern while I loaded another clip. As I launched another curtain of bullets, a deafening explosion illuminated the scene. Falling plaster and dust churned the air.

Alarmed voices rushed down the stairs and surrounded me. Their weapons were drawn; their helmet lights illuminated the carnage.

"Ruslan, are you all right?" they yelled.

That entrance from the tunnel was permanently sealed and would never be accessed again.

The fateful day had come at last. The mood in the terminal became more somber.

Artem approached me and said, "Word has come. Tomorrow we'll be attacked in force."

"What word?"

"The Orcs brought in fresh reinforcements. They are at full strength to hit us hard."

"How do we know this? Maybe it's another lie to demoralize us after the beating they got last time."

"How do we know this? Our spy network, that's how."

"Like we had in Ilovaisk?"

"All right . . . all right . . . let's not get bitter. As of now, you are relieved of guard duty. Get your equipment ready and relax. Get a good night's sleep."

Under the cover of darkness, Artem and I made our way to a crater that was further out from the previous location. It was more exposed, but it provided a clearer view of the target area. We dozed for some time, exchanged few personal tidbits, and had some tea. Toward sunrise, we listened for the ominous "Allahu Akbar."

No "Allahu Akbar". No Chechens.

We were facing Russian "volunteers" or as they had been telling their families back home, they were enjoying a vacation in some out-of-the-way location. They did not rush in a frenzy; they did not scream to the high heavens at the top of their lungs. They moved like seasoned combatants.

"They're on the move," said Artem.

I attached my silencer and focused my scope. The rat-a-tat of gunfire was my signal to pull the trigger, one precise shot at a time. As before, the assault was repelled. Artem and I settled in waiting for the signal from *Sokil* to return.

It did not take very long for RPGs to zero in on our position. Each explosion was one step closer than the last. If only the walkie-talkie would buzz, if only the smokescreen would appear, and then the blast landed in our foxhole.

I was clinging to the wall in a spread-eagled stance. The grenade landed behind me. I felt a terrible pain in my left leg. Shrapnel and frozen dirt tore apart my leg around my knee.

Artem screamed into the transmitter, "Medic, stretcher, serious injury." He then cut the laces and removed my boot. He slit my pants and slipped on a tourniquet above the knee. He took out a container of powdery antiseptic from the kit that he carried with him and spread it on the wound.

I passed out.

27

Brighton Beach

The Second Avenue cacophony blared at maximum intensity. The day's noise pollution was reaching its steady state. It was time to conclude Asher's astonishing tale of self-sacrifice and heroism.

Asher did not expect an all-night interview and was not prepared with a change of clothes for him to go directly to work. He asked Terry if he could borrow a white shirt. He shed and bundled the embroidered shirt and put it into his backpack. He donned the workday white, which was somewhat oversized. But when he tucked it into his trousers and rolled up the sleeves, it would do.

Terry remained in his sweat suit and slipped on his sneakers. His loyal companion Blackie was comfortably snoozing in his favorite cushioned chair. Terry did not want to disturb his pet; he merely refreshed his bowl before leaving. Maya would come in a few hours and let him out on the terrace.

Terry carried his gym bag with him when they left the apartment. It was still too early for Asher to be going to work, so he suggested breakfast at *Veselka*.

Surprisingly, at this ungodly hour, the restaurant was abuzz with patrons. The owner saw Terry enter and waved him to come forward.

A young couple was paying the bill and was on their way out. A waiter cleared the table and returned momentarily carrying glasses of ice water.

"The usual, Mr. Adamchuk?" he said as he set the water on the table and handed a menu only to Asher.

"Asher, what strikes your fancy?" Terry said. "Everything here is top-notch, so say the *New York Times*. My usual, in which I dare not overindulge, is corn beef hash and hash browns topped with eggs over medium—an insidious conspiracy to harden your arteries. How does that sound to you?"

"It does promise to be rather filling. But I will join you and have the same," he said and handed back the menu to the waiter.

"Two of my usual, Stefko. Lots of coffee, orange juice, and whole-wheat toast. That should hold us for the rest of the day."

After the sumptuous breakfast, Terry accompanied Asher up Saint Mark's Place to the subway station on Broadway across from the Cooper Union, reassuring him that his family's safety would be his top priority. Meanwhile, he should remain calm and not deviate from his normal routine.

He continued up Broadway toward Union Square at a fat-burning pace and then marched further uptown to the health club located on the ground floor of his office building. He dwelled on the extraordinary events and heroism recounted to him during the all-night session and how best to approach resolution to Asher's predicament. The first step seemed obvious. An absurd scheme to burglarize a building in the diamond district could only spawn in the warped minds of the Brighton Beach mobsters. If indeed that was the case, then Mustafa Chubarov would be in the know.

The brisk walk soaked his undergarments and sweat suit by the time he reached the gym. A quick body wash, muscle-soothing steam, and a scrub-down shower dissolved the cobwebs from the previous night. He dressed formally in his office from the wardrobe which he maintained well stocked for such occasions. He was ready to tackle the day.

As usual, Sol was already in his office.

"Come on in," Sol replied to the knock on the door. "Ahh . . . It's you, Taras. How goes it?"

"Hey, Sol, you have a few minutes?"

"For you, my friend, my time is yours. Our new client is not due for at least an hour . . . By the way, how was the festival?"

"It was excellent, as usual. It seems the atmosphere and the entertainment get better each year. And then, of course, there is the food, food just like Mother used to make. The dance groups were outstanding—almost professional. I could honestly say that my heritage is flourishing with every new generation . . . But actually, I did not stay very long. I met with Asher."

"You did? That's great . . . What do you think?"

"What do I think? I think we are dealing with quite a patriot and a true hero. Under no circumstances can we let him down."

Sol did not expect such a reply. He was taken by the lavish tribute to his distant relative. He did not interrupt. He just sat there dumbfounded.

"I thought it would be a friendly get-together for an hour or two, more to relieve his anxieties than to add to what I already surmised. And then, as we chatted over the food that I brought from the festival and steins of chilled Brooklyn ale, he mentioned Maidan in passing. My ears perked up.

"It so happens, he was there in the midst of the revolution, and Zinaida and Asher took an active part in it. She attended the wounded at Saint Michael's infirmary, and he was engaged in a self-defense Sotnia. I could not believe my good fortune to be face-to-face with an eyewitness to history. I quizzed him on every minute detail. Later, I did the same with his service in the Dnipro-1 Battalion and his misfortune at the Donetsk Airport . . . Before you know it, it was daylight."

Sol said, "It's hard for me to imagine how such a mild-mannered individual would sacrifice in time of danger to defend his motherland. This puts his plight on an entirely different level . . . How can I help? My wallet is at your disposal. What do you need to get started?"

"At the present time, I don't know what it will take. But rest assured, my time and my wallet will do their part. As much as it pains me, I must start with Brighton Beach. Then we will see where it takes me."

"Keep me informed and let me know what you may need. Meanwhile, I will maintain closer ties with the Feldmans."

"Will do. See you at eleven."

Terry went to his office and called for an appointment with Chubarov.

"Mustafa Ahmetovich, thank you for seeing me on such short notice."

"Taras, I am always delighted to see you. We don't have to be so formal. This is America. We are all equal." He chuckled. "We're all Democrats . . . How's business . . . You know you can always come work for me. I can use a man with your skills."

Terry appreciated the sentiment, but he knew better. This type of individual demanded respect. By no means was he in a position to deal with him on a first-name basis. Underestimating the reality would cost him in the future, especially if he was foolish enough to transgress in the presence of others.

"Thank you for your confidence, Mustafa Ahmetovich. I value your friendship . . . I do need your opinion on a situation in which I am involved."

"Let's talk about it over a light lunch. My wife and I came here today by boat. She is off somewhere shopping in the city . . . We can relax and enjoy the fresh sea air. I am sure my chef Ghenadij is preparing something seaworthy for us."

As they were crossing Emmons Avenue, Chubarov said, "I assume you did not drive. Next time I can have Timur pick you up. He likes driving you."

"Oh, I don't mind the subway. The ride is like reliving the past—gives me a chance to reconnect with my youth."

Chubarov veered left. A white canopy bearing two marine antennas was visible above the embankment. In a few minutes, they came to a stairwell where the boat was moored.

"This is certainly not some trivial boat, Mustafa Ahmetovich," Terry remarked. "It is more a yacht than a boat."

"It happens to be the largest boat that I can sail myself and not need a full-time captain. It is our family boat that we use for outings with our children and grandchildren. It has a sporty look and this canopy is perfect on a sunny day. The cockpit can be wide open to circulate fresh air, just as it is now. Come let me show you around."

They stepped on the extended swim platform and from there up onto the cockpit. The cushioned seating was moved together to one side into a U-shaped booth. A table was set in the center covered with linen and place settings for two.

Chubarov said, "The grandchildren love that swim platform. We would anchor in the sound, and they would frolic in the water to their heart's content."

The door to the galley was wide open. The sizzling from a hot skillet could be heard from within.

"How goes it, Zhenia?"

"Your timing is perfect, Mustafa Ahmetovich. Everything is ready."

"Good. We'll be seated in a moment . . . Taras, first let me acquaint you with the heart of this beast."

They moved forward to the custom-built helm, its modern flat-screen control panel, and leather-covered steering wheel.

"The boat is powered by powerful twin Mercruiser V Drives. There's enough horsepower to pull the grandkids on water skis. It handles easily like any luxury car . . . Below deck are the galley and sleeping accommodations . . . Now enough yachting for a day. Let's relax and have a bite to eat."

Ghenadij brought to the table a bottle of chilled Sauvignon Blank and poured it.

"To your health, Taras Grigorovich." Chubarov raised his glass. "You notice we are breaking tradition. We are becoming gentrified."

"And to your health, Mustafa Ahmetovich. Sto Liat, as the Poles would say."

The glasses clicked.

The chef filled the table with condiments, slices of toasted whole-wheat garlic bread (*bruschetta*), Sicilian olive oil, a pepper grinder, and a bowl of garlic shrimp.

"Enjoy!"

The fare was an unexpected surprise to Terry. He anticipated the usual lamb dish that Chubarov knew was his favorite—and wine, not vodka? It must have been the influence of his new toy.

Noting the quizzical expression on Terry's face, Chubarov said, "My darling daughter is trying to convert me to be a Mediterranean bumpkin. Next thing you know, she'll convert me to be a Roman Catholic . . . children!"

Ghenadij returned to the table, cleared the appetizer dishes, and returned with plates of crab cakes, French fries, and side dishes of coleslaw.

"Mustafa Ahmetovich," he said. "If it's okay, I should return to the restaurant. They will need help with the lunchtime crowd. I have another bottle of wine in the fridge. Just leave everything as is. I'll return and clean up. Enjoy the crab cakes. Let me know how you liked them."

"Thanks, Zhenia, go on ahead. I am sure the crab cakes will meet your high standard.

"That Zhenia is my best chef," he continued. "He's been with me from the very beginning. He loves experimenting with new dishes. He has quite an imagination, a magician with herbs and spices . . . What do you think of the crab cakes?"

"They are outstanding, as tasty as I ever had in the Chesapeake."

"I am glad you like them. We bring in the crab meat fresh from the Chesapeake. Actually, Zhenia surprised me today. I thought he would prepare his special shrimp dish. We only use Gulf shrimp, by the way. I'll make sure we have it next time."

Terry appreciated the bonhomie, but he had enough goodwill for one afternoon. He was ready to discuss his business. Yet it was not his place to start the ball rolling.

With the meal concluded, the host cleared the table, including the empty wine bottle. He returned with a new one and poured.

"How do you like this wine? My daughter bought me a case from a local vineyard on Long Island."

"Very refreshing—compliments to your daughter. A perfect choice for the crab cakes."

"I am pleased to hear it. I will have to tell her that. Now, how can I be of service?"

"I am trying to help a fellow countryman who finds himself in a very difficult situation. Let me tell you briefly his background so you can appreciate my concern and commitment to his safety. He hails from Kyiv. He and his wife were on the frontlines of the Maidan Revolution. He faced the gunfire along with his Sotnia and survived the slaughter on Instytutska Street.

"In the aftermath of Putin's annexation of Crimea and the warfare in Eastern Ukraine, he joined the Dnipro-1 Battalion. Eventually, when the need arose, he volunteered to defend the Donetsk Airport. He was struck in the leg with shrapnel from a rocket-propelled grenade, and his leg had to be amputated. He was flown to the Walter Reed Hospital in Washington for rehabilitation.

"Right now, he lives in Brooklyn with relatives until his leg is fully recovered, and he can be fitted with a permanent prosthesis."

Terry knew that Chubarov would be moved by Asher's chronicle and heroism. He let the words sink in and cleared his throat with a sip of wine.

"This is an incredible story. It needs to be told." Chubarov chimed in with enthusiasm.

"I agree with you, Mustafa Ahmetovich. But first things first. This fellow, his name is Asher, is a jeweler by profession, and a highly skilled one at that. In the interim, he took a job with a retailer on 47th Street. Several weeks ago he was approached by several toughs and told to provide them with the security details of the building. I assume their intention is to burglarize the place . . . Besides overtly trailing him and harassing him on the telephone, they threatened the lives of his wife and children."

"That is absurd!" Chubarov exclaimed angrily. "Who in his right mind would attempt such lunacy? Don't they understand that the jewelry district is a fortress protected not only by the police but by their own army of round-the-clock security?"

"That is exactly my point. They must be some rogue group, some young, ill-informed amateurs, driven by lack of experience and stupidity."

"How can I help?"

"Before I can proceed, I need to know what I am up against. Who is behind this?"

"I can assure you right now that none of my people are involved. There are too many opportunities that pose no risk whatsoever. This is foolishness."

"I gathered that much. I was hoping that you might find a lead through your contacts. After all, these assailants spoke Russian."

"I will look into it right away. Let's talk in a few days . . . I will be going to Florida on Monday. Let's do this. I will be at my daughter's on Sunday afternoon. I'll have Timor pick you up, say at two. I should have some news for you then."

28

Fundraiser

Timur was punctual to a fault. At five minutes to 2:00 p.m., Terry saw an unfamiliar black sedan pull up and double-park below his window. He assumed it was his ride and went downstairs.

"Timur, Zdorov, long time no see!"

"Good afternoon, Taras."

Terry slipped into the passenger seat, fastened the seat belt, and put on his favorite wraparound *Wiley-X* sunglasses.

Timur turned left on Saint Marks, then left again on 1st Avenue on the way to the Midtown Tunnel.

"Since when are you driving a Tesla?" Terry said. "I thought you were wedded to the Beamer for life."

"It's not my car. I am breaking it in for the boss. He likes the latest gadgets. It's not exactly to my liking. It feels like a hyped-up golf cart. You don't feel the connection with the drive train like you do with the Beamer. And I prefer driving with the stick even in city traffic."

"Have you considered Gymkhana racing? Sounds like that would exercise your Beamer to its limits."

"I seriously considered that once. The problem is, to be competitive, you cannot use a plain passenger car. You need a vehicle dedicated to racing, not only with a more robust engine but also with durable suspension and safety features. That also means having a trailer and something to tow it with. Add to that the demands of my job and the dream becomes impossible."

"What is your job exactly? I could never figure it out. You seem to be all over the place."

"That's exactly what I am, all over the place, wherever Chubarov sends me. There are times I feel like a glorified gofer. But I do enjoy the variety of assignments and the first-class travel . . . And no complaints about the money."

Once they cleared the tunnel, Timur stepped with a heavy foot on the pedal for the next few miles until the LIE slowed to a crawl.

"Where exactly are we heading?"

"We are going to Lloyd Neck to his son-in-law's home. He is having a campaign fundraiser for his bid to Congress."

Terry was startled.

"He didn't say anything about a fundraiser. I thought it would be a family picnic. I brought a bottle of Sapphire Gin as a present. Looks like I'll be giving it to you."

"If you insist, I would certainly appreciate it. That's for sure."

"I would have dressed more appropriately for the occasion."

"You are dressed just fine. It's one of those casual Gatsby outdoor picnics that the well-healed Long Island swells like. You'll fit right in."

"Fundraiser. If I knew, I would have brought my checkbook."

"Not to worry. I can lend you the money, up to the IRS limit. You can give me a check when we return."

"Thank you, Timur. I hope it won't be necessary. I usually carry an extra check in my wallet. I hope I didn't forget to replace it the last time I used it. I'm sure, if push comes to shove, plastic will work."

They crossed the Cross Island and Timur opened up the golf cart well above the speed limit and attacked the road aggressively.

"Are you familiar with the problem that I asked Chubarov for his help?" Terry asked.

"Yes, I am."

"What has he found out?"

"I would rather that he tell you himself. He is a very particular man when it comes to trust. If I told you anything in that regard without his approval and it slipped out in conversation, my trust would be compromised forever. The only thing I can say . . . No, I think I may already have said too much. I better say no more. You'll know it soon enough."

They left the expressway and meandered through various roads until Timur came to a full stop.

"This is the infamous Snake Hill Drive. Many a foolhardy soul failed to abide by the fifteen-mile speed limit and wound up losing the front end. And it's such a short stretch to boot. Oh hell."

A few curvy miles later they approached a viaduct.

"It's a peninsula?"

"Yap."

"Slow down, Timur. This breathtaking view will be the highlight of my day."

Timur pulled over and stopped. "Get your fill," he said.

Terry exited and walked over to the water's edge. Timur joined him.

The day could not have been more perfect. Cotton puffs drifted leisurely across the pale-blue sky. Clusters of picnickers lined the bank with their makeshift fishing poles angled in the sand in hopes of a catch. A light wind barely rippled the bright-blue water. Sailboats expertly harnessed the breeze, effortlessly crisscrossing the Long Island Sound.

"You see that colorful walled compound." Timur pointed toward the end of the viaduct. "That was Billy Joel and Christie Brinkley home when they were married."

"Looks impressive."

In less than a ten-minute meandering drive along the shoreline brought them to a speed bump and a posting, Sound Bay Estates. After several turns, parked automobiles lined the road. By no means was this a simple row of pedestrian vehicles. These were Rolls-Royces, Bentleys, Maseratis, and home-grown limousines—the princely carriages of the anointed elite.

Timur turned slowly into the cobbled driveway flanked by massive wrought iron gates and proceeded to the parking garage. Along the way was a tent with sizable buffet and refreshment stands. Small tables and outdoor chairs extended the hospitality to the chauffeurs.

Surrounded by majestic oaks stood the manor house. Classic red terracotta roof tiles accentuated the brick façade topped with six brick chimneys like sentinels rising above the proud residence. Above the entrance was a stars-and-stripes banner proclaiming "Shawn Bradford for Congress." On the right side of the entrance hall was a reception table beneath a smaller banner. Two ladies were on the greeting committee for the fundraiser.

Terry verified earlier that he had a check in his wallet. He approached the greeters.

"Good day, ladies," he said. "If I may, I would like to contribute to the campaign."

"We would certainly appreciate it."

"What exactly is the statutory maximum that I can contribute without transgressing the rules and how do I endorse my check?"

"It is $2,700. You can simply write 'Bradford for Congress' and sign the ledger."

A wall-to-wall, scrolled glass patio door opened out to the backyard. To the left was a tennis court overlooking the Sound. To the right was an expansive tent bustling with energetic conversation. Straight ahead was a sprawling, two-level deck. Chubarov's sporty launch was moored at one side. Other craft were also tethered to the platform.

Timur guided Terry to meet the host. He was a forty-ish, athletically built man, pumping hands and thanking for the support with a sincere smile on his round, lightly tanned face.

"Shaun," Timur broke in between handshakes. "I would like you to meet Terry Adams, a good friend of Mustafa Ahmetovich. He came here from the city to offer support for your candidacy."

"I am delighted to meet you and thank you for your support," chimed the candidate while enthusiastically shaking his hand. "Any friend of Mustafa is a friend of mine."

Chubarov approached the threesome and placed his hand on Terry's shoulder. "I am glad to see you, Taras. You met the politician of our family. As usual, he's off and running. Timur, why don't you and Taras have a bite to eat. I'm sure you'll find the food to your liking. It's not healthy to discuss important business on an empty stomach. I'll catch up to you in a while."

The quality of food was not unexpected. What was unexpected, however, was the welcoming greeting from Zhenia from behind the bountiful buffet table. He was dressed from head to toe in chef's white, including a stove-pipe hat—quite unusual for an outdoor event. Somewhere there was a message to the contributors that this was not merely an ordinary Sunday afternoon barbecue. At his side was another chef similarly dressed but wearing a less distinctive head covering.

"Taras Grigorovich, this is a pleasant surprise. Your timing is perfect. I just roasted racks of lamb. If you would like, I will save one for you. Meanwhile, you and Timur can enjoy the hors d'oeuvres and champagne. I will bring it when you are ready . . . I suppose a medium-rare marbled steak would be to your liking, Timur?"

Once they were seated, a waitress asked for their beverage preferences.

"The chef recommends champagne," Terry said. "How about you, Timur?"

"I'll have the same."

Chubarov approached the table as the meal concluded.

He said, "I hope you left some room for dessert. Taras, let's talk first. Come with me where we can have some privacy."

They entered a room that appeared to be Bradford's office. Technology dominated the work space. Three oversized computer screens were set in an arc on a semicircular desk. Two TV monitors were hanging on an opposite wall along with clocks indicating the time in New York, London, Hong Kong, Beijing, and Singapore.

"Shawn is an investment banker," said Chubarov. "He splits his time between home and the city and he also travels quite a bit. It's a twenty-four-seven commitment. He is ready to follow another path . . . By the way, I do appreciate your support."

A wise investment—duly noted, Terry thought.

"Let's sit down and I'll tell you what I found out," he continued. "First of all, let me apologize for dragging you way out here. I will be flying to Miami early tomorrow morning and will remain there for several weeks. I did not want to keep you in suspense for that much time. As a rule, when it comes to serious matters, I only deal in person—one-on-one."

"I appreciate that very much, Mustafa Ahmetovich. Actually, I am glad to have come. It has been a memorable experience for me in many respects."

"I grilled my own troops, as well as my colleagues. The reaction was the same from everyone that this is amateurish stupidity. It will not succeed and will only anger the authorities at us. I also verified that no one provided protection for these people . . . We neutralized the three individuals who were harassing your client. They are no longer in town. Timur can fill you in on the details.

"This absurdity was cooked up in Kyiv. Some petty hoodlum is behind the scheme. The perpetrators were recruited by someone named Bobrov who is most likely a mere foot soldier. That is all we could find out on short notice. Your man is safe for now. I can assure you it will only be for a short time. Others will be sent as long as the head man is not dealt with . . . Any questions?"

"None that I can think of right now. You have given me an important answer that this is not a stateside attempt. So I will focus on Ukraine. The name Bobrov, even though it is a somewhat common name, it is a solid lead. Timur may be able to give me a first name. That will help."

"Unfortunately, there is no first name."

"Well, at least we know he is from Kyiv. That narrows it some . . . Mustafa Ahmetovich, you have been of great help. I am in your debt."

"I was glad to help. You have my mobile number. If anything comes up while I am away, please let me know . . . Now, why not enjoy dessert. I understand it is outstanding."

"I must make a slight detour," Timur said as he exited Snake Hill Road on the way home. "I have to drop off the Tesla at Mustafa Ahmetovich's house in Glen Cove and pick up my Beamer. We'll be taking the scenic Hempstead Turnpike instead of the LIE, a drive which you will enjoy and I can fill you in on the details."

“Glen Cove, isn’t that where the Soviets, I mean the Federation, has its consular retreat?”

“Yeah, they all seem to bond with their own kind, don’t they?” Timur cackled.

“It all seems interconnected.”

“About those three young men, they were street toughs like those titushky on the Maidan. They were approached by a man named Bobrov and offered three months in the States with a per diem and a bonus at the completion of their assignment. The demand was for the security provisions of the facility. They would not carry out the actual burglary. They were given throwaway cellphones. I took a look at them but could not find anything obvious. I have them in my Beamer and will give them to you.

“I dispatched them out of town, one to Miami, one to Chicago, and one to Las Vegas. As far as Bobrov is concerned, they did not know more than his last name. All they had was his mobile number, which, I am sure, is also a throwaway.”

29

Preparations

Terry called Asher on his cellphone as soon as he entered the apartment.

"Asher, zdorov. This is Taras. I have some good news. The threat has been diffused. Have you recently seen any of those hooligans or received any menacing calls?"

"Good day to you, Taras. No, I have not, not since midweek."

"I am glad to hear that. That vermin will no longer trouble you. I have been told that these thugs were not from the stateside but from Ukraine, specifically from Kyiv. I need to find the source and put an end to it before they resurface. I must travel to Kyiv to do so. Can we get together for lunch tomorrow?"

"I can come over right now."

"No, I need some time to get my thinking straight and figure out where I will need some help from you. Tomorrow around lunchtime will be best. Can you make it?"

"I certainly can."

"Do you know the Second Avenue Deli on Thirty-third?"

"No, but I can find it."

"It's on Thirty-third Street, between Lexington and Third Avenue. There is a subway station nearby. Better yet, you might consider walking and keeping an eye on anyone following you. What is a good time for you?"

"I'll be there any time you say."

"Let's do it at a quarter past one. By then the lunchtime crowd will thin out. See you tomorrow."

Next morning Terry settled in behind his favorite corner table at the Starbucks across the street with his iPad connected to the restaurant's free Wi-Fi. He sipped a café mocha grande while searching for historical points of interest in Kyiv and the most convenient hotel from which he could tour the city on foot in his spare time. At intervals, he kept thinking how to best exploit the Bobrov lead.

He dialed his office number on the cellphone.

"Terry Adams office, can I help you?" was the automatic reply.

"Good morning Maya, it's me," he said sarcastically. "Didn't you see my name on the caller ID?"

"I was busy feeding Blackie and answered sitting on the floor. You left early and forgot to feed the cat . . . How was your outing? Where are you?"

"I'm across the street. I'll be right over and tell you all about it."

He finished the coffee, disconnected from the internet, and walked back to the office.

"Hi, Maya. Sorry about Blackie. I had a rough night after all that rich food and got up early. Blackie was still asleep and I forgot to fill his bowl."

The cat was making loops between his legs and purring contentedly. Terry rubbed gently below the chin to his pet's satisfaction.

"Well, how was it?" Maya asked.

"It was like being in another universe, limousines, chauffeurs, yachts, sailboats—crème de la crème, as they say. It also turned out to be a fundraiser for Chubarov's son-in-law. He is running for congress. Can you imagine? These gangsters are hand-in-hand with the cream of society. Amazing what money will do . . . By the way, I had to contribute a check for twenty-seven hundred dollars. Please make a note and let me have a blank one for my wallet."

"Did he get you there just to get your money?"

"No, not at all. That's not even pocket change to him. No . . . But he may have been testing me because I felt that he had verified my contribution before he spoke to me. To men like him, things like that are an indicator of a man's character."

"How was the food?"

"Hot dogs and hamburgers." Terry laughed. "Simply put—spectacular. By no means was this a simple backyard cookout, high-quality food, top-of-the-line liquor, and the desserts . . . I think the desserts kept me up all night. Chubarov even had his own chef prepare the banquet."

"What did you have?"

"For starters there were the out-of-this-world hors d'oeuvres and champagne, then there was the rack of lamb with Brooklyn's best, and then were the Napoleons washed down with more champagne. It makes me shutter how much I overindulged, but, for once, it seemed worth it. I will try to walk it off.

"I did find out some useful information and a possible lead. The lead happens to be in Kyiv. That is where I must go next. I would like to leave in two, three days, preferably Thursday, but no later than Friday. Please book me a business class seat with an open return, direct flight only. Verify if I need a visa. I believe it is no longer required. See how many traveler checks we have in the safe. I will need nine thousand. If not, get some. More than ten in cash may be a problem with customs. Last thing, please go to Barnes and Noble and get a tourist guide to Kyiv. I'll study it on the plane. I'll be uptown if you need me. I'll be in touch."

"Come on in, Taras. How did it go yesterday?"

"Overall, it was a good day. The immediate threat to Asher has been eliminated. Unfortunately, the threat is from overseas, and I was advised that it needs to be halted at the source before it rears its ugly head again."

"Can I assume you are talking about Ukraine?"

"Yes, and more precisely, Kyiv."

"That would make sense."

"I also suspect it may revolve around his father-in-law's jewelry business. So I'll be going there by the end of the week. If you need me to start digging further on the current divorce case, I can spend full-time on it for the next two days."

"It will not be necessary for the present. You supplied enough information for the husband to realize that he cannot hide his offshore holdings and is conceding to a more equitable settlement. We are now negotiating with him in earnest. He, no doubt, has other assets that he doesn't want to come to light. He will settle on our terms."

"Good . . . I will be meeting Asher for lunch in preparation for the trip. You can reach me in Ukraine on my cellphone. I have the international SIM chip."

"Where do you stand with the expenses?"

"So far the only expense is the contribution to Chubarov's son-in-law's campaign to congress. The rest should be travel expenses."

"You donated to what?"

"You heard me right. And that was a wise investment for the future. I was in the company of the ruling class."

"Zdorow, Asher. Have you been waiting long?" Terry said. "As you can see, I also decided to walk today after yesterday's festivities."

"Good day to you, Taras," he replied. "No, I just got here. I made my way slowly, stopping at display windows and watching for anyone following me like they do it in the movies. But I did not see anything suspicious."

"I am sorry to have put you through this ordeal, but I needed to verify whether some replacements have been sent for the three that are no longer in the city to bother you."

"This was not an ordeal by any means. I needed the exercise. I sit all day concentrating on the gems and don't build up my stamina. In a way, I should be thanking you."

"When you get back home with that natural bedside manner, you should run for office . . . Let's go in. I see there are several booths that are open where we can have some privacy."

Once they eased into a booth, Terry said, "This restaurant used to be on the corner of Second Avenue and Tenth Street. That's where the name comes from. When the lease ran out, the owner of the building tripled the rent. Other people's money moved in. Who else but a bank could pay thirty-five thousand a month? I used to frequent the deli when it was in the neighborhood."

As the waiter set a crock of pickles on the table, Terry said, "What I liked most about the place, believe it or not, were these half-sour pickles. Try one. See what you think . . . The portions here are enormous. Whatever we don't finish will be takeout dinner—at least it will be for me.

"I'll be impolite and start the ball rolling. Waiter, I'll have a hot pastrami sandwich on rye with coleslaw and a Brooklyn ale. How about you, Asher?"

"It will take me all day to go through this menu. I'll just have the same."

"That was easy," Terry said.

When the waiter left, he said, "Now let's get down to business. There were three men that were assigned to intimidate you. They were green recruits and were easily scared off. All three are no longer in the city. I don't think they were foolish enough to report their sudden departure to their handler. So as far as I suspect, in his eyes, they are still active on the job. That gives us some time to find the head man and convince him of his error. Unfortunately, I need to do this in Kyiv . . . Do you know or have you heard of someone named Bobrov?"

"No, not offhand."

"That's all right. It's not important," Terry dismissed it casually. "In any event, I will need to start with your father-in-law."

"That's not a problem. As a matter of fact, you can stay in our apartment. We live in his house."

"Thank you for the offer, but that would not be very practical . . . Is he aware of your situation?"

"No, we did not want to worry Zina's parents. They are already anxious about us as it is."

"I would like to meet with him as soon as possible. I will be arriving at Borispol on Friday morning. I'll call you with the flight information when I return to my office. Are you going back to work?"

"No, I've taken the afternoon off. I'm going home."

"Are your in-laws very religious? Do they adhere strictly to the Sabbath?"

Asher was caught off guard and hesitated.

"Let me tell you why I ask. If they are strict, I will not force myself on them and create a difficult atmosphere. Your father-in-law may feel intimidated and hold back."

"Rifka, my mother-in-law, is very strict. Isaac will make exceptions when necessary. He is the one who turns on the appliances on Saturdays. But, I am sure, they will accommodate you if I ask them."

"From what you said, it would be wise to set up the initial meeting for Sunday afternoon, say at two o'clock . . . I was thinking of staying at the Radisson by the Golden Gates. It seems centrally located to many points of interest. What do you think?"

"It's more of a businessman's hotel. There are better ones around Independence Square. It all depends on what you want to see. Keep in mind that taxis are not very expensive. I could ask Boris to show you around. He is sort of guard, messenger, and driver—a very reliable all-around hand."

"I would rather walk. But you could ask him if he could pick me up at the airport. That would be helpful."

"Consider it done."

"Let's see what else. You have my cell phone number. Send it to Isaac. Also, take a snapshot of me and send it along. Remember, I am your good friend touring Kyiv for the first time. Don't mention anything else. And don't mention the name Bobrov . . . I will call you later in the day."

30

Kyiv

Terry landed at the Kyiv Borispol Airport on Friday in the early afternoon. Regrettably there were no direct flights from JFK. The Lufthansa Thursday flight connecting through Frankfurt seemed the shortest in duration. The business class comfort and service made the trip bearable. He had more than enough time to digest the travel guide that Maya had gotten him. His reservation at the Golden Gate Radisson placed him within walking distance of the sites a first-time visitor would want to see.

Boris approached him without hesitation at the customs exit.

"Taras Grigorovich, I am Boris," he said. "Isaac Leibovich sent me to pick you up."

"Pleased to meet you, Boris. How did you recognize me?"

"I have your photo on my cell phone . . . You have no luggage?"

"I am here for a short visit. My carryon will be sufficient."

"Let me help you with the suitcase. We can proceed to my limousine."

Boris drove Terry to the hotel entrance and waited until he was checked in. He gave him his cell phone number and offered to take him wherever he wished at any time.

The Radisson catered to businessmen and leisure travelers. The accommodations were spacious and quite up to date. His premium suite was on the upper floor with an unobstructed view of the city. He unpacked, washed his face, and shaved. There was still enough daylight left for him to walk off the kinks in his tendons. He was appropriately dressed for the exercise since he always preferred traveling on extended trips in his tracksuit and sneakers.

As Terry stepped out on Volodymyr Street, a solemn awareness came over him that he was about to traverse sacred ground. He would be retracing the footsteps of the fallen heroes, the *Heavenly Hundred,* who made the ultimate sacrifice for their motherland in the final days of *Maidan*. Those events were enshrined in his heart from Asher's accounts, videos, and publications which he religiously studied when they occurred.

He turned onto Sophievska Street on the way to Independence Square. He saw no evidence along the way of the considerable destruction that took place during the *Maidan* insurrection. Even the cobblestones underfoot, the protesters' weapons of last resort, were restored and the bitter memories were since washed away. The Trade Union's Building was a tragic site of the carnage. It was set ablaze from the roof by the police on the night of February 18. Numerous deaths of trapped occupants occurred there; some, out of desperation, leaped headlong to their deaths. No visible scars from the atrocity were evident.

Earlier on that Tuesday, the massive gathering on *Maidan* formed a peaceful procession and proceeded down Instytutska Street to the parliament, which was in session at the time. Their aim was to underscore previously issued demands for government reform. The marchers comprised a mile long cross-section of concerned citizens, including some future voters wheeled in baby carriages and strollers, and some septuagenarians relying on walkers and canes for support.

They did not reach their destination. A wall of helmeted riot police backed up by drunken street hooligans, *titushki*, intercepted them. They sprayed them with tear gas and attacked them in full force, whipping them indiscriminately with metal batons. The defenseless multitude had little choice but to scatter and take flight and be butchered along Instytutska.

He lingered for some time below the Performing Arts Center at the entrance to Instytutska Street. In front of him was the notorious elevated footbridge from which Berkut snipers had a field day massacring at will the panicked petitioners. He pictured the desperate scenes that were captured in the video images. They triggered in him chills and speckled his brow with perspiration. He took a deep breath and whispered the requiem chant *Memory Eternal* in their remembrance.

Sunset interrupted his reverie. His body clock beckoned him to reality. He retraced his steps to Khreschatyk, the capitol's main thoroughfare. There, he sat in a booth of a busy outdoor restaurant. A pretty young waitress dressed in an embroidered blouse welcomed him in Ukrainian and handed him a menu.

Terry said, "I think I am in the mood for something light, something our own."

"I can recommend our varenyky, holubtsi, kovbasa *i* kapusta," she enumerated.

"I think I will have a portion of holubtsi [stuffed cabbage]. Are they with meat?"

"If you would like, we serve them with either tomato or mushroom garnish, whichever you prefer. I would recommend the mushrooms. They are my favorite."

"Good. Then I will have them with mushrooms."

"And to drink?"

"What is your favorite domestic beer?"

"All our domestic beers are world-class. Obolon is brewed here locally. I can bring you a six-beer sampler. That may be your best choice."

"That sounds good. A sampler it will be."

Terry woke up the next morning refreshed and ready to continue exploring the city. As he always did after an extended flight, he stayed awake on the first night until late in the evening as a means of resetting his body clock overnight to local time. In this he succeeded with rare exceptions.

After the customary hygiene and prolonged shower, he dressed and called the monastery for an appointment with Bishop Ahapit. His relationship with the monastery, more specifically with St. Michael's Golden-Domed Cathedral, dated back to the years following Ukrainian Independence. In their zeal to destroy the remnants of the imperial past, the Soviets demolished the century-old house of worship in the 1930s. The Ukrainian Diaspora undertook the funding of its reconstruction; Taras Adamchuk was one of the contributors.

The breakfast buffet at the hotel was a pleasant surprise. It abounded with Western-style foods including a yogurt station with assorted toppings and a made-to-order grill station. He could very well have been eating at the Plaza or at the Waldorf.

He set out on his excursion once again. He was dressed casually on the seasonally warm day, an open-collar shirt, linen slacks, and custom-fitted walking shoes. He turned left on Volodymyrska and proceeded northward to Saint Sophia Square.

Terry stopped to pay his respects at the grave of Patriarch Volodymyr, the second primate of the united Ukrainian Orthodox Church in the post-Soviet era, which was located to the right of the entrance gate to the Saint Sophia compound. Moscow's surrogates made every effort to undermine the independent Ukrainian church in favor of their own fifth column. When His Holiness died, the faithful set off a funeral procession to inter the patriarch in the Saint Sophia cemetery. Berkut was set upon the mourners with truncheons causing countless head and shoulder injuries. The entrance to the compound was blocked. The infuriated crowd took up shovels and dug a grave in the pavement and laid their pastor to eternal rest. They marked the burial site with a carved marble crypt.

Years earlier, Terry met then reverend Vasyl Romaniuk in person on his visit to Manhattan. He was familiar with the reverend's thorny maturation under intense Soviet repression. Romaniuk became an outspoken member of the Ukrainian nationalists, the OUN, for which he was hounded and eventually sentenced to seventeen years in the gulag. He recounted to anyone who would listen that the only reason he survived the harsh labor camp environment was that he was protected by his fellow imprisoned Bandera followers whom the guards feared.

Terry solemnly crossed himself and bowed his head in prayer, then he continued across the square to the monastery for his appointment with Bishop Ahapit. Two memorials flanking the west wall of the complex came into view. The first was a monument dedicated to the victims of the artificial famine imposed by Stalin in the years 1932–1933 on independent-minded Ukrainian peasants who resisted joining the communist collectives. In excess of ten million innocent lives perished from starvation at the hands of the monstrous dictator and his henchmen. The extent of the atrocity is recorded forever in history as the *Holodomor.* In its heart-wrenching simplicity, the memorial is highly symbolic. A massive block of stone projects a stately presence with only the dates 1932–1933 carved across its crest. The interior is hollowed in the form of a cross. Within the cross stands the profile of a woman with arms open wide and cloaked in black—mother Ukraine in mourning. Her bosom is perforated with the shape of an innocent child. The haunting allegory of God, mother and child conveyed all that needed to be stated.

The wall adjacent to the *Holodomor* monument was dedicated to the fallen heroes in the climactic days of the Revolution of Dignity. The hundred patriots were honored as the *Heavenly Hundred* and their memory has been celebrated throughout the nation. Their portraits have been enshrined at the site for posterity.

Terry was deeply dismayed by the youthful faces whose life was extinguished so needlessly and whose brothers and sisters were still in a deadly fight in the east to underscore that their lives were not sacrificed in vain.

He went into the monastery grounds. Several inquiries led him to the bishop's chancellery.

An acolyte greeted him at the entrance. "Glory to Jesus Christ. Can I help you?"

"I am Taras Adamchuk. I have an appointment with Bishop Ahapit."

"Oh yes, he is expecting you. Please follow me."

"Taras Grigorovich," the bishop set down his pen and came around from his desk. "I was looking forward to meeting you in person. Welcome."

He embraced Terry with a brotherly greeting.

"Afanasi, please bring us some tea and biscuits . . . Taras, please join me at the table."

Afanasi brought in a tray with steaming cups of tea, sugar and utensils, and a tin of assorted biscuits.

"This is an unexpected pleasure. What finally brings you to our shores? Can I be of assistance?"

"I appreciate your offer. I am here on behalf of my good friend to resolve a problem that needs some doing here in Kyiv. It should take a day or two and then I will return."

"Well, don't hesitate to ask . . . Do you have an adequate place to stay? We can gladly accommodate you."

"I am at the Radisson, just up the street. It seems ideally located for my first-time visit."

"In the spirit of your first visit then, may I acquaint you with our monastery and our cathedral, which, I must say, you had a generous hand in restoring."

"That was the least I could have done at the time . . . I still am amazed how you managed to purchase three ambulances, fill them with food, and dispatch them to the warfighters for the pittance that I sent you later on."

"In Ukraine you learn to be very resourceful from the moment you stand on your own two feet. Take for example the broken-down Jeeps America sent us as foreign aid to combat the Russian aggressor when we desperately needed anti-tank javelins. Yes, we were disappointed. But even those relics did not go to waste. Every scrap was used one way or another. Engines, transmissions, fuel tanks, they were all repurposed. As for the ambulances, we bought German ambulances that were obsolete by their standards. Our boys refurbished the engines, reinforced the suspensions to cope with the potholes, upgraded the interiors, and touched up the exteriors. Those ambulances will be in service for decades to come."

"I am glad it worked out well," Terry said as he laid down a stuffed envelope on the table. "I brought you another installment of ten thousand for aid to Donbas."

"Once again, we very much appreciate your generosity. Your timing is excellent. Bishop Serhij, the bishop of Donetsk, will be in town next week. I can arrange for you to meet him and give him the money yourself."

"That will not be possible. I will be leaving in a matter of days."

"The situation in the war zone is dire, especially for the residents in old people's homes. In some cases it's bare existence. Your money will go a long way. I can tell you that your dollar will buy two to three times more produce than will our hryvnia . . . Now, let me show you the cathedral."

The bishop pointed out various facilities in the compound as he led him to the eastern wall of the cathedral and pointed to a large marble panel pinned to the surface. Two columns of names, in alphabetical order, were inscribed on it in gold letters.

"These are the contributors to the reconstruction of the cathedral when Ukraine's independence was declared. Up there near the top in the first column you can see the name and patronymic initials АДАМЧУК гр ТАРАС—ADAMCHUK gr TARAS. Your generosity will forever be remembered."

Saint Andrew's Descent winds downhill from Volodymyrska Street to Podil, the city's commercial and mercantile district. On weekends, the cobblestone roadway transforms into the nation's largest open-air market. Vendors from far and wide flock there with their wares occupying every bit of space and spilling out onto the roadway with their displays. More aggressive artists mount their creations on lamp posts, railings, and window shutters.

For Terry the atmosphere and the merchandise were reminiscent of an outdoor mélange of Delancey Street markets, the Seventh Street Festival, and street art exhibits at Washington Square. Tables overflowed with name brands from Rolex watches to Nike and Adidas footwear to Levis and designer blue jeans—none authentic, most of them Chinese counterfeits. Ukrainian embroidery abounded in every shape and form: shirts, table cloths, pillowcases, ceramics, and wood carvings—most hand-crafted but some machine-made. And the artwork had classical themes, as well as copies of world-famous paintings and ultra-modern colorful perspectives.

Terry eased slowly through the bazaar. He was not a shopper by nature. Nevertheless, he devoted much time to the domestic handiwork, especially to the hand embroidery and ceramics that were not yet available back home. His quandary was where he would put it in the apartment that was bursting at capacity. Gifts were one tempting answer. He would not forget Maya or Vika, for that matter.

It was late afternoon and the morning buffet had long run its course. "Solomyanska Bravaria" placard drew his attention. He went in. Like the mini breweries stateside, this one did not disappoint in the atmosphere, homebrew, and its menu. He chose a tall glass of unfiltered wheat beer and a drinking man's platter of assorted, homemade sausages with potato bits seasoned with garlic. It was a place worth remembering, recommending, and revisiting.

He walked back uphill to buy what he decided on while he was enjoying a second glass of beer. On his mind was an unusual linen shirt that he had seen, which was hand-embroidered in blue and yellow yarn. The traditional shirts have patterns in vibrant red, green, yellow, and black. The blue and yellow colors were patriotic; he could wear it on special occasions. With the market approaching the end of the day, the vendor was anxious for another sale and offered his bottom-line price. As he noticed Terry pull out US dollars from his pocket, he cited a price so reasonable that Terry opted to forgo the customary bargaining.

The next stop was at a stand manned by a proprietor wearing an elaborately decorated peasant shirt and a sleeveless woolen coat of rich Hutsul design. His costume attracted much of the passing crowd and he seemed to do brisk business even at the late hour of the day. His attire placed him in the Transcarpathian region of Western Ukraine, which is known for its woodworking craftsmanship. An ample variety of crucifixes, candle stands, plates, and carved boxes was spread on the table before him. Terry purchased two lacquered music boxes, each inlaid with eye-appealing semiprecious stones and coral beads.

At the hotel, Terry stopped at the concierge and asked him for some bubble wrap as the Hutsul only had newspaper and a flimsy plastic bag.

"I can have them gift wrapped for you if you would prefer."

"I appreciate the thought, but the security at the airport will insist on removing the wrapping and examining the contents before they would let me carry them on the plane."

"I will have the bubble wrap and a sturdier bag sent up to your room right away, Mr. Adamchuk."

"By the way, is it too late to get a seat at the opera for tonight?"

"There are usually premium seats held in reserve for special guests. I will see what could be done."

"Good. That would be the highlight of my trip."

The next morning Terry hurried to Saint Michael's to attend the Sunday divine liturgy. The golden-domed cathedral façade was reconstructed in the Baroque style, the style dominant during the seventeenth-century Ukrainian renaissance while the interior maintained the Byzantine influence in every aspect. Terry was mesmerized by the mystical environment in which he found himself. The focal point was the altar separated from the faithful by an icon screen, the Iconostasis. The screen is extensively carved and gilded in grapevine motives. Five tiers of icons populate the surface with three access doors to the tabernacle: the Royal Doors in the center are used exclusively by the clergy and the Deacons' Doors on either side are used by the deacon and altar boys. The nave and the adjoining apses are adorned from the floor through the dome by iconographers with mosaics and frescoes of the biblical themes and the saints.

When the liturgy began and the choir chanted the responses, his Sunday school teachings came to mind how Prince Volodymyr selected Greek Orthodoxy when he decided to convert his realm to Christianity. His emissaries must have attended the liturgy in Constantinople and related to their sovereign the spiritual uplifting they experienced, the same experience Terry was feeling at the moment.

It was no surprise that the cathedral did not have pews like the churches back home. The faithful remain standing through the service except during the Eucharist and the Lord's Prayer when most are kneeling. The nave rapidly filled to capacity. He was glad not to have overdressed as the temperature crept up. He was drawn into the solemnity of the moment. His thoughts drifted to the memory of his beloved Alicia. He prayed in her remembrance, and at the conclusion of the service, he lit a candle.

As he approached the hotel entrance, he recognized the Mercedes parked at the curb. He came up to the driver's side of the limousine.

"Boris, good day to you. Are you early or am I late?"

"Good day to you, Taras Grigorovich. I suppose it's a bit of both. Isaac Leibovich was getting anxious."

"I attended the liturgy in Saint Michael's this morning. The service is quite long when a bishop is officiating . . . Let me go upstairs and freshen up. I'll be down in a few minutes."

Isaac Stein opened the limousine door and greeted Terry with a firm handshake.

"Welcome to our home, Taras Grigorovich."

"I am pleased to meet you, Mr. Stein. Let us forgo the formalities. I am simply Taras. I am not used to the patronymics."

"Consider it done. I am Isaac . . . Let us go in and I will acquaint you with our enterprise."

He led Terry to the showroom and introduced him to Nina, the bubbly showroom attendant. Mostly touristy trinkets were displayed on Sundays unless a wealthy buyer was expected. The custom jewelry was stored in the basement safe. The work area in the rear was silent except for the computer-operated *Sarines* roughly cutting gemstones round the clock. They did not descend to the less interesting work space in the bowels of the establishment.

They crossed the lobby and took the elevator. On entering the apartment, Isaac introduced him to his wife.

"Rifka, this is Taras, our children's good friend in America."

"I am happy to meet you, Taras. Welcome to our home."

They sat down in the living room.

Isaac said, "Would you like a cup of tea or perhaps, a glass of wine. I can offer you an excellent Georgian wine."

"A glass of wine will be fine."

Rifka said, "What brings you to Kyiv?"

"Some minor business of a personal nature."

Bottle of wine and glasses were brought. Wine was poured. Mutual health was toasted.

Rifka said, "Tell us, Taras, how our children are faring. We Skype with them every week. But you know how it is. Everything is always good . . . Are they having difficulties? They seem awfully homesick."

"From what I could see, they are doing just fine. Everyone is healthy and occupied with their daily routines. The boys are attending school and have lots of friends. Zina is working in a hospital. And Asher is plying his specialty in the diamond district . . . His leg is healing well and in a few months, he will be receiving his permanent prosthesis. Once the rehabilitation process ends, they should be on their way home . . . I must say that you could not tell from his gait that he has an artificial leg."

Isaac interjected, "Mama, why don't we continue this at the table. I am sure Taras is famished . . . I can taste your special stew from here."

The rich aroma that dominated the senses was an exceptionally rich beef stew. The dining table was not lacking in amenities including crystal glasses, a bottle of local vodka, and silver candlesticks. Rifka dominated the conversation, questioning every nuance in Terry's responses.

Terry was careful not to accidentally even hint that he was here on Asher's behalf. That would only cause an unnecessary stir. He only volunteered that he was a private investigator working for a law firm specializing in divorce.

Isaac and Terry returned to the living room after the meal while Rifka remained in the kitchen.

"A drink?"

"A glass of tea perhaps after that very delicious meal."

Two glasses of tea in silver holders were brought on a tray.

"Asher told me that I may be able to help you in some way. He was not very specific."

"I am trying to find someone named Bobrov. It appears to be a common name, but there is an outside chance he may be known to you. At least that was Asher's feeling."

"I do know an Ivan Bobrov . . . I don't have any direct dealings with him, but I could get you in touch with him if you are interested. He works for one of my colleagues . . . Is there a specific reason you need to see him? Does it have anything to do with Asher?"

"It does and it doesn't. I am just making inquiries," he replied in an indifferent tone.

Neither did Terry's demeanor change at the mention of a "colleague". Yet he was excited that he found a solid lead.

"That colleague of yours that you mentioned, Bobrov's boss, perhaps he may be more helpful. What is his name?"

"Nikita Filipovich Grushev."

"This Nikita Filipovich Grushev, how can I get in touch with him?"

"If he's in town, I can ask him to see you. I assume you would want to meet him as soon as possible."

"Yes, it would shorten my stay."

"Give me a minute. I'll use the phone in the kitchen. It has his number on a speed dial."

Terry relaxed sipping his aromatic linden tea. He kept repeating in his mind Nikita Grushev. Progress was ongoing in the kitchen by the sound of the conversation.

Isaac returned with a smile of accomplishment on his face.

"He will see you tomorrow at eleven thirty in his office. He lives a few steps from the Radisson in the western corner of the Golden Gate Square in a high-rise apartment building. He occupies an entire floor, where he also maintains his office. You just identify yourself to the guards at the gate and they will direct you."

"Sounds impressive. I am very grateful to you . . . What is your relationship with Grushev, if you forgive my asking?"

"He provides security for me and my enterprise."

"Your facility looks like a fortress. What can he add to your security?"

"Ahh, Taras Grigorovich, I can see you are not familiar with life in our democracy. I am safe, to a degree, within these walls. But what happens when I or anyone in my family steps outside? We are at the mercy of every hoodlum in town. He provides protection for which I pay a heavy price."

"Forgive my ignorance. Once again, I must thank you. You have been of considerable help . . . I thank you and your wife for your hospitality."

"It has been our pleasure. Please relay our love to our children."

On the way out, Terry enthusiastically thanked Rifka for the outstanding reception. Isaac took him down to the entrance and told Boris to drive him wherever he wished.

"Where to, Taras Grigorovich?"

"Could you drop me off at the funicular? I may as well experience yet another tourist attraction Kyiv has to offer."

When he returned to his room, he noticed the time stateside to be close to ten o'clock in the morning. He dialed Maya's number.

"Hi, Taras. What's up?"

"Good morning, Maya. Am I calling you too early?"

"No, I've been up for some time. I am getting ready to go to church."

"I need a favor. Could you stop at the office on the way and look up something for me. It's important."

"Can do."

"Remember the flash drive I brought back from Nicosia. I need you to see if it lists a Nikita Grushev—G-r-u-s-h-e-v. If it does, let me know and how much is in the account. I'll be waiting in my room to answer your call. Thanks."

He was hoping that Grushev was like the lesser oligarch wannabes who flocked to their comfort zone in Cyprus and have not yet discovered the Seychelles or Caymans as the more sophisticated robber barons did.

The phone rang. Maya was on the line.

"Yes, he's on the list and has quite a sum."

"Oh, that's great news. Thanks . . . I hope I did not disrupt your plans."

"I was glad to do it if it helps. When are you coming back?"

"If it goes as I expect tomorrow, I will fly home on Tuesday."

"Good. I can't wait to hear your adventure. See you. Gotta go. I'm running late."

The guard verified Terry's appointment over the cell phone, then accompanied him to an elevator and escorted him to an upper-level floor.

"The office is on the right," he said as he waited for Terry to go in before leaving.

It was a functional reception area with a functional secretary—not a glamorous maiden that Terry expected.

"Mr. Adamchuk, please have a seat. Mr. Grushev will be with you shortly."

Terry timed ten intimidating minutes before the buzzer rang and the secretary said, "Mr. Adamchuk, please go in."

Terry had a knowing smile on his face. He knew with whom he was dealing.

Grushev stood up but remained behind his important desk.

"Taras Grigorovich, welcome. Won't you sit down?"

No handshake—'you snake!'

Grushev appeared quite short in stature. Perhaps to compensate for his height, he projected an image of a bodybuilder with broad shoulders and a thick neck, a bulldog not to be tangling with. He was dressed in a hand fitted blue-striped suit and a designer necktie. His hair was professionally trimmed to highlight an oblong face with raised cheekbones.

Terry was sure he was facing someone with a strong Napoleonic complex—a self-important martinet.

"Isaac tells me you are a good friend of his son-in-law Asher, and you are here investigating a matter related to a divorce."

"That is not entirely true. Isaac Stein may have misunderstood me. I am a forensic investigator for a law firm specializing in divorce. But I am here to find out who is responsible for the activities of Ivan Bobrov to burglar a jewelry establishment in the diamond district in New York. I was led to believe that he actually works for you."

Grushev sat motionless for a moment. His blinking eyes were indicating a rapid assessment of his options.

"Yes, Ivan Bobrov is one of my lieutenants," he finally said. "I will speak to him and get back to you."

Terry did not expect more than that, neither did he want to pursue the issue any further as a supplicant. He needed leverage. For that he needed to return home and ask Vika for her help. For the present, he was done.

"Nikita Filipovich, I am grateful for your help. You can reach me at—"

Nikita interrupted dismissively, "Leave your number with my secretary on the way out. If there is nothing else, I am running late for an appointment."

"No, there is nothing else. I look forward to your call. Have a good day."

He left, no pleasantries, no handshake.

On his return to the hotel, Terry stopped at the service desk and made a reservation for the morning flight. There were no business class seats available. But he could have the last available first-class seat, which he took and upgraded his open-ended return ticket.

In his room he shed the suit and tie and dressed casually. It was too early to call Vika. He would call her later in the evening and set up a get-together for Wednesday.

He decided to return to the brewery for the same meal he had on Saturday, which he enjoyed very much. After all, he was a creature of habit.

Gone was the weekend fair atmosphere from Saint Andrew's Descent. There were open shops, restaurants, and some historically interesting buildings that he stopped by and read the descriptive plaques. He had time on his hands and was not in a hurry.

Out of nowhere, a pair of arms grabbed him from the back and brought him down to the pavement. “Don’t move,” the assailant shouted in his ear.

In a moment the hold was released and Terry stood up. A small crowd of bystanders gathered.

“Timur?” he said in confusion. “What is going on? What are you doing here?”

A broken light pole lay in the middle of the roadway. Shards of plastic were scattered along the sidewalk and a hubcap with the Mercedes logo.

“Let’s leave quickly before the police come and ask a lot of useless questions,” Timur said.

Further down Andrew’s Descent, beyond the sight of the incident, Terry said, “What is going on? Where do you come from?”

“What is going on? I just saved your life. That’s what is going on.”

“I am confused. You just saved my life? What do you mean you just saved my life?”

“Do you think that was an accident? Let’s go sit somewhere where we can talk.”

“I was on my way to have some lunch. We can talk there.”

“You mean at the Solomyanska Bravaria?”

Terry looked quizzically at Timur, but he only replied, “Yes.”

They both ordered the homemade sausage dish and craft beer.

“Okay, why are you here, Timur?”

“The chief felt responsible for steering you to Kyiv. He suspected that the people you would encounter may deal with you in a harsh way. The supposed accident happened too quickly after your meeting with Grushev. He did not wait for you to slip out of his grasp. He actually smashed up a new Mercedes.”

“How do you know all this?”

“I’ve been tracking you from the time of your arrival. Nothing unusual happened to you until you met this Grushev. That is your man.”

“I will deal with him.”

"Not while you are in Kyiv. He will try to kill you once again. Every hour you are here, you are in danger. For your own safety, I am glad that you are leaving tomorrow. He has no reach in the States."

Terry did not ask how he knew his plans. He just listened.

"I have been staying at the Radisson from the beginning, just a few doors from you. You can rest easy. I am armed. The night surveillance will alert me when anyone sets foot on the floor. As for tomorrow, I will have one of our people drive us to Borispol. Once you are boarded, I will have to make a quick stop in Moscow and then head home."

31

Reckoning

Andrew, Terry's accommodating Starbuck barista, rushed across Second Avenue carrying an oversized carton of freshly brewed coffee and an assortment of baked specialties including several chocolate croissants straight from the oven. Terry opened the door, let him into the office, and relieved him of the package.

"Thank you, Andrew," he said. He paid the bill in cash and as usual, added a generous tip.

"Looks like you will be asking for a big commitment from Vika with all this caloric inducement," Maya quipped sarcastically.

"Is it that obvious?"

"But it's okay. After all, we're all good friends. It won't matter. She'll sense your urgency."

Vika walked in. "What is that delicious aroma in the air? You got back in one piece?"

"Nice to see you, Vika. I did come close to meeting my maker. I'll fill you in later. But first, have a cup of coffee and your favorite croissant."

"Oh, oh . . . this sounds serious."

Terry's cat Blackie was not to be left out of the bonhomie. He meandered between everyone's legs, purring contentedly as he was being cuddled. Meanwhile, Maya refilled his bowl.

"Well, don't keep us in suspense," Vika said. "What is the urgency of this gathering?"

"In due time. In due time, my dear. First, I brought you a small present. I hope you like it."

He handed her the music box wrapped in Christmas foil.

Vika's eyebrows arched and a broad smile graced her face—the same reaction he observed from Maya earlier in the day when she received her present.

"Don't ask. That is all I had in the apartment last night. At least I did not wind up using last week's newspaper though I can assure you I was surely tempted."

The music box was a hit and elevated the friendly atmosphere to the refrains of Lara's theme.

"Where do I start? Asher's in-laws were very gracious. Boris, their majordomo, picked me up at the airport and brought me to the Golden Gate Radisson, which is in the center of the old city, conveniently located within walking distance to many points of interest . . . On Sunday, I had a lavish luncheon with the Steins. Later, I asked Isaac if he knew a Bobrov. He did and identified his boss, Nikita Grushev. He then was able to set up an appointment with him on the following day.

"Our instincts were correct. This stupidity with a burglary in the diamond district had to be somehow connected with the jewelry business in Kyiv. It turns out this Grushev is a racketeer supplying protection to Isaac Stein. I guess he thought of exploiting Asher's access to the facility in Manhattan and pulling off a major robbery.

"I received a cold shoulder from this arrogant, self-important gangster. I suppose he tried to impress me with his brusque demeanor. I realized at once that it made little sense to deal with him any further without having some leverage. I let the insult slide and left him on friendly terms. His bank account in Cyprus should provide that leverage. We'll get to that in a bit.

"Later in the day, I found out the hard way that I must have struck a nerve in the brief encounter with this petty hoodlum. I was walking leisurely down Saint Andrew's Descent to a mini brewery for lunch when someone grabbed me from behind and brought me to the ground. It turned out to be Timur, of all people. He was sent by Mustafa Chubarov to keep an eye on me. Thank God he was there. He saved my life. Next to us was a smashed light pole and shattered parts of a Mercedes. Apparently Timur was tracking me from the moment I set foot in Kyiv. He must have strong ties with the Ukrainian mob. He told me he was armed and the next morning, his friend drove us to the airport.

"So there you have it . . . Fortunately this lowlife is not as clever as he thinks he is. He is behind the times. He keeps his hoard in Nicosia and we easily found his account. I would ask you Vika to help me transfer, say five million euros to my account in Dubrovnik."

"You have an account in Dubrovnik?"

"I have accounts in several places overseas. It makes it more convenient for me when I have business in Europe and need cash on hand. I intend to hold on to the money for a number of years as a guarantee for Asher's safety and then return it intact."

"We'll have to see if it can be done. There may be new controls on his bank accounts."

Vika engaged her cell phone and speed-dialed a number. It took a while for an answer.

"Pasha, Zdrastvuj. Where are you? It took forever to reach you."

"Costa Rica."

"Costa Rica? You on vacation? When will you be back?"

"Monday."

"I have a rush job for you. So call me when you return. See you then and don't get too sunburned or whatever else you can catch over there. Those innocent young maidens can reward you for life. Have fun."

Terry took a clean flash drive and loaded the necessary information.

"Thanks, Vika. I owe you."

"You'll pay dearly. And next time take me along. I'd like to explore my heritage."

Terry was back in the uptown office getting caught up on his open cases. He briefed Sol on his experience in Kyiv and the measure he was taking before he would tighten the grip on Grushev.

He met with Asher on the previous evening and assured him that his threat would be resolved in a matter of days. Asher confirmed to him that no one was watching nor threatening him. Terry commended the reception he received from his in-laws and the valuable lead he received from his father-in-law.

His cell phone rang. An unexpected number appeared on the screen. He answered.

"Good day to you, Mustafa Ahmetovich."

"Taras Grigorovich, welcome home. I hope your trip was fruitful."

"Yes, it was. And thanks to you, I am forever in your debt for saving my life."

"May you prosper for a hundred years! I would like to talk with you. Are you available tomorrow?"

"I will make myself available."

"Good. Timur will pick you up at noon."

On the next day, the Tesla pulled up at noon. Terry was ready and walked out at once.

"How goes it, Timur?"

"Okay, no complaints."

They headed to the Brooklyn Bridge, crawling with the traffic.

"You know it would have been faster by subway. But I did not want to contradict the boss."

"I don't mind. It will move on the other side of the river."

Timur eventually pulled up near the inlet where the boat was moored. They were met by Chubarov as they stepped down to the platform.

"Welcome aboard!" said the captain cheerfully.

Terry noticed that the table was set for three. Toward the back stood Zhenia, the master chef, dressed in formal whites. Something was sizzling in the galley. From the aroma, it could only be his favorite lamb.

"Please make yourselves comfortable. May I serve you an aperitif? I have an excellent Bordeaux. I am sure you will like it."

Crystal glasses were filled with deep-red vintage elixir. Terry's instincts were alerted.

"I asked Timur to join us. After all, he has done all the legwork. A job well done, Timur! I raise my glass to your health."

"I gladly join your sentiment," Terry said as the glasses were raised and clicked.

The chef came up from the galley. "Ahmetovich, the food is ready to be served."

"Gentlemen, please join me at the table. Take your drinks with you unless you prefer something more potent. Zhenia promised us a surprise."

Surprise indeed: grilled baby lamb rib chops with Provençal dressing on a bed of roasted vegetables and potato fritters—mint jelly on the side. Zhenia served the mouth-watering plates with pride. "Bon appetite!"

"Thank you, Zhenia."

The dish brought back to memory the exceptional rack Terry enjoyed at the fundraiser on Long Island, but this dish was definitely enhanced a notch. There seemed to be too much of an effort to please him. He wondered what would come next. He may as well, as the old proverb suggested, sit back and enjoy it.

Other than flowing praise for Zhenia's wizardry, nothing noteworthy was being said during the meal.

With the culinary extravaganza consumed, Zhenia cleared the table, not at all embarrassed by the compliments.

He said, "Would anyone like dessert? I have my own tiramisu. Perhaps some tea?"

"Thank you, Zhenia. We'll have cognac while we talk."

They remained at the table imbibing from their snifters.

"Why did I ask you to come here today rather than speak to you over the phone and to whoever might also be listening? Out of respect for you, I wanted to speak to you eye to eye. I felt responsible for instigating you to go to Kyiv. I did not anticipate that an attempt would be made on your life. That possibility was furthest from my mind . . . I did send Timur to Ukraine, but it was strictly for personal business reasons. Keeping an eye on you was his own initiative . . . I was surprised that you did not spot him following you."

"I had no reason to suspect that someone would be following me. I was just another tourist until my meeting with Nikita Grushev. I thought I left him on good terms," Terry replied.

Timur said, "I stayed far enough away to be noticed. I found out from the guards whom you went to see. That was my assignment . . . What made me suspicious was when you left the hotel in the afternoon, a black Mercedes that was parked in the street began trailing you at a safe distance. I honestly did not think someone would try a hit-and-run on the sidewalk. That was the assassination method practiced twenty years ago. No one uses it nowadays. But there it was . . . I kept close to you. And when the Mercedes accelerated, I ran and pushed you out of the way."

"Thank God you did. I am forever in your debt."

Timur nodded.

"Let me explain to you my motivation," said Mustafa. "I am a firm believer in order and discipline. Never mind the stupidity. This upstart ventured into our territory without our knowledge or permission. That cannot be allowed . . . The most expeditious way for me to find out who was responsible for this absurdity was to help you and let you identify the culprit."

Terry showed no emotion even though he felt used to some degree.

"I am happy to tell you that the issue has been resolved."

Terry could not hold back. He said with some sarcasm, "Did he accidentally leap out of his office window?"

Mustafa replied, somewhat surprised, "Taras Grigorovich, what made you say that? Are we living in the nineteen thirties? Must everything end on a slab? Of course not! Your nemesis decided to return to his home grounds in Kharkiv. He will not set foot in Kyiv ever again. As far as Asher's father-in-law is concerned, he will be contacted shortly by a highly reliable individual who will provide him with security at the same terms he had before."

He refilled the snifters, "So problem solved. No one injured. To your health, Taras Grigorovich."

On the way back Terry said to Timur, "Please drop me off at the subway station. I want to make some urgent calls from the office before the day is up. It will be much quicker and less strain on you. I suspect you would have to return the Tesla."

"I appreciate it. My Beamer is parked at the restaurant."

Once in his office, Terry called Vika. "Hi, Vika, slight change in plans. I just returned from a very interesting lunch with Chubarov. I can tell you the details over dinner tomorrow if you are available."

"I get to pick the place?"

"Of course."

"Is seven good for you? I'll make the reservation."

"Good. I no longer need to deal with our protagonist. He is gone for good . . . So I need to change the money transfer situation. It should be more manageable. Have Pasha transfer ten thousand euros to Dubrovnik. That will provide another donation to the orphans in Donbas. Also have him transfer ninety-nine hundred dollars to my checking account. That will cover the expenses and won't red flag our favorite Uncle Sam. Thanks . . . See you tomorrow."

Wolodymyr Mohuchy is a retired technologist specializing in electronic, microwave and phased array design. He is the author of ***From the Ashes,*** a biographical novel of survival and redemption under the brutal Soviet and Nazi regimes. ***Terminal Payback*** is the initial Terry Adams adventure which delves into a web of conspiracy and corruption on a global scale.

He is a philanthropist and a community activist.

Lightning Source UK Ltd.
Milton Keynes UK
UKHW011842060921
390144UK00008B/525/J

9 781664 191648